FAR AWAY

FROM

HERE

BY WILLIAM
PANZARELLA

FAR AWAY FROM HERE

© 2008 By William Panzarella

ISBN: 978-0-615-24675-8

Dedicated To:

Everyone who has wrestled with addiction;
both those that have survived
and those that have not.

This book is also dedicated to all those
family and friends that have
unwillingly been affected
by their loved ones addictions.

TABLE OF

CONTENTS

PREFACE

Michael Patterson, age 24, was born into your average, middle-class, nuclear family. They lived in desirable area of Long Island, New York, seemingly a world away from the gangs and crime of the inner-city. His parents loved and supported him and there was never any physical abuse in the household. Besides the inevitable trivial arguments, there were never any heated or long-lasting quarrels. Mike even had a close relationship with his younger sister, Melissa. But it is here, beneath the Brady Bunch-like façade of suburbia that lays the true ground zero of the never-ending, pandemic known as drugs. And Mike Patterson has become but one of the tens of millions of victims of this nondiscriminatory demon.

As is often the case, Mike's experimentation with drugs started off as teenage curiosity. Even when Mike first started getting into trouble, it was all seemingly, harmless fun. But like with so many others' stories, what started off as curiosity and harmless fun, morphed into something more serious. Smoking joints and cutting class turned into snorting cocaine and dropping out of school, then came selling drugs and getting arrested. Before he knew it, Mike had been cast into an all-consuming black hole. At the other end of that black hole laid prison and a lifetime of regrets. For after a drug-laden, anarchic journey, cumulating in a dark night that would haunt him for the rest of his life, Mike was arrested and would spend five years in a New York State penitentiary.

While in prison, Mike Patterson had plenty of time to delve into his soul and into the past, which ate at him like a cancer. He thought long and hard about the choices he had made and how they had not only affected his life, but the people closest to him: his family and ex-girlfriend that died the night he was arrested. But it was through this soul searching that Mike decided to turn his life around. He made a promise to himself that once released he would walk the straight and narrow and try to make amends for some of the things he had done. Now, after serving four years and eleven months, the time has come to put that promise to the test.

Upon release from prison, Mike Patterson is ready to put the past behind him and start anew. He is ready, even eager, to get a job and become a productive member of society. But perhaps most of all, he is ready to finally reunite and reconcile with his mother and teenage sister, with which he will now live. However serious Mike is though, he will find out that the ghosts of the past are not so easily relinquished and that some things cannot be atoned. He will also learn that even if he might be able to survive his own battle with drugs, the war wages on, always eager for its next victim. And its next victim might be closer to him than he ever could have imagined.

This is a novel, but to file it under pure fiction would be a mistake. Though the characters in this book are, for the most part, factious, they very well could be your neighbor, co-worker, brother or sister, friend, son or daughter. And the story itself, with perhaps only minor changes is being played out everyday, not only throughout America, but across the globe. Those that have battled addiction – whether it is narcotics, prescription drugs or alcohol – as well as their loved ones that have become unwilling participants in their plight do not need statistics to know how easy, and sometimes quickly these demons can rip a family apart. They do not need statistics to tell them how often there is no climbing out of rock bottom. They also know all to well that even if there eventually is light at the end of the tunnel, it is almost always a long and arduous journey.

However, it is important to note that this is not just a story about drug addiction, but also about life in general. It is about the choices we make, the way they affect not only ourselves but the ones around us and the price that everyone is left to pay. Like life itself, it is a story of love and loss; happiness and pain; survival and defeat; beginnings and ends.

Chapter 1

COMING HOME

C hoices. If life can possibly be summed-up by one word, it would be "choices". In fact, only two things are certain in life: first is that one day you will die; and the other is that you will be forced to make many choices along the way. Sometimes we wish that we did not have to make them. Sometimes we do not even notice we have them. But they are always there. The choices that we make shape us into what we are – and what we will become.

Most choices are trivial: what to wear; what to have for lunch; or where to go on a Friday night. Some choices seem insignificant at the time yet turn out to be anything but trivial. Maybe you chose to get behind the wheel of a car after having one too many drinks. Maybe you decide to stop on your way home from work to buy a lottery ticket – and it winds up having the winning numbers. Maybe you decided to take a later flight – and the flight you were originally supposed to take crashes. Sometimes however, it is apparent when a certain decision may affect the rest of your life. Sometimes it is as clear and profound as being at the proverbial fork in the road. It is a place that all of us will find ourselves. Some will stand there more than others. Sometimes it will be clear which path to take. Other times it will not. Sometimes we will know which one is the wrong path, but take it anyway. Yet one thing is for certain: we can choose the path, but not the destination it leads to.

Perhaps no place is the importance in the choices we make more evident than prison. Of course many people are there not because they made a bad decision or two along the way. They are there because they are career criminals: thieves, rapists and murderers. They lead a life of crime. These people are well aware of the consequences of the choices they make, but deliberately make them anyway. However, prisons and jails are also filled with those who, for whatever reason, just made a bad decision or walked down the wrong path once in their lives. Maybe alcohol or drugs clouded their judgment. Maybe it was rage that made them do something that they would normally never have done. It doesn't make whatever they did right. It does not give them an excuse or mean that they should not have to face the consequences of their actions. It is just an unfortunate fact of life that sometimes we choose to do something without ever even noticing that there are other choices.

Mike Patterson – inmate 773420 – was not a bad person. He was not an evil person. Yet there he was, in a small cell; a place that he had called home for the past five years. There he was with the murderers and child molesters, sharing the same yard – the same showers. Maybe Mike's biggest crime was being young and stupid. He was only nineteen when his sentence started. For five years Mike laid in that cell thinking of the choices he had made and how differently he would have chose if only he could go back. However, he also spent five years trying to come to terms with the realization that there was no going back. There was no changing the course of time – and knowing that killed him. It ate at his every thought. It ran through his veins and stuck to his skin. There would be no future or present without the constant reminder of the past. Sometimes Mike even wished he could be more like some of the murderers or rapists, because at least they had no conscious. Nothing haunted them. Nothing kept them up at night. Mike however had a conscious. He knew right from wrong. He knew that things could have turned out so different. Sometimes regret is the greatest punishment of all.

They call being in prison "doing time", because that's all there is – time. Mike had time to think about a lot of things over the past five years. He thought about his mother and sister that waited for him back home. He thought about his late father. He thought about his girlfriend that died the day he was arrested. There were so many "what ifs". He had changed much over just five years. He had turned from a careless boy, into a mature man – but at a very heavy cost. Of course, being in a controlled environment was very different than being on the outside, where all of life's temptations were constantly being flaunted right in your face. There was nothing that ensured that once on the outside Mike would not return to his old wild ways. There would be no guards to watch over him. There would be no locks to keep him from life's medicine cabinet of imminent evils. On the outside, everything would be right at his fingertips or just a phone call away. However, the day to test whether Mike had truly turned his life around had come. The long awaited day for the twenty-four year-old to step back into the outside world had finally arrived. Mike Patterson was going home. The freedom that had drifted into myth some time ago had finally turned back into a reality.

As the guard walked Mike from his cell down the narrow corridor, his heart began to beat faster and faster. It was not nervousness, yet rather overpowering anticipation. Suddenly, the loud and constant clamor that filled the prison fell eerily silent. For the first time, Mike could not hear the voices of inmates reverberating off the walls. In fact he heard nothing but the beating of his own heart. He saw nothing but straight ahead. It was so surreal that he wondered if it was just another cruel dream. Was he going to awake only to find himself still in his cell – as he had many times before?

After stopping in a small office to sign some papers, receive some long forgotten, personal belongings and get some last minute instructions regarding his parole, the time had finally come. With prison issued blue jeans and a white t-shirt, a sole guard led Michael Anthony Patterson to the same tall, ominous, barb wired gates that he had walked through five years earlier. Only this time he was on the inside walking out. For endless days he had fantasized about climbing over those gates and running to freedom. He had dreamt about them being plowed-over or broken open in a daring escape. Now, they would open for him. Now, he did not have to run to freedom. All he had to do was take two small steps. With his heart still racing Mike held back tears as the gates slowly rolled open. Oh what a glorious sound they made, he thought to himself. "Well, there you go Mike" was the only thing that the guard said as he pointed towards the outside world. Then, with a simple nod of acknowledgment Mike slowly put one foot in front of the other and just like that, had once again become a free man.

As the steel gates closed behind him, Mike could no longer hold back the emotions. While inhaling a deep fresh breath of the September air, a tear streaked from his eye followed by another and yet another, until five years worth of suppressed tears flowed freely down his face. He cried not just for the joy of finally being freed or the sorrow for time lost or for the pain that he had kept bottled up inside. Rather, he cried for all those reasons and standing there outside those walls, he could feel an enormous weight being lifted from his shoulders; a weight that piece by piece dissipated into the gray September sky.

Mike's mother and sister were supposed to be there at the gates waiting for him, but were obviously running late. Not that it bothered Mike. After all, he had waited five years, what was another fifteen or twenty minutes? Besides, he was just happy not to be on the other side of the gates. Enjoying his long awaited return to freedom, Mike stared down the barren stretch of road that once led him to the prison. His tears now subsided a smile grew on his face. Kneeling down, his hands sifted through the loose dirt and pebbles. Letting out a laugh that drifted into the air, Mike made a mental note that dirt had never felt so good. The air had never been so fresh. The sky had never looked so endless. Everything seemed so real, so tangible. That long, narrow road was no longer confined to an image in his dreams or a view from the prison's yard. It was something that he could touch, could stand on. It was a road that he could walk down if he wanted. No one was going to stop him or give chase.

Mike strolled in silence down the poorly paved road, as a slight mid-September breeze softly combed along his skin. Five years earlier, he had gone down that same road, though it was in the opposite direction. He was also a different person then. Though only five yeas had passed it seemed a lifetime and a world ago. In fact it felt so distant that in a strange way it seemed like it didn't even really happen at all – like it was all some bad dream. Yet there he was on that same road, walking back down it under very different circumstances. He was walking back to where he had come from. However, because time changes everything, Mike Patterson was not walking back into the past, but rather into the future. The road may have been the same, but time had inevitably altered where it lead. Though Mike wished more than anything that he could walk down that road into the past and change everything, he knew that was not to be. It may have been the first day of the rest of his life, but he unfortunately knew that some things would never begin again. He knew that some roads led to places that people never come back from.

Mike Patterson grew-up in a suburban part of Long Island, New York called Massapequa. There he lived in a three-bedroom, middle-class house along with his parents and younger sister Melissa. There was never an excess of money, but the family always had enough to pay the bills. There were never any times of dire straits. Mike's father, who was the sole income of the household worked as a foreman for a bottling distributor. It was not a glamorous job, but it always paid for the roof over their head and three good meals a day. It was a good upbringing. There was never any abuse or talk about bankruptcy or divorce. If Mike's parents argued it was usually about petty things. For the most part they were a normal healthy family.

Mike, however, always had a knack for getting into trouble. As early as the fourth grade he started getting called to the principle's office followed by the inevitable calls home to his parents. But it was never anything serious back then. It was usually a case of butting heads with his teachers or getting into scuffles with other kids. His father would scold and lecture him, but as long as Mike had respectable grades, he brushed off the often-minor altercations with his teachers and classmates as just "boys being boys". Mr. Patterson wanted his son to get a good education but neither did he want him to grow-up to be a sissy. So through grade school and junior high Mike kept his grades respectable and tried to keep his trouble making to a minimum.

As Mike entered his sophomore year in high school, everything changed. It started with the death of his father, John, who had died of a heart attack. As far as everyone knew he had been a healthy man and his untimely passing at the young age of fifty, came as a surprise. For the first four months Mike stopped getting into any trouble altogether and stayed home almost every night with his grief stricken mother and sister. However, he soon jumped back into getting into trouble headfirst. He started drinking, smoking pot, cutting classes and getting into fights. Perhaps Mike was not doing anything different than many of his peers, but he just seemed to push the envelope a little further than most of the other kids. There was a certain sense of bitterness and angst to everything he did. Sure, all teenagers are pissed-off about something or someone, but his anger seemed a little deeper, a little more concentrated. Mike didn't just hang around a bad group of kids – he was the leader. And it didn't take long before the parties became wilder, the drugs heavier and the fights more frequent. By his junior year Mike was selling pot and acid. It also became regular for him to cut half of his classes and not return home sometimes for days at a time. Mike's father was not around to discipline him and his mother, who was still trying to cope with the loss of her husband, didn't have the strength to deal with him. She also was not aware of the full scope of her son's troubles.

Halfway through his senior year, Mike dropped out of high school. Although still living at home for the most part, he was making enough money, dealing pot and acid and throwing keg parties to buy himself whatever he wanted. By this time he had a fake I.D. and was hanging out with an older crowd at local bars. For Mike, life had become one big party. The invincibility of youth was much too strong for him to consider any consequences and time was something that appeared to have no end. However, the bitterness that he had worn like a badge of honor was about to be retired. It was at this time that Mike met Katie Fuller, a sixteen year-old sophomore. After meeting her at a party, he instantly fell for the slender, blue-eyed brunette and knew that she was "The One". She was the one that was going to change his life forever. He was right. Things would never be the same – for either of them.

As Mike walked down that desolate road, still waiting for his mother and sister, he could not help but think about Katie. Not a day went by when her soft, pale face didn't flash before his eyes. Not a day went by without her image coming alive in his head as clear and real as if she was standing right there in front of him. Mike wished that the road he walked down would lead back to her, but he knew that it would not. The road back to Katie had been erased.

As soon as Mike and Katie met there was a spark that instantly turned into flames. Yet it was clearly not a case of opposites attracting. To the contrary, it was more like two peas in a pod. Katie, a year younger than Mike, shared his sense of living on the edge. Also, like many teenage girls, she was attracted to the bad-boy image and what better person to fit that image than Mike. Almost instantly the two were inseparable. Mike would sneak Katie into his room for the night. Sometimes they would rent hotel rooms for days at a time with the money Mike made selling drugs and throwing parties. There was the occasional misplaced jealousy, which usually ended up with Mike getting into a fight with some guy, but it only seemed to add to the excitement of their relationship. With each day, each week, each month their obsession with one another grew. It was no longer Mike or Katie – it had become Mike *and* Katie. They were always together and seemed made for each other. Mike, although he had many friends, had always thought of himself alone in the world. Now he had finally found someone who felt the same and together neither of them would ever have to feel alone again.

In February of 1980, Mike was driving one of his friends' cars. He and two of his other friends had just come from the bar where they had been drinking for a couple of hours – though it was only two in the afternoon. Once behind the wheel, the drinking continued. They were also passing a joint around. On their way to another friend's house, Mike overlooked a stop sign. Somehow he managed to swerve out of the way of a pick-up truck crossing his path. However, in doing so, Mike piloted the car through a wire fence, across a front yard and straight into someone's living room. Luckily no one was home. Not luckily, the police happened to be only three cars behind theirs and saw the whole thing. Before the young men even had time to come to their senses and check to see if they were all in one piece, two police officers had guns pointed in their faces – and more patrol cars were already on the way.

After spending the night in jail Mike was bailed out by his mother. However, he faced myriad of charges: DWI, driving without a license, possession of marijuana, possession of false identification, minor in possession of alcohol and criminal damage. It seemed as though the party was over.

Surprisingly Mike had never been in trouble with the law before so although the charges before him were serious, with a good lawyer the court may have granted him some leniency. However, Mike began to panic. He thought about spending time in jail; yet most of all he thought about being separated from Katie. Katie was Mike's whole world. She was everything. The thought of being separated from her – even if it was just for a couple of months – weighed on him more than the thought of actually being locked-up. In fact even thinking about it crippled him with fear. Mike loved Katie and trusted her, but she was young and beautiful. He wanted to believe that she would she would wait for him, but it was a chance he was not going to take.

At that point in time Mike Patterson did not see the choices in front of him. Going to court and facing being separated from Katie was not an option. So he and Katie decided to run away together to California. He knew that doing so would make him a fugitive – they both knew it – but they just could not bear to let each other go. There was no future for Katie or Mike besides the one they would share together. It was a fate that would forever bond them together – in life and after.

Suddenly Mike's concentration was broken, snapping him out of the dark corridors of the past and back into the present. It was a car approaching. Mike stopped almost in the middle of the street as it drew closer and more into focus. Apprehensively he stood by the side of the road, straining his eyes to see if it was them, but it seemed like the car was taking forever to get to come down the road. Then finally, as Mike could start to see the blurry images of the driver and passengers, the car beeped its horn. It was them! The moment had arrived! Excitedly Mike waved his arms in the air.

As the car carefully pulled off to the side, Mike ran to it like a child running to the tree on Christmas morning. All three doors flung open at the same time, but Mike's mother rushed to him before anyone else. "Michael", she yelled in sheer elation as she wrapped both arms around him, "I thought this day would never come!"

"Me too," he replied, embracing his mother. It was five years, but it seemed more like twenty. His mother and sister had visited him in prison, but it was not the same. No longer did a plate of Plexiglas separate them. He could touch them. He could hold them in his arms. He could finally go back home with them. As Mike loosened his bear hug, he could see the tears rolling down his mother's slightly wrinkled face. "C'mon ma, don't start crying now."

"What are you doing on the side of the road," she asked, fighting back further tears.

"Well when they finally let me out, the last thing I wanted to do was stay around there. I didn't want them to get any second thoughts about letting me go," he joked. "Seeing how there's only one damn road in and out of this place, I figured I'd start walking down it and run into you guys sooner or later."

Betty wiped away another tear. "Sorry we're late. There was so much traffic."

Mike smiled. "It's alright. Don't worry about it ma. It was actually a great feeling to be able to walk around."

Before she could say another word, Mike turned his attention to his younger sister. With a smile that stretched from ear to ear, he ran over and wrapped his muscular arms around her slender frame. "Missy," he yelled in jubilation, "it's so good to see you. God, it seems like it's been forever!"

Melissa immediately broke into tears. The two had always been close. Unlike many brothers and sister that constantly bickered, they had always shared a close bond. When Melissa was born, Mike boasted to everyone that would listen, almost as if he was the proud father. There was never any jealousy about who was getting more attention. When she was a toddler, he used to read her bedtime stories. Then when she became older he used to help her with her homework.

"Oh Mike", she said in a quivering voice as her tears continued to pour, "I missed you so much. It was so different without you being around."

Mike gently wiped away the tears that rolled down her cheeks. "God…do you realize that it's been nine months since I've even seen you."

"I would have visited you more but…"

"It's o.k." he interrupted while wiping another tear from her face. Mike could not stop staring at her. She looked so beautiful and pure. Her face was so innocent; such a complete contrast to everything he had come to know in the last five years. "I can't believe how much you've grown. Even when I saw you last March, it was just from across the table. I bet you're driving mom crazy with all the boys calling the house."

Melissa blushed. "Yeah right," she replied. "Besides, forget about me. Look at you. My God," she said as she tried to grip his bicep with her small, slender hand. "What have you been doing in there – lifting Volkswagens?"

Mike laughed. "Well, you have to work out a little. There's not much else to do in there."

"Work out a little? Damn, the last couple of times I visited you, you had a long sleeve shirt on." Melissa couldn't get over how muscular her older brother looked. Mike, who was six foot, had always been a skinny kid. He was still slender, but cut. His body wasn't overly bulky like that of a professional bodybuilder, but rather finely chiseled.

"Yeah Michael, you look great," his mother added.

Melissa gave her older brother another hug. "It's just so good to have you coming back home again."

"Yeah," he replied. "It's gonna be good to do things together again Missy."

"I've been looking forward to it," Melissa said almost in a whisper as a smile burned brightly on her face. Mike just stood there looking at her for a while – her blonde hair against the cool gray Autumn sky. To him, Melissa represented innocence. She was the purity and the youth that he had never found for himself. She was a symbol of hope and the untainted road still ahead. She was the opposite of everything he had come to know – and everything he had been.

Mike then turned to face his friend Brian who had driven his mother and sister to pick him up. The two had been friends since seventh grade. Brian was also the only friend that had visited Mike while he was locked up.

"Thanks for coming to get me and especially taking my mom and Missy," Mike said as he gave his old friend a handshake and a hug.

"It was my pleasure. It's just good to see you finally out", he replied.

"No really man, it means a lot."

Brian cracked a smiled along his slightly unshaven face. "You're not gonna get mushy on me now Mike, are you?"

Mike shook his head. "The only thing mushy is that crap they call food in there that I've been forcing down for five years. I've been dreamin' about eating some real food since the day I stepped into that hellhole." Mike turned to face everyone as he pointed his finger down the road. "So lets get the hell outta here and get some burgers or something!"

"I knew the first thing you'd want to do is get something real to eat," Mrs. Patterson proudly said. "That's why I made you your favorite – lasagna." Mike walked over and kissed his mother on the head and said she was the best. Mike would have been ecstatic eating a Big Mac or box of fried chicken. Lasagna however, sounded like edible gold.

So with that, they all piled into Brian's Ford Impala and journeyed down that road that Mike had come-up five years earlier. It was a long car ride home and everyone was understandably eager to talk to Mike; to fill him in on whatever was going on. They talked about the old neighborhood. Brian talked about his new job doing roofing, working for his older brother's company. Melissa talked about high school and her friends. They talked about a lot of things. Though Mike was half-listening and joined in the conversation at times, he could not help but fade in and out of thought. He looked closely at the moving landscape, mesmerized by every passing car, tree and signpost. These were all things, albeit trivial to most, which he had not seen in years. Sure, he had been able to watch television while he was locked-up and saw the prison buses roll in and out of the front yard almost everyday, but this was different. These were all things he could get out and touch. He could have Brian stop the car and could walk out into the open fields if he wanted. He could climb one of the tall trees. Soon they were driving down populated areas, with billboards and store signs. There were

McDonalds and Burger Kings. There were homes. Mike tried to pay attention to the conversation, but was too busy watching strip malls and houses roll by. These were the things he had dreamed about for the past five years, only to have them stolen away every morning he awoke. These were all the things that he never even noticed before being incarcerated.

Mike began pointing out to everyone the grocery stores and people walking down the sidewalks. His words filled with excitement, as if he was a visitor from a distant planet. It was as if he was seeing all these things for the first time. That is when they all realized the significance of freedom. That is when the harsh reality of confinement hit them and as joyful as the moment was, they all had just a little sinking feeling in their stomach because they knew that the world he so blissfully pointed to was the world that they took for granted everyday.

The ride back to the home he had left some time ago symbolized Mike's strange and arduous journey from one chapter in his life - that he hoped to leave behind - into a new, but uncertain one. He knew not where the future would lead, but was convinced that wherever it was, it was a better place then where he had been. There was no going back down the paths of the past to see where he had made wrong turns. There was only hope that the path ahead was more lucid and better paved.

Almost on cue, everyone stopped talking as they approached the old neighborhood. Everything looked eerily the same as when he left. It had only been five years but Mike somehow thought it would look different. He watched silently as they passed his old high school. His eyes fixated on the small strip-mall he used to walk to almost everyday; the pizzeria he used to eat lunch at; the bar he used to sneak into with his fake I.D.; the bakery his mother used to take him to when he was a boy. Five years was not long enough to dilute the memory as visions of days past came back into crisp focus.

Mike could not understand why, but with every block that brought him closer to their house, the more nervous he felt. Saying nothing he sat uncomfortably in the passenger seat as they drew near. Soon a small bead of sweat helplessly escaped from his brow. Why was he feeling this way he wondered? Why was he so uneasy? Was it that he was afraid to face the future? Was it the uncertainty of what lied ahead? That's when it hit him. Maybe it was the past that he was afraid to face. Mike had thought about the past every single day while in prison – the things that went wrong, the lost chances, the regrets – but now he had been driven back to it. Now it was right there, in his face, something tangible. That was the high school where he had met Katie. That was the corner bar that he used to get so drunk in he couldn't even remember what had happened the night before. That was the pizzeria that he used to meet people in to sell drugs. They had driven right past the house that he used to snort cocaine in with his friends. In prison he used to think about these things, but they were all so distant and detached. Now they were all right there, waiting for him, talking to him – staring back at him.

The moment arrived as they pulled-up into the driveway. Mike was home. "Well Mike," his mother said as she crouched over from the back seat. "You're home now."

Mike exhaled a long, deep breath. "Yeah…yeah, I'm home."

"It still looks the same, huh bro?"

"Yeah man," Mike replied as he slowly climbed out of the car. "It still looks the same." His words were no longer coming out as easy, as a dry lump logged in his throat.

There it was in front of him – the old house. The house he had grown-up in. The house he learned to walk in. That was the porch where he used to sit and wait for his father to get home from work. Those were the hedges that he used to help his father trim. Mike remembered how his father used to watch over his every move, making sure they were cut just to the right specifications. His father would grab the sheers from his hand and show him the right way to do it. Mike would get frustrated and storm into the house, only to be summoned back out again to finish the job. So many arguments they used to have in that front yard. Now Mike would give anything to have one of those arguments again. He would do anything to help his father trim those bushes one last time.

At first everyone just watched as Mike examine the outside of the house. They watched in amusement as he inspected the grass, the old tree that stood in the center of the small front yard, the paint on the house. They watched as he looked up to the second floor to his bedroom window.

"Well listen man," Brian said, finally breaking the silence, "I know the three of you have a lot of catching up to do, so I'm gonna head home."

"No Brian. Please, at least come in and have some lasagna", Betty pleaded.

Brian put both hands out in a politely declining gesture. "No, thanks Mrs. P. I appreciate it, but the three of you should be alone. I believe you all have some catching-up to do." Brian then turned his friend, giving him a light punched on the shoulder. "I'll see ya soon and we'll do some more catching up."

"Thanks Brian, I appreciate it. And thanks again man, for picking me up."

"It's just good to have you back man." Then, after giving Mike another quick hug, Brian bid farewell to Betty and Melissa and jumped back in his car. "Give me a call later," he yelled through the opened driver's side window before slowly pulling away.

Then, without hesitation, Mike walked up to the front door; a door that he had not walked through for quite some time. Apprehensively, he watched as his mother turned the locks and slowly pushed it open. With a deep breath it was time for him to once again walk inside. Mike noticed that some things were different, but for the most part, it looked the same as it did the day he left. The colors were the same. Most of the furniture looked the same. He walked by and touched the couch that he had spent countless hours on watching television. His eyes roamed around the dining and family room like a curious visitor, fascinated by it all. He smiled at all the familiar surroundings and stared at anything new as if deciding whether or not to give his stamp of approval.

Mike then walked straight to his old bedroom. To his amazement it looked just like it did the day he had saw it last – only cleaner. His Black Sabbath, AC/DC and Led Zeppelin posters were still on the wall. His collection of records and tapes were still on shelves by the stereo. The bowling-pin lamp he made in shop was still on the wooden dresser. So was the framed picture of him with both his parents and sister when Melissa was first born. It all seemed strange. He had never given his room much thought, but just figured all along that his mother would have at least taken down his posters.

With his mother and sister standing silently in the doorway, Mike walked over and sat on the bed. "It feels weird," he blurted out, as if they understood exactly what he meant. "It's just like I left it."

Betty smiled at her son, glad to see him back home again, back where he belonged. "Well how did you expect it to be?" She asked.

"I don't know," Mike replied, shrugging his shoulders. "I guess I figured that you'd at least take down my posters."

Still in the doorway, Melissa walked into the room. "Well I did borrow some of your albums and tapes, but I returned them."

"Some of my albums," he said in a surprised voice. "When I left, I kind of remember you listening to the Bee Gees and Abba. I don't think I have any of that in my collection."

Melissa laughed. "Well, my taste in music has changed a lot since I was twelve."

"God… You were twelve years old huh?" Suddenly, those five years seemed much, much longer. Mike thought about when he was twelve. A lifetime had passed before he turned seventeen, the same age Melissa was now. Twelve and seventeen were two different worlds. There were so many changes within that time period he could have written a book about them. Mike realized just how much of Melissa's life he had missed. He practically missed her whole teen years. Sure, Mike had been away from his mother for five years too, but for the most part she was the same as before. People do not change much from fifty-two to fifty-seven. But between twelve and seventeen - a person goes through more changes in that short span sometimes than the entire rest of their life. Mike had missed so much. He had missed his sister grow, develop. He had missed her go into high school. He missed her go from ABBA to Black Sabbath.

After Mike finished his getting re-acquainted tour around the house it was time to eat. For the first time in a long time Mike would have a home-cooked meal. Yet it was more than that – it was his mother's famous lasagna. He had spent countless days and nights dreaming about just being able to eat a slice of pizza or a hamburger from McDonalds. Homemade lasagna though, was in a completely different stratosphere. Since Mike walked out those gates hours earlier, he had felt and seen freedom – now he was ready to taste it.

The exact recipe was a closely guarded secret that had been passed down for who knows how many generations. All Mike knew was that it took all day to make – at least the sauce anyway. Mesmerized, Mike watched as his mother brought the lasagna to the table in an almost ceremonious fashion. A touch of steam was still rising from the lightly browned mozzarella. The fresh, vibrant aroma of garlic and basil permeated through the air filling the entire house. Mike could tell by the smell and look alone that it was a masterpiece. "Oh ma," he exclaimed, "I don't know if I can handle this."

"I can always make you a hamburger," she shot back jokingly.

Mike responded with a you-must-be-crazy look. "Just give me the spatula." Then, without further ado, Mike began to cut into the creamy pasta as his mother brought out the other food. Lasagna was undoubtedly the main attraction, but it was never served just by itself. The family name may have been Patterson, but Betty's maiden name was Cirellio and the family grew-up on good Italian cooking.

With all the food on the table Mrs. Patterson said a short prayer thanking God for the food on the table, the fact that Michael was back home and that the three of them could be a family again. It was not routine for them to say a prayer before dinner except maybe on Thanksgiving or

Christmas. However, it was a special occasion. It felt like Thanksgiving and Christmas wrapped into one.

All eyes now shifted to Mike as he went to take his first bite. They watched with smiles and great enthusiasm as if they were waiting to see a baby take his first steps. Mike hammed-it-up as he cut off an oversized piece of lasagna. With the creamy ricotta cheese dripping from the fork, he placed the entire piece in his mouth. After swallowing, he let out an exasperated moan of pleasure. "Oh ma... You have no idea how good this is."

"I'm glad you like it," his mother responded with joy.

In between moans of pleasure, Mike talked loosely with his mother and sister. Each of them wondered to themselves the last time they had sat down and had dinner together. Even before Mike went away, it had been quite some time since he had dinner with them, as he was never home. It was a comforting feeling, to have them all at the table again. There was a sense of normality to it – even knowing all the hardships they had endured over the years. They talked about their mother's job at Macy's. Melissa talked about her new friends and recent movies she had seen. Mike asked about old friends and people who lived around the neighborhood. It was the typical things that normal people talked about when they met at the dinner table. It almost seemed too normal. For a moment – just a moment – it was as if all the bad that had come to them had never happened at all.

At one point, Mike looked at his mother and sister. Their lips were moving, but somehow their voices fell silent. A warm, comforting feeling flowed through his body from head to toe. Right there, right then, he wished he could freeze everything so it would never change. Right there in that moment, at that table, he felt something that he never remembered feeling before; it was the feeling that everything was going to be o.k. Most special moments are not realized at the time they are happening, but rather in hindsight as one looks back and reflects. This however, was one of those rare moments when a person realizes how special it is as it is happening. And like most of those moments, there was nothing spectacular about it. It was not a moment dressed in bright lights or special surroundings. There was no big party. It was just a simple moment – a simple moment in time.

After dinner both Mike and Melissa helped their mother clean the dishes. Then Mike adjourned outside to the backyard patio. His mother wanted to stay up all night, but Mike saw how exhausted she was and assured her that they would now have plenty of time to sit together and talk about whatever they wanted. So with her son's assurance and a kiss on the forehead, Mrs. Patterson reluctantly went upstairs to bed.

Melissa however, followed her big brother outside. Together, they sat on a swinging love seat that had been part of the backyard since their father was alive. Its wood had faded and cracked and its metal frame was rusted, but the old swing that Mike and Melissa used to sit in as kids still held them up. It seemed fitting that after the years it was still there for them to sit on together, almost as if it had been waiting for them. Both the seat and frame seemed like they should have broken and been turned into scrap some time ago.

The cool, gray September sky had faded peacefully into a black, starry night. A crescent moon hung silently in the distance like an eerie guardian of the stars. All seemed so still and calm yet so alive. Summer had slipped away into memory, but it had not yet turned too cold to sit out and enjoy the nights. In fact, the air was crisp and refreshing.

Melissa gently swung back and forth next to her brother, as if they were kids again. Under the stars they sat and talked in a tone as calm and soft as the night itself. "So it must feel great to finally be out?"

Mike sighed, as if that was a good enough answer. "Yeah," he paused, "it sure does." There were so many things he wanted to say to describe how good it felt to finally be home, but just could not seem to put them into words. The again, perhaps there were no words to describe it.

"I can't believe that this damn swing still works," he said, grabbing its rusted chains. "This thing has been here forever."

Melissa smiled as she looked at its withering frame. "Yeah," she replied, feeling the wood as if it was a family pet. "This thing has been out here almost as long as I can remember."

"I remember when dad first put it up," Mike said, his words fading into the cool, brisk night. "You must have been only six or seven years old." Suddenly Mike could see a picture of that day as clear as if he were watching a film of it playing against the backdrop of the sky. "It was just before the summer – May. We were going to have a barbeque the next month for your birthday and Mom was getting on Dad about fixing up the back yard. She said there was no place for people to sit. So Dad brought home this love seat and that old patio set we used to have. I remember helping him put it together." Mike let out a fleeting laugh. "I remember him getting so pissed. Man he was pissed, but you know dad always refused to read directions. But after a couple of hours, we finally managed to figure it out. I remember it was still daylight when he called you and Mom from the house to see the finished swing. Mom smiled and clapped and you – you jumped right on it. I remember Dad watching you there, swinging back and forth. He had such a proud look on his face. I mean he completely forgot about being so mad at the damn thing. He just seemed so happy watching you swinging there. In fact as strange as it sounds, I never remember seeing him with such a smile on his face."

Melissa listened intently as her brother narrated their past. "You remember that day that well, huh?"

"Yeah. Yeah I do. I can remember the look on Mom and Dad's face. I remember how clear and blue the sky was – how it was an unusually warm day for May. I remember how simple it all felt – how clean."

Suddenly, Melissa started to recall a distant, hazy memory that she never realized she had. "It's funny how you can sometimes remember one day in particular that stands out from all the rest... Especially when at the time it seems so insignificant."

"Yeah, I guess it is kind of weird," Mike replied. "Especially how vivid it can be, as if it only happened yesterday. So, are there any days that stick out your head?"

"Yeah sure", Melissa answered without pausing. "It was the night of dad's funeral. I was sitting out here on this same swing. There were so many stars in the sky that night. I don't remember a moon, but there were a million stars. Anyway, I was out here by myself crying and you came out to tell me about how everything was going to be o.k. You let me put my head on your shoulders and cry. Finally, when I couldn't cry any more, we sat on the swing and looked-up at the sky. Then suddenly, out of all those sparkling stars, we both saw the same shooting star."

"I remember that!" Mike shouted with enthusiasm.

Melissa pushed his arm. "Get out of here."

"No, no, really," he replied. "We both happened to be looking up in the same direction. It was so bright and seemed so close."

Melissa was shocked that he remembered, but continued with her story. "I remember that after it faded into the night you told me that it was a sign from Dad in heaven telling us that everything would be all right." Melissa stopped for a moment to stare into the sky, as if she was waiting for that same star to streak across the night. "I actually felt better after you told me that." Through the corner of his eye, Mike could see a small tear seep from his sister's eye. "I remember that was the first time after Dad had died that I smiled. I remember that night as if it was yesterday. I believed you when you told me that. I believed that everything was going to be all right."

Mike bowed his head towards the ground. "I'm sorry Missy."

"Sorry for what? I don't want you to be sorry," she quickly interjected. "In fact I want to thank you. I mean you made me smile at a time when I didn't think anything was ever going to make me smile again. If you hadn't been there for me then it would have been a lot harder to handle. I mean Mom was there, but... well I'm just glad you were there."

Mike shook his head. "No, I mean I'm sorry for not being here for the past five years."

Still gently swinging back and forth, Melissa looked into her brother's eyes. "Mike, I'm sure you've been through enough without having to feel sorry for not being here for me. I've been fine. It's just good to have you back home again."

"No, I mean it." Mike knew that the last thing his sister wanted him to do was feel sorry for anything. He knew she was not mad at him; but he was mad at himself. "Just here me out Missy – please. I know that right after Dad died I was here, but after that I don't know what happened. I don't know if it was the anger I had built up. I don't know if it was just the times, but I just went off the deep end. I put myself before everybody else. I didn't give a shit about anything and the thought that what I did might effect you or Mom never even crossed my mind."

Melissa put her small, cool hands on his face. "It's all right Mike," she whispered.

"You might say it's all right and you may think it's all right, but it's not. I missed out on five of the most important years of your life. I mean look at you. You're no longer the little girl I knew. You're a young woman. I've missed out on so many things. I've never met your best friend Allison that you were telling me about or your boyfriend. I wasn't there for your first day in high school. I never realized you started listening to the same music I like or…"

Melissa put her finger over Mike's lips before he could say another word. "It's o.k. Mike, you're here now. They'll be plenty of time for you to meet Allison and Tom. They'll be plenty of time for us to talk about what music I like. And they'll be plenty of time for us to do things together. The important thing is that you're here now and you'll be here tomorrow and the next day."

"I know. I just wanted to say I'm sorry. If I had just known then how much my stupidity would affect everyone…I just wish I could do it all over."

Melissa knew that he was not only talking about her and their mother, but also about Katie. She understood how responsible her brother felt for what happened to Katie. She wanted to tell him that it was not his fault, but that was a conversation for another time. They had had enough therapy for the night.

The two reminisced some more before Melissa finally went off to bed. Although she could have stayed up all night talking, Mike convinced her that she needed to wake-up for school in the morning. After all, she had already taken that day off to go pick him up.

Mike, however, stayed outside. He had not been outside at night in quite some time. It had been too long since he basked under the stars; since he inhaled the crisp, night air; since he had emptied his mind into the quiet, still of the darkness. It all seemed so calm and peaceful. No one was yelling from their cells. There were no guards walking around. There was no stench of prison air. Most of all however, there were no walls, no ceiling. There was just the endless sky that stretched into infinity.

Finally around one o'clock, Mike retired to his old room. It felt strange for him to be alone in the room almost the same exact way that he had left it. It was as if nothing had changed. Still feeling restless, Mike began to unceremoniously take all his posters off the wall and roll them up. His taste in music had not changed. It was just that Mike was ready to re-enter the world as a responsible adult and it just didn't seem like responsible adults would have posters of rock bands and half-naked girls hanging on their walls. So one-by one they went down: Led Zeppelin, then Black Sabbath, then AC/DC, then Bo Derek and Dorothy Sratton.

When Mike finally finished he laid wide-awake in bed, looking around at the room. It was a place of many memories. Mike remembered all the times he would sneak Katie in to spend the night. He remembered them trying not to make too much noise, but somehow always managing to knock over something or laugh too loud. He knew that they must have waken-up his mother and sister on a few occasions, but for whatever reason, nobody ever came to the door. It was as if the room was their own little house for the night. God those were great times Mike thought to himself. Katie never got mad or complained about having to sneak around. She didn't care. She was just glad to be there with him. They were just glad to be with each other.

Looking back Mike wondered how something so simple and innocent could have become so fucked-up.

So many nights in that exact same room, Mike held Katie in his arms as they fell asleep. So many times they made love there. Sometimes it all seemed like a lifetime ago and yet sometimes it felt like just yesterday. There was not a day that went by that Mike didn't think about her, dream about her. Yet being in that room made it feel so real. It was as if he could still smell the scent of her shampoo. It was as if at any minute she was going to come through that door. Mike would have given anything for that to happen. However, that could never be. Katie was gone and his hands would never again brush along her gentle skin. He would never again be able to look into her sparkling blue eyes or lay beside her. They would never be able to keep the promise they made to each other: to grow old together. The more Mike thought about her the more pain he felt. He tried to think of good memories they shared together, but that just seemed to make it worse. Mike had always blamed himself for what happened to Katie. It did not seem fair that he was there and she was not. He never seemed to get mad at her though, for leaving him behind. His anger was always directed towards himself. Their time together and the fact that she was no longer there was something that he thought about everyday, some days more so than others. He knew it was something he had to face and was determined not to put it behind him, but come to grips with. For years Mike had been preparing himself not to forget, but to move on.

Mike woke-up early the next morning. Although only getting about four hours of sleep, it was the best sleep he had in over five years. To say he felt revitalized was an understatement. It was more like a feeling of rebirth. Right after waking up, Mike enjoyed a long, hot shower. It was the first shower in years that he was able to take by himself. It was like going to a spa. Mike could have stayed in there for hours. The steam cleared his lungs and the hot water seemed to wash away all the years of confinement.

After the shower, Mike put on a pair of blue jeans and sweater that his mother had bought for him. In fact she had bought him a whole new wardrobe. Not only was Mike five years older, but also he had become more muscular and none of his old clothes would fit. Sitting on the bed Mike rubbed his fingers along the soft cotton v-neck sweater. It felt so soft, so new. It was certainly a drastic departure from the prison issued blue jeans and rough, denim shirt he had come so accustomed to wearing. As he pulled it over his head he marveled at how comfortable it felt. Now, not only did he feel like a new man, he also looked like one.

Betty and Melissa awoke to the smell of breakfast cooking on the stove. As they wandered out of their respective rooms, they followed the tantalizing aroma to the kitchen, where Mike had eggs, toast, bacon and orange juice waiting for them on the table. "Michael, what are you doing?" His mother asked. "I was going to cook breakfast."

Mike stood over the table pouring a glass of orange juice. "No, ma, that's all right," he replied with a smile on his face. "Believe it or not I've actually been dyin' to do this. I wanted to surprise you guys."

"Cool. Can you do this every morning?" Melissa asked jokingly as she brushed back the hair from her face.

"Well, it smells delicious," his mother proudly proclaimed as she sat down.

Melissa, who was not used to starting the day off with a complete breakfast, also gladly grabbed a seat. "Yeah, it really does smell good," she added. "Usually I just grab a bagel or something at the school cafeteria before class. I think you're going to spoil me Mike."

Mike looked at both of them with a sense of pride. Seven or eight years ago he would never have thought of cooking a big breakfast for his family. To the contrary, Mike could never get out of the house fast enough. Now however, he could not think of anything he would rather be doing or anyplace he would rather be. "Well c'mon, don't let it get cold," he said with a smile.

The morning before Mike was eating steaming slop from a plastic tray with a hundred smelly, angry men. He had to force down each bite as fast as possible while keeping one eye on the inmates and another on the guards. Now, one day later, he was taking his time eating fresh eggs and bacon sitting alongside his mother and sister. What a difference one day can make.

"So Mike, what are you going to do today," his sister asked.

Mike finished swallowing a piece of bacon before answering. "Well, Mom's offered to drive me to the unemployment office on her way to work. As part of my parole, I have to find a job." Mike then paused as he gulped down some more orange juice. "Well hell, I mean I want to work anyway. I spent the last five years being locked in a room. The last thing I want to do is sit around and do nothing. I'm anxious to get out there and put in an honest days work. I mean they put you to work in prison but you make like a buck a day." Mike laughed. "Can't buy much with that."

Melissa reached over for a piece of toast as she asked what kind of work he was looking to get into. However, before he could answer, their mother cut in. "I tried to get you a job at Macy's."

"I know ma, it's alright," he replied.

"I also talked to my friend Phyllis, who runs a catering business, but…"

Mike leaned back in his seat and gave his mother a look. "It's ok ma, really. I told you that you don't have to do that. I'll find a job on my own. It may not be glamorous, but I'll find something."

Not wanting to press the issue, Betty backed off. "I know, I know," she replied as she patted her son's hand. "We're just so glad to see you back home. That's the only thing that matters. Everything else will work out."

"Yeah," Melissa joined in, "as long as you're back home with us. Hey, maybe you can get a job as a bouncer or in a gym with all those muscles you put on."

Mike laughed. "Get outta here."

"No really, I mean it. When I saw you wearing that t-shirt yesterday I couldn't believe how big you got. Here," she said while reaching for his arm. "Roll-up that sleeve."

Mike pushed his sister's hand away. "Com on stop it will ya."

"So Mike, after school, I want to bring Tommy over so you can meet him."

"Yeah, that'll be great."

After breakfast, Mike cleaned-up as his mother and sister took their showers and got dressed. Before Melissa left the house for school, Mike gave her a kiss on the forehead and said to be careful. Then, almost as soon as Melissa left, it was time for Mike and his mother to start their day. Walking to the car Mike looked-up at the sky. It was a beautiful day. Mike noticed how alive everything seemed. Gone was the layer of clouds that had lined the sky the day before as an infinite sea of pristine blue coated the mid September morning.

Mike rolled down the passenger side window to let in the fresh air, not seeming to get enough of it. "So ma, are you gonna be late for work?"

"No, I should make it there on time. It doesn't matter anyway. I'm never late. Some of these people – you should see them – they come in late all the time."

"Don't they get in trouble?"

Betty laughed. "Na, they just kiss-up to the boss. That's what it's all about Michael."

Mike just nodded his head. "I appreciate you dropping me off."

"Don't be silly." Betty let go of the steering wheel with one hand and patted her son on the knee. "I'm just sorry I wasn't able to get you a job at…"

Mike interrupted before his mother could finish the sentence. "Ma, I told you that's all right. I know you tired. It's ok, I'll get something."

"I know," she replied.

Staring out the window at the moving landscape, Mike nonchalantly changed the subject. "I'll tell ya', I can't believe how much Missy has grown."

"She's real happy that you're home. You know she really looks up to Michael."

Mike let out a subtle, but cynical laugh. "Yeah, what a good role model I am."

"You know what I'm talking about Michael."

"Yeah, I know," he grudgingly acknowledged. "How is she doing in school?"

Betty paused before answering. "O.K. I mean she's not an 'A' student, but she gets pretty good grades."

"Is there money for her to go to college?"

Betty was somewhat caught off guard by his question. "Well I have a little money saved-up, but it's not much. Your father's life insurance didn't really provide for that. But Mike, she'll be able to get a student loan. I don't know if they'll pay the entire tuition, but probably most of it."

"Well she's going to go to a good school," Mike proclaimed. "She's a smart kid and she's gonna have a bright future. I'm not gonna let something like tuition get in her way. I'll work seven days a week if I have to, but I'll put money aside for her."

Betty laughed. "Michael, I told you, she'll probably be able to take out a student loan. I know you want to be there for her and I couldn't be happier about that, but you also have to think of yourself. There's nothing wrong with watching out for your sister – in fact I think that would be good for her – but you also have to get yourself back on your feet. I know it won't be easy but remember you are still only twenty-four. I think it was great that you were able to get your GED." Mike had dropped out of school his senior year, but was able to get his GED while in prison. "In fact, I thought you might think about going to college yourself."

Mike shook his head. "I know, I know. It's just that Missy hasn't blown her chances like I did and..."

"Michael, you messed-up before that's true, but you've paid your dues. Now it's time for you start over. There's no going back to change what happened. There's nothing you can do about that. Having you gone for five years was horrible and I'm sure it was even worse for you, but I can tell you're a changed person. Look…" Betty's voice grew softer. "You're still young enough to have a bright future ahead of you."

Their conversation was cut short as Betty pulled into the parking lot of the Unemployment Office. "Look," she said as she stopped the car. "I'm just glad you're home, o.k." She then leaned over and gave Mike a kiss on the forehead.

Mike smile. "I know ma. I'm glad to be back. Everything will work out."

"I know it will," his mother replied.

After waving goodbye, Mike turned his attention to the disheveled looking building and started his adventure with the Unemployment system. He had no idea what to expect, but knew it entailed a lot of red tape and paperwork. However, it was something that had to be done and he had been through much worse. So in he went. While filling out forms, he noticed how differently people were dressing. He was happy to see that the glitter and gaud of disco fashion, which was already dying when he started his sentence, appeared to be finally extinct. However, some of the new fashions also seemed pretty disturbing. Mike noticed that not only did longhair stay in style, it was everywhere. It was also apparent though that hairspray had crossed genders. Not only did girls have their hair sprayed five inches above their head, but so did a couple of guys. What the hell were they thinking, Mike wondered. He was all for guys having long hair - he did himself before they chopped it off in prison - but these guys looked like girls –and not the way David Bowie looked like when he was Ziggy Stardust. No, these guys were trying to look pretty or something. Some of them were wearing suede boots and pounds of silver bracelets. There was also something else that was catching Mike's eye however – women. Not lost in the happiness of being freed and urge to start a new life was the fact that he had not even seen a real woman in five years. Mike may have become more responsible, but he certainly did not forget what women were all about. He still had a pulse.

After Mike finished at the Unemployment Office – it was a three and a half hour affair – he grabbed a cab back home with some money his mother had given him. Later on that night, Melissa brought home her boyfriend Tom. Mike had always been protective of Melissa and was even more so now. He knew Melissa had grown-up, but was still not comfortable with her dating. It was not that he did not trust his sister. It was the *other people* that he didn't trust and to his defense, there were very good reasons. For the past five years Mike had been surrounded by rapists, murderers, pedophiles and every other breed of predator. He had heard horror story after horror story, confession after confession. There was no longer any hiding from the overwhelming realization of the evils of which men were capable. There was also no hiding from the realization that not every murderer or rapist was covered with tattoos or had scars on their face. Not every monster looked like a monster. Some of them looked like the next store neighbor or the clerk behind the counter or the kid with whom you went school.

Knowing what he knew, seeing what he had seen, was both a blessing and a curse. It was a blessing because it kept him on his toes. However skeptical it made him, it made him alert of his surroundings. Mike had learned how to read between even the most deceptive of lines. He knew the many masks that the monsters wore. On the other hand, he hated knowing what he knew, seeing what he had seen. Mike did not want to believe how cold and dark the human psyche could be. The realization of how cheap the cost of life could be was haunting. The comprehension that remorse was something that some people were incapable of feeling was a hard pill to swallow. Mike did not want to believe in monsters, but he knew they existed and knew that no one – not even Melissa – was immune from their presence.

His thoughts and prejudices aside, Mike tried to meet Tom with an open mind. In fact, Mike greeted him at the door with a warm smile and friendly handshake. As skeptical as Mike was, his first impression of Tom was that he was an ok guy. With his short brown hair and somewhat stocky stature, he looked a little on the jock side. Yet Mike did not sense that ignorant, stuck-up jock vibe. Tom seemed to have a laid back swagger to him. After meeting Mike, Tom said hello to Betty, whom he had met a few times before.

Exchanging loose words, they all sat around the table to indulge in left over Lasagna. Tom told Betty how delicious it was, but did not overdo it with the kissing up. He was respectful, but at the same time it did not seem like it was an act. Mike was getting a good first impression and to show his approval, he did not grill Tom with twenty questions.

After dinner Betty stayed in the kitchen to clean up while Mike, Melissa and Tom circled around the TV in the family room. Both Mike and Tom had offered to help clean up, but Betty told them go and relax. Mike would have stayed behind anyway to help his mother, but did not want to be rude to Melissa's boyfriend. After all, he was a guest in their house. Adjourning to the family room Mike sat on the love seat sofa as Tom and his sister sat on the larger couch. Although they sat next to each other, Tom made sure not to get too close while in the presence of her brother. He didn't want Mike to get a bad impression of him, especially when things seemed to be going so smoothly. He also didn't want Mike to kick his ass.

"I'll tell you, your mom sure knows how to cook a good meal," Tom felt obliged to say again.

"Yeah," Mike agreed, "she always did."

"It must be good to finally be able to eat real food again huh?" Melissa gave her boyfriend a stern look as he suddenly realized that maybe being locked-up was not something that Mike wanted to talk about. Tom immediately felt like an ass for saying it, but certainly meant it as nothing more than innocent conversation.

Mike did take it as innocently as Tom meant it to be. "Yeah, I'll tell you," he said in a strong but relaxed voice, "It's amazing how much you take good food for granted." After a second's pause, Mike let out a soft, brief chuckle. "It's amazing how much you take a lot of shit for granted."

Tom laughed along with him, however uneasily. "Yeah, I guess so."

"So Tom, Melissa tells me that you're also a senior."

Tom was glad that Mike changed the subject. "Yeah, that's right."

"So what are your plans for college?"

Now Melissa gave her brother a look. Mike immediately felt her eyes peering into him. "What? That's a natural thing to ask."

"No it's alright," Tom replied, obviously not missing the look Melissa had given her brother. "You know I'm not really sure. I definitely want to go to college, but I may want to wait a year. You know, take a year off. Lately I've been thinking about going into management, but I see how much these lawyers make and I'm thinking maybe that's the way to go. I guess I just haven't figured it out yet."

"That's alright, at least you have some idea. That's a start. Me, when I was your age I didn't know what the hell I wanted to do." Mike laughed at himself. "In fact, I still don't have any idea what the hell I want to do."

Feeling the atmosphere switching to a more serious side, Melissa decided to change the subject altogether. "It's almost eight o'clock," she said "let's see what's coming on TV."

"Yeah, here's the remote control" Mike replied as he gently tossed it to her. "I'm the last person that would know what's on TV. They let us watch the tube in the can sometimes, but it was mostly educational programs and old re-runs of I love Lucy or Gilligan's Island. Don't get me wrong, that Gilligan is pretty damn funny, but after a while it gets old."

Tom stayed over for another hour as the three of them relaxed on the couch and watched television. The conversation stayed light, mostly focusing on TV. Mike was intrigued by the A-Team, a popular sitcom at the time and used the commercial breaks to have Tom fill him in on the plot and the characters. Mike had never seen Mr. T before and couldn't seem to get enough of him.

Mike spent the rest of the week trying to find a job. He knew that an ex-con, even at his young age, would not be an employer's first choice - or second or third choice for that matter. It also did not help that he had no specialized skills. Mike knew that whatever job he could get would most likely involve manual labor and would probably start at minimum wage. However, he was realistic and knew that everyone had to start somewhere.

Mike also spent time just enjoying his freedom. He joined a local gym and worked out for about an hour each day. Around 4:00 he would start cooking dinner, usually sticking to something he knew how to make, like pasta or hamburgers. Melissa normally arrived home around 3:30, but Mike would make her wait to eat until their mother came home from work. This way they could all eat together as a family, like they were supposed to. Mike also enjoyed spending time with his sister, whether it was watching TV or just talking about nothing in particular. He had waited years to spend time with Melissa and now he was taking advantage of it.

By Friday though, Mike was beginning to get a little frustrated with not being able to find a job. It had not even been one week, but he was getting anxious to start work. He was eager to start earning an income. He also knew that that getting a job would be one of the final steps towards being a responsible adult. A real job was something he would not have even fathomed eight years ago – especially if it may have meant working for minimum wage. Now though, holding down an honest job and being responsible was something that he wanted to do more than anything else. He needed to do it – not just for his parole officer, but also for himself. He needed to prove to himself that he *was* a changed person.

Chapter 2

MEMORIES AND GHOSTS

Right off the bat Saturday started out as a good day. In the morning Mike received a phone call that would cut short his quest for work. His friend John, who he had not talked to since being incarcerated, had apparently heard from Brian that he was looking for a job. The moving company that John worked for needed to hire someone and he arranged it so Mike could meet with the boss.

Later that afternoon, Mike met John and his boss at the neighborhood pizzeria, as they had planned. After telling Mike how good it was to see him out, John introduced him to his boss Dave, who looked to be in his early forties. It turned out that Dave, who ran the company with a silent partner, had done time himself when he was younger for grand theft auto. Fortunately for Mike, this translated into Dave being sympathetic towards his current predicament. The three talked informally over a fresh pie about Mike's ambitions as well as Dave's own experiences.

"Well, Mike," Dave said in between bites, "I think it's really good that you're trying to turn things around. I finished up my six year stint ten years ago and never looked back. I had done a short stint before that – about nine months – but I guess I didn't learn my lesson the first time around. But while I was doing my second stretch I told myself 'No fuckin' way, this shit ain't for me'. Prison ain't no fuckin place to be. You know that."

Mike let out a sigh. "I sure do."

"You do realize though that most guys – once they get out – they're worse than when they went in. Some guys say they want to turn their shit around, but…"

Politely, Mike interrupted him. "No way. I mean I know you're right and I would be skeptical too."

"No, No, I don't mean to come off as skeptical," Dave replied "I'll tell ya' what. I know that I just met you, but you seem to be sincere about getting your shit together. Not to mention that John over here, who I put a lot of faith in, vouches for you. If you're interested, you come work with us and we'll see how things turn out."

Those were the words that Mike was waiting to here. "Listen you won't regret this. I mean it. I know you've probably been bullshitted by the best, but…"

"Yes I have, but if I thought you were bullshitting me at all, I wouldn't have made you an offer. Listen, if anyone can understand how hard it can be tryin' to find work when everyone thinks you're a fuckin criminal, it's me. Believe me, it took me months to find a job after I got out and even then it was like people wanted to look up your asshole to make sure you're not stealing anything. I mean I had a job as a dishwasher. What the fuck was I gonna steal – dishes?" Everyone let out a quick laugh at Dave's expense, including himself. "I know it's like you against the fuckin' world. It's an uphill battle, that's for sure. Listen Mike, I don't really know you and none of us knows what will happen tomorrow or six months from now, but if you really do want to turn your life around then as someone who's been in your shoes, I'll try to help you out."

Mike knew that finding some one like Dave was like finding the golden ticket. "Well listen," he said as he extended his hand towards Dave, "I really appreciate it. I really do."

Dave gave him a firm handshake. "Well hell, I guess it's the least I could do. I mean what we do isn't rocket science. All I ask is that you show-up for work on time, work hard and be professional. Oh yeah, and try not to fucking break anything."

Mike smiled. "Will do."

John gave his friend a firm smack on the back. "Congratulations man."

"Hey listen, thank you too John I won't forget this buddy."

"Don't worry about it man. It's just good to see you finally out."

The three spent about another half hour at the pizzeria going over the details of job. It was a couple dollars more than minimum wage, which was a pleasant surprise to Mike. It was a small operation, which only had three trucks and ten employees, but what mattered most was that it was a legitimate business. It was a real job that Mike would receive real paycheck from. He had never received a real paycheck before. He didn't even know what they looked like. Dave told Mike that he would have to come in Monday morning and fill out employment and tax withholding forms before he could start work. It may sound strange, but Mike was looking forward to filling out those forms. They might as well have printed on them: "By signing here you have now been declared a responsible member of society." Mike was also happy about the job itself. He had known that whatever job he found would probably involve manual labor, but had envisioned digging ditches or washing dishes. Being in the moving business did not have the same stigma attached to it as those jobs. No one ever said, "If you don't get a good education, you'll wind-up working for a moving company." Sure, it was not glamorous or prestige, but it certainly didn't seem too bad for someone that had just been released from prison not even a week ago.

After Dave generously flipped for the lunch tab, he left John and Mike. The next time Mike would see him would be Monday morning, when he reported for work.

"Hey listen John," Mike said as the two stood outside in the parking lot, "thanks again man for everything. I really appreciate it."

John gave Mike another pat on the back. "I told you man, don't worry about it. Hey, you remember when that punk Tom Mcfarlen was giving me shit in the park by the school. He thought I stole some weed from his locker."

"Yeah, I remember," Mike replied as he watched two pretty girls walk by.

"A whole group of us were over there hanging out and smoking weed as usually. Anyway, you walked over there and got right in his face. He kept talking shit so you kicked his ass, right there."

Mike laughed. "Yeah, thank god that guy was a pussy. He used to talk tough, but I never remember him getting into any fights before that. I think he was one of those guys who was a bully in elementary school and thought that he could still bully people around in high school. But anyway, that was no big deal man. Believe me, that guy was an asshole; it was a pleasure to kick his ass."

"I know it wasn't a real big deal at the time, but you gotta remember shit like that. I know it was high school, but you don't forget that shit." Suddenly, John realized that he was starting to ramble so he changed the subject. "Hey man, I'm sorry Dave started laying all that bullshit on you."

"What do ya' mean?" Mike asked.

John pulled a pack of cigarettes from his coat pocket. "You know, about flying straight and turning your life around. It sounded like he was preaching."

"Ah, don't worry about it," Mike replied.

As John lit the cigarette, the two watched another couple of girls walk by. "So what are you doing now?"

Mike looked at his watch. "I don't know. It's only five o'clock. I mean I don't have to be anywhere. Why?"

John blew out a cloud of white smoke that faded into the September air. "Well I'm gonna meet some of the old crew at six."

"Like who?"

"Kevin, Dan, Fat Joey..."

Mike smiled as he could see all their faces flash before him. "Fat Joey, no way."

"Yeah, Linda's gonna be there. So is Diane Webster. Brian said he might come, but if he knows you're gonna be there, I know he'll show up." Suddenly John paused as the expression on his face changed from enthusiasm to hesitation. "Wait a minute man."

Immediately Mike sensed the change in his friend's demeanor. "What? What's the matter?"

"I'm gonna meet them at Baxter's." Baxter's was the neighborhood bar that they all used to hang out at. "I wasn't even thinking about it being a bar and everything."

Mike thought for a brief moment before answering. "It's cool. What am I never gonna step foot inside a bar again. It'll be good to see everyone. I'll probably stick to club soda though. I mean there's nothing that says I can't drink alcohol - it's legal — but I don't want to start getting drunk already, not even a week after my release."

"No, hey man, it's cool. That's totally cool."

Baxter's was in the same shopping center as the pizzeria, so since it would still be an hour before any one showed-up, they decided to walk around the parking lot and reminisce. They talked about the time a group of them were kicked out of the library, which was right next to Baxter's. They were all tripping on acid and Mike was chasing them through the isles with a book about the devil yelling that they were all going to hell. The guys were taking books off shelves and throwing them at Mike while the other people in the library started freaking out. Finally, a security guard chased them out and they were all banned from the library for life. They also talked about how they used to smoke pot behind the dumpsters and how on a few occasions cops would chase them through the parking lot. Then John brought up how they used to ride their bikes around the parking lot when they were little, pretending that they were in some sort of gang. They couldn't have been more than twelve years old then, Mike pointed out. Some would think it strange that they had spent so much time over the years in a parking lot, but that was all part of growing up in Long Island – especially at the time.

After about forty minutes of walking around and laughing about the past, the two ventured into Baxter's. After grabbing a table, their walk down memory lane continued. Mike and his friends had been fixtures at the neighborhood bar. Although most of them were at least three years shy of the legal drinking age when they first started coming, the bartenders never seemed to mind a good fake ID.

As Mike sipped his club soda, he looked around at what used to be his favorite hangout. Baxter's looked no different than the hundreds of other neighborhood pubs that littered Long Island from the North to the South Shore. There was nothing fancy about it. It didn't have a theme or decorative memorabilia hanging on the walls. It looked just like an ordinary bar. It had the customary one pool table and dartboard. However, the pool table was too close to the walls so on some shots you had to use your stick like some kind of contortionist, with one end on the table and the other straight up in the air. It never stopped people from playing though. In fact there was always a line of quarters on the edge of the table from people waiting to play the next game. Like all other neighborhood bars in Long Island, it was always the usual suspects. Some of the bars catered to an older crowd. Some catered to an underage crowd. But it was almost exclusively the same crowd. You rarely saw new faces when you walked in other than the occasional patrons who wondered in while they were waiting for a train, since many of the bars were in close proximity to the Long Island Railroad. Most of the bars had Irish names like O'Malley's or O'Brien's, but few of them were as authentically Irish as some of the pubs in Queens, Brooklyn or the city.

Many nights Mike stumbled out of Baxter's. Some nights he didn't even remember being there. It was always a wild time. You could score drugs as easy as you could buy a beer there and usually Mike was one of the ones selling. He would buy enough beer and shots to fill a swimming pool and yet always managed to walk out the door with more money than when he came in. Now there he was, sipping on club soda with his short hair and button down shirt.

One by one the old gang started to roll in. Mike used to hang out with a variety of people from his various escapades, but these were the people from the neighborhood. You see in New York, with maybe the exception of Manhattan, you grew up with kids from your own neighborhood and even though you may meet other people and make other friends, you always kept in touch with at least some of the guys from the old neighborhood – even if you moved. That's just the way it was.

It was the first time in a long time that Mike was able to see some of his old friends and they all appeared as happy to see him, as he was to see them. It felt great for Mike to be able to talk to everybody and catch-up on things. He was even a little tempted to have a beer, though not tempted enough. Mike knew his mother, who he had called earlier to say where he was going to be, was probably already worried. What was he going to do though, go from work to home for the rest of his life and never go out again? She had to know that he was going to eventually run into some of his old friends.

"It's fuckin' great to see you Mike," his friend Dan exclaimed before pounding his Budweiser.

"Yeah Mike, it's good to see you out," replied Diane, who was also from the neighborhood. "You look good."

Although Diane had always been like one of the guys, her comment made Mike blush. "Thanks," he replied, noticing how good she looked.

"Yeah man, you sure put on some muscles," added Fat Joey.

With a cigarette hanging out of his mouth, their friend Dan reached over to grab one of Mike's biceps. "No shit man. Let me feel those fuckers."

Mike quickly pulled his arm away. "Get the fuck outta here."

"So," his friend Kevin said as he motioned the waitress over for another round, "does Baxter's still look the same?"

"Yeah, pretty much. Only it's missing me over there in the corner falling down drunk." Everyone chuckled. "It looks like a different crowd though," he said pointing to the people standing over by the bar.

"Yeah," replied Dan. "You still get some of the old regulars, but now it's filled with new underage kids that just got their fake IDs."

Mike laughed, remembering his old fake ID, which said his name was Raul Montgomery and that he was twenty-seven. "They never got fuckin busted, huh?"

Kevin shrugged his shoulders. "Apparently not. Who knows, they probably give the cops a fuckin' envelope every month."

"We don't even come here that often anymore," added Kevin. "These new kids, they're all fucked-up."

John pointed to the growing crowd at the bar. "Yeah, most of them look like faggots. And look at the chicks, they're all pigs."

"I like pigs," exclaimed Dan as he raised his mug proudly in the air.

Diane slapped the back of his head. "You should, they're your own kind."

"Hey yeah, that's what I've been meaning to ask you guys. You see that guy standing over there with the long, frizzy hair." Mike pointed to a kid standing by the bar drinking a beer. "What the fuck's up with that. I mean what the fuck is up with that look. He looks like a girl." Everyone at the table looked over and laughed. "What is that hair spray in his hair? And what's with all the frigin bracelets?"

Dan nearly spit out his beer from laughing. "That's the new look man."

Mike shook his head in disbelief. "I know. I've been seeing guys looking like that all over the place."

"He looks prettier than me," added Diane.

Mike's jaw dropped as he pointed once again. "Holy shit, what's that? Are those fuckin blue boots that he's wearing?"

Everyone at the table started to crack-up. "That's nothing. You think that's fucked up, you should see some of the girls," replied Dan. "Now that's fucked up! There's this new bitch Madonna that sings this pop crap and all the girls are trying to look like her."

Diane gave Dan a dirty look from across the table. "I like some of her stuff."

"Oh get the fuck outta here Diane," Dan snapped back. "You can't be fuckin serious. That shit sounds like ten year olds should be listening to it. And she looks like a fuckin whore on Holloween."

"Well at least we don't have to worry about disco anymore," Mike proudly proclaimed.

Everyone gave a "here, here" as they raised their glasses in a toast.

Suddenly Kevin leaned towards the middle of the table and pointed to a group of people standing by the bar. "Holy shit man! Do you know who that is?"

John looked over. "Who?"

"That's fuckin Joe Corella," Kevin responded.

"Get the fuck outta here."

"Hey, that name sounds familiar," added Mike.

Kevin polished off the remainder of his beer before turning to Mike. "We went to high school with him. He used to go out with Cindy Swanson."

Suddenly a light bulb went off in Mike's head. "Oh yeah, I remember him. In fact I had a class with him. That guy always had chicks hanging over him. What the fuck happened to him? He looks all scraggly and shit." Trying not to stare, Mike looked through the corner of his eye at the guy they were talking about. He was wearing a pair of faded jeans with a rip in them and a yellow t-shirt that looked like it had not been washed in a while. His face was unshaven and his hair looked like it had not been brushed all day. "I remember that guy used to always be so worried about how he looked. He never had a fuckin wrinkle in his clothes." Mike gave him a closer look, not believing that it was the same guy. "He used to carry a comb in his back pocket and whip it out every five minutes to make sure he didn't have a hair out of place. What the hell happened to him?"

"I heard he got hooked on dust," Kevin replied.

Mike looked at Kevin who was still leaning over the table. "Angel dust? Get the fuck outta here. That guy?"

Kevin shook his head while pouring himself a beer from one of the pitchers on the table. "Yep. He started smoking the shit and the next thing you know..."

"His fuckin brain is fried," John said, cutting-in. "The guy is fuckin gone man. He doesn't even know where he is anymore."

Diane then jumped into the conversation. "I remember running into him a couple of months ago. I was in the parking lot of the Sunrise Mall. I went over to say hello and he didn't even know who I was. I mean I had three classes with the guy in high school."

Mike shook his head. "That's messed up man. Hey, didn't he used to have a crazy older brother that everyone said used to carry a gun?"

"Yeah," replied Fat Joey. "His older brother was the one who got him started on the dust. He used to sell it." At this point, everyone at the table was listening to the story. "His brother's doing hard time now for trying to kill his girlfriend."

Diane waved her hand at Joey in disbelief. "Get outta here."

"No, I'm serious. One night his brother was so fuckin whacked out on dust and whatever else he was taking, he thought his girlfriend was possessed by the devil. No shit – the devil! Anyway, he came home and bashed in her head with a baseball bat." Everyone at the table cringed. "Yeah. He thought he fucking killed her so he panicked and just left her there in the living room."

"Get outta here," replied Diane. "We would have heard about something like that."

Joey leaned back in his chair. "I'm telling you, it's for real. My cousin Pete knows one of his cousins."

"No wait," Dan jumped in. "I think I heard something about that. It happened almost a year ago right?"

While still drinking his beer, Joey nodded his head. "Yeah. I told you, it's for real."

Intrigued, John put down his pint. "So how'd he get caught?"

"One of the neighbors heard screaming and called the cops. When they got there they kicked down the door and found her there bleeding. They put out one of those APBs for him and picked him up at some bar a few hours later."

"Wait a second," John said as he put up a hand in Joey's direction. "You're telling me that he bashed his girlfriend's head in, left her for dead and then went to a bar?"

"I told you man, he was whacked out on dust."

John shook his head in disbelief. "That's fucked up! Man, that is really fucked up."

"What happened to the girl?" Mike asked.

"She had to have a shit load of stitches, but fortunately she didn't have any brain damage or anything."

At that point Brian walked in with Linda Torrelli, who was not from the neighborhood, but still knew everybody. Everyone stood up and greeted them. Linda gave Mike a big hug and said how good it was to see him out. Both Linda and Brian asked how long they had all been waiting for them, in which Dan replied " a couple of pitchers". Then Brian asked what they had all been talking about. Instantly everyone at the table looked at each other with a blank stare.

As the night progressed everyone grew louder, speech started to slur and the atmosphere became more festive. The bar started to get more crowded. The drinks started to go down faster and the one-liners started to come out. After all, it was a Saturday night. Mike played a couple of games of pool for the first time in a while and it showed; Fat Joey, who was a notoriously bad pool player, beat him. Still, Mike was having a good time hanging out with the old crew and catching up. He also found the whole scene amusing. It was the first time he was sober in a bar, other than if he had just arrived. It was also the first time being around his friends when they were drinking and he was not. There was no doubting that a part of Mike wanted to join in on the fun, but another part was just content watching the show. It was interesting to be able to see what it was like being drunk through the eyes of a sober person. Now Mike realized how cops were able to tell that a person was drinking even if they only had a couple of beers. No one was falling down or hanging from the ceiling, but they certainly didn't look or act the same as when they first walked in. There was a change in their voices. Instead of everyone talking one at one time in an orderly fashion, they shouted their words all at once as if they were fighting to be heard over each other. Words slurred into each other and sometimes made little sense. Their appearance also changed. Their faces were flush and their eyes glossy and fighting to stay open. Also, everyone suddenly became more affectionate, hanging on to each other's shoulders as they talked into one another's ears. Like a scientist watching an experiment, Mike just looked on as he drank his club soda.

After a few games of pool and a couple of games of darts, Mike sat back down at the table with Diane, Linda and Kevin. The four of them talked for a while amongst themselves as more and more people started coming into the bar.

"So", Linda yelled, "It must be so good to be out." It was the third time in the last hour that she had asked Mike that same question.

"Yeah," he replied as he did the two other times.

"I'm so sorry about Katie," she yelled back. Suddenly, a dead silence fell at the table as Diane and Kevin shot Linda with a stare. Before that moment everyone had consciously reframed from bringing up Katie's name.

It was something however that Mike knew would have to come up sooner or later. "Yeah," was his only reply as his demeanor instantly changed.

They could see Mike's facial expression morph into an introverted stare. Suddenly the whole atmosphere around the table changed as Diane gave her friend a kick under the table. Linda just looked back, finally realizing what she had said. There was nothing wrong with giving your condolences to some one who had lost a loved one. But this was different. Katie had not died of natural causes or in a car accident. "I'm sorry Mike. I didn't mean to..."

"It's ok." Mike replied before pausing. "She was a good person."

Linda and Diane managed to change the subject, but the damage was already done. Mike could not go back and play another game of pool and have fun with Katie on his mind. Besides, it was probably time for him to leave anyway. "I think I'm gonna head out," he said as he stood up from the table.

Kevin gave his friend a look. "Are you serious man?"

"Yeah. It's getting kind of late and I know my mother's probably worried about me."

Diane, who was still sitting at the table, was worried about Mike. She knew that although he pretended everything was ok, it probably was not. She could see it in his face. "I'll walk home with you Mike." Diane, who still lived with her parents, lived only a few blocks from Mike.

"No that's ok, you don't have to. It looks like things are just getting started over here."

"No that's ok. I was going to head home soon anyway. I've been feeling a little under the weather. I mean unless you want to be alone."

"No, not at all. I guess I could use the company." Mike knew that she was lying about not feeling well. He knew that she was just concerned and although the last thing he wanted was sympathy it did make him feel good. It was good to be cared about. So the two made their rounds saying goodbye to everyone as hugs and handshakes were exchanged all around.

Mike made a special point of saying goodbye to Linda. The last thing he wanted was for her to think that she had offended him. He knew that her comment was meant innocently.

The evening was cool and crisp. Diane wore a thin, leather jacket around her slender frame. Her long black hair waved peacefully in the subtle breeze. The fresh air was a welcomed change to the stagnant smokiness of the bar as their lungs could finally breathe freely again. The two walked slowly, taking their time as they strolled down the residential streets. Even though it was a Saturday night, Massapequa was a quiet community, in contrast to the constant clamor and glaring lights of the big city. Houses shared the landscape with surrounding woods that served as natural playgrounds for neighborhood kids. It did not look like what people think of as New York, especially in 1985. There were no subways, no bodegas on every corner. There was no steady stream of taxicabs. Graffiti didn't litter every storefront and wall.

"I really appreciate you walking home with me," Mike commented.

"It's all right. It was getting too crazy in there anyway. In fact the fresh air feels good."

Mike inhaled a deep breath. "Doesn't it."

"Listen, I'm sorry about Linda back there. She didn't mean any…"

"No it's all right. I mean you all knew Katie." Mike stopped in his tracks as an uneasy silence befell the air. Combing his hand through his hair, Mike stared up towards the starlit sky. Suddenly the memories were too much to bear and began flowing freely as if some one had opened up the floodgates. "It's just that it feels like it was just yesterday," he said after clearing a dry lump from his throat. "It's just not right."

Diane looked at Mike. Seeing him choking back tears made *her* want to cry. It was hard for her to see him that way. She always remembered him being so strong and full of life, always laughing and having a good time. Now here he was in front of her, crippled by his own emotions. As tears began to swell in his eyes, Diane put her hands on his shoulder. "It's not your fault Mike."

"It is my fault." Letting out a deep breath, Mike quickly rubbed away his swelling tears. "It's all my fuckin fault Diane. If it wasn't for me, she'd still be here today." Mike looked back up towards the stars as if he was looking to them for answers. "I fucked up her whole life."

"Now wait a minute Mike," Diane replied, fighting back her own tears. "I knew Katie and she loved you more than anything. You made her happy. I don't know what happened that day, but I know whatever it was, it wasn't your fault."

Mike tried to compose himself. "How can you say that? If I made her so happy, why would she take her own life?" Closing his eyes, Mike began to journey back to that fateful day. "She wouldn't have even been there if it wasn't for me."

"What happened that day? No, never mind – it's none of my business." Diane turned her head, feeling uncomfortable for asking the question.

"No, you have the right to know," Mike quickly countered. "You knew Katie. In fact, if you don't mind, I need to get it off my chest. I need to talk to some one about it. I mean I had to talk about it to my lawyer and the court when it first happened, but that was different. I think I was still in a daze when I went through all that shit."

Diane looked at Mike, who had worn his memories like a crown of thorns. "Sure", she said in a gentle voice, "you can talk to me about it." Although her intentions had not been for Mike to divulge what happened, she had heard different versions and was always curious of the truth. She would soon find out that the old saying was right: be careful what you wish for.

As they walked down the sidewalk, Mike began the story that he had discussed with very few people before. "Well you heard about the whole incident about me getting arrested for driving Fred's car into that house and then me and Katie running away."

"Yeah," Diane quietly replied.

"Well it was a fuckin stupid thing to do. I mean becoming a fugitive because I was maybe facing a year in jail – that's fucking as stupid as it gets. I should have never been drinking and driving anyway." Mike paused for a breath of air. "Anyway, we had this crazy plan about running away together and going to California and living happily ever after. You know, like some fucking crazy fairytale or something. The problem was though, that we only had three hundred bucks between us." Mike looked for a place to sit or a wall to lean against, but there was none, so they continued to walk. "Anyway, I knew this guy Vinny, who I used to get all my coke from. He knew all these crazy fuckin people – I mean real bad dudes. He knew my predicament and supposedly had this big score he was going to let me in on. Katie and I would fly out to Boston to meet this guy and drive two kilos of coke to Chicago. Supposedly the coke was already paid for. The guy in Boston was supposed to give us twenty-five hundred bucks for transporting it plus a half ounce of coke for our troubles. That would be enough we thought to get us to California and find a place to stay."

"Damn," uttered Diane in disbelief. She had heard so many versions of the story; everything from them going to Boston to sell a couple of sheets of acid to them hiding out in Mexico.

"Of course, things didn't go as planned," Mike continued. "In fact they got real fucked up right from the start." Mike spoke almost in a trance as if he was there five years ago, narrating the story as it happened. "We made it to Boston all right, but as soon as we got there and hooked-up with Vinny's people, things started getting real fucked up. We wound up staying at this drug house for a week as the plans kept on changing. First it was that they were just waiting for the coke to get delivered to them. Then it was the guy who we were going to meet got arrested so we had to meet some one else. I started getting real paranoid, as you can imagine. I mean being fucking up on coke for days didn't help. Katie was already heavily into blow. In fact, she was into it way more than I was. Staying at that place was like being in a candy store for her." Mike paused for a moment and shook his head in disgust. "I'll tell ya' Diane, that place was like fucking hell itself.

There were all kinds of characters coming in and out of that place night and day. People had guns and were shooting up in the bathroom. It was fucked up. Katie was popping pills and as if we weren't messed-up enough, we started freebasing. Now bare in mind that neither of us had ever smoked coke before. It was almost too much for me, but Katie loved it. Man she was in bad shape."

Diane grabbed Mike's hand, searching for words of comfort, but there were none.

"Anyway, finally the coke we were waiting for arrived. The difference was that now we would be transporting one kilo and we would be getting paid a thousand bucks instead of the twenty-five hundred. Also, we would have to meet the guy in Albany, not Chicago. And on top of it, we wouldn't get paid until we dropped off the blow. I was pissed of course, but what could we do? By this time we were completely fucked out of our minds – especially Katie. We had been at this place for a week, snorting, freebasin, smoking hash and drinking booze. I mean we hadn't even left the house in a week. This was the first time that we would even be gong outside in the sunlight."

Mike blew out a deep breath and combed his hands though his short black hair. "I'll never know how, but somehow we made it to Albany. Looking back, it's amazing that I was able to drive one block, let alone all that distance. I mean I had been up at that point for about three days straight. Somehow though, we made it without crashing or getting pulled over. It was crazy. There I was on the run from the law with over a kilo of cocaine in the trunk and a thirty-eight that they had given me in case anyone tried to rip us off. I never carried a gun before. What the fuck was I gonna do with a gun? I wasn't going to shoot anybody. I should have thrown that fuckin think over the first bridge we crossed. But I didn't." Mike paused again to catch his breath. "Of course, when we finally got to Albany, things got even more fucked up. The guy we were supposed to meet showed up, but didn't have our money. I immediately called up our connection in Boston, who told me that it was ok. He said to just give him the kilo and he would wire me the money the next day. I was too fucking strung-out to argue with anybody. I could hardly stand up at that point, so Katie and I rented a room in some Motel Six or something like that. We had been given two hundred bucks for traveling expenses. So there we were, in Albany at some roadside motel. We had about twenty bucks left, a half ounce of coke that they had thrown in for our troubles, a loaded gun and a car that I would later find out was stolen."

Diane tried to imagine the situation, but couldn't. She freaked out when she was pulled over for a speeding ticket.

Still walking down the sidewalk, Mike continued his tale of horrors. "I was bad, but Katie was much worse. I mean getting fucked up was nothing new for her, but we're talking about beyond fucked up. Neither of us had ever smoked coke before. I can't believe how out of control things got in only one week." Mike stopped for a second to try to collect his composure. "Now she started to get all fuckin freaked-out. She started saying crazy shit like now we were never gonna get to California and we were going to spend the rest of our lives in jail. It was bad Diane. It was real fucking bad. At that point, she had probably been up for four days straight. I told her I wasn't going to let her have any more coke, and she started freaking out. She started screaming at me; throwing shit at me. I was afraid she was going to make so much noise that some one would call the cops. Still, I couldn't let her have any more. Even as fucked up as I was, I knew that if she smoked any more coke or took any more pills she would have a goddam heart attack or something. But that didn't stop her from trying to get it. After she finally stopped yelling and throwing a tantrum, she started begging and pleading." Mike said in a trembling voice.

Diane also felt sick to her stomach, not believing what she was hearing. She had tried cocaine a couple of times and knew people who had become addicted, but had never seen anything like Mike was describing. Seeing him there, shaking as he walked, his voice crackling, she could almost feel the horror. It was as if Mike was going back to that motel room and was taking her along. Diane couldn't stop thinking of Katie, seeing her there, begging on her knees for drugs. She couldn't stop thinking of the pain Katie must have felt. It was too horrific to even contemplate.

"That evening I was finally able to go to sleep," Mike went on. "I completely passed out. I guess my body just couldn't take it anymore. Anyway, when I finally woke up, it was six o'clock the next evening. Still pretty much out of it, I could smell the stench of cocaine when it's smoked. Oh man," he said shaking his head. "I'll never forget that god-awful smell. It's just a smell you'll never forget. Katie had taken the keys out of my pocket while I was passed out and went into the car where I had locked-up the coke. Apparently, she had made a pipe out of a coke can – I had smashed the glass pipe we had – and stayed up all night again, smoking and snorting the shit. There she was, sitting at this tiny table that was in the room, with an open bottle of pills and a giant zip-loc bag of coke in front of her. She had gotten a bloody nose and had let it just dry up there right on her face. She was a complete fuckin mess. She looked like one of the zombies from Night of the Living Dead." Mike stopped to wipe away a tear that rolled down his cheek. "That was the first time since we had left Long Island that I actually felt scared. I mean I was terrified. I couldn't believe what I was seeing. At first, I jumped out of the bed pissed-off as I could be, but then when I went over to her I started to break down. I couldn't believe that it was Katie in front of me. I knew I had to get a handle on the situation. I told her right after we got the money wired to us from Boston we would drive straight to the airport and buy one-way tickets to California."

Mike stopped and stared up at the night sky, which seemed as infinite as the hole left in his heart by the memories of that dreadful April day. "She liked the sound of that," he continued in an eerily calm voice. "She actually started to come around. At that point it was almost as if everything was going to be ok. It was like we had been sidetracked from our original plan, but we were about to get back on path. I had no clue what we were going to do once we got to California, but I knew we just had to get the hell out of there. Somehow, it was like as long as we got to California, everything was going to be all right. After we sat there and talked about it for a while, I went into the bathroom to take a cold shower to sober up some more." Mike paused to clear a lump in his throat. "That's when all hell broke loose."

Suddenly a haunting silence besieged the night. It seemed as if even the breeze had come to a standstill. As Mike prepared to delve even further into his pain, Diane waited in fear of what was coming next. "As soon as I went into the bathroom and turned the shower on," he hesitantly continued, "I heard someone pounding at the door. It was the cops. Instantly I went into a complete panic. I dashed out of the bathroom and jumped over the bed to where the coke was. Katie was freaking; 'what are we gonna do, what are we gonna do?' She kept screaming. I didn't say anything. I just grabbed the bag and ran back in the bathroom to flush it down the bowl. At this point they're yelling that they're gonna kick down the door. There I was, standing right over the toilet about to dump the whole fucking bag in their and I hesitated – just for a moment. I don't know why. That's when I heard the shot." As the words left his mouth, tears started to pour from his eyes. "Oh what a horrible sound," he cried, putting his hands over his ears. "I just dropped the bag on the floor and stood there, paralyzed. It must have been only for a second, but it felt like eternity. It was like time just stopped. The next thing I know, the cops are in the bathroom cuffing me. Everything was so surreal. Then, when they brought me out of the bathroom, I saw her there." No longer able to contain his emotions, Mike clutched Diane and wept unabashedly into her shoulder. "God Diane," he cried, choking on each word. "She was just laying there on the floor next to the bed with all that blood. Oh god why? Everything was gonna be ok! Why did I have to leave that stupid fucking gun under the mattress? Why didn't I just take the bullets out? I mean I knew she wasn't doing good, but I never thought – I never thought…"

Mike stood there for the next ten minutes holding onto Diane, sobbing as she tried to inconspicuously wipe away her own tears. He held on to her like a child clutching his mother after being awakened from a nightmare. And like a mother, all Diane could do was hold him and say that everything was going to be all right. She was feeling her own pain, her own fear. She couldn't stop thinking about Katie; seeing her there in that motel room lying on the floor. But somehow she found the strength to pull herself together and be there for Mike.

After a while, the two began walking again. Diane, still horrified by the whole story, tried to assure Mike that it was not his fault. The more they walked, the calmer Mike began to feel, until he could breathe slowly again. Finally, they arrived at Mike's house. A now composed Mike stopped and turned to Diane. "I want to thank you for being there for me," he said in a low voice.

"It's o.k. Mike," she softly replied, gently taking hold of his hands.

Feeling embarrassed, Mike bowed his head towards the ground. "I'm sorry I had to put you through that. I mean I haven't seen you for five years and here I am..."

"Mike," she said in a soft, soothing voice, still holding on to his hands, "don't worry about it. This is just between me and you."

"Thanks. I appreciate it," Mike said with a smile. "I can't believe my eyes are probably all red. I mean here I am making sure to be good and not to drink anything and I'm gonna walk in the house with my eyes bloodshot."

"Here," Diane said as she went into her small, black purse and pulled out a bottle of Visine.

Mike thanked her before squeezing a few drops in each eye. "This is so embarrassing."

"I told you Mike, this is just between you and me. Besides, I think it was something that you needed to get off your chest."

After wiping away the excess drops, Mike gave Diane back the small, plastic bottle. "You're right, it was something I needed to get off my chest."

"Are you sure you're going to be all right?" She asked.

Mike shook his head. "Yeah I'm fine. I'll be o.k."

"Well if it's ok, I want to call you when I get home to make sure you're all right."

"Really Diane, you don't have to."

Diane smiled. "Please."

"OK, sure." With that, they gave each other a hug and Diane went on her way.

What a strange path the course of time sometimes takes, Mike thought. Five years ago he had known Diane as a pretty brunette that was fun to drink beers with and hang out. He would have never imagined that five years later he would be baring his soul to her. Life was full of twists and surprises.

Once inside, Mike's mother greeted him, asking whom he had been talking to on the porch. Mike told her and then went into who was at Baxter's; making sure to emphasize that he didn't have anything to drink. However, Betty could tell anyway. Of course Mike did not go into the whole ordeal of how he told Diane about Katie, seeing no need to worry his mother.

After about a half hour, Diane called. Mike took the call in the living room as his mother went upstairs to go to sleep. Sprawled out on the couch, Mike talked to Diane for almost an hour, but didn't go into anymore about Katie. Instead, he talked about how glad he was to be back home with his mother and sister and how he couldn't wait to start making a new life. He told her about the new job he would be starting. Diane talked about what was going on in her life. She talked about her job as a bank teller and how the guy she had been seeing for three years left to take a job offer in Texas. Apparently he had asked her to go with him, but she decided to stay in New York, mainly because of her family.

After the call was finished, Mike lay on the couch and watched TV while waiting for Melissa to come home from a night out with her friends. Like a worried mother he wanted to make sure she arrived back safely, but as the clock persistently moved further into the night, the harder Mike fought to stay awake. Then finally, around one in the morning, Melissa came through the front door. She was surprised to see her brother still up on the couch. "Hey Mike, what are you still doing up? What were you waiting up for me?" She asked half-jokingly.

"No," Mike lied.

"So, whatcha' watching?" She asked as she walked over to the couch.

"Oh, just flipping through the channels," he answered. Mike could immediately tell by his sister's voice and bloodshot eyes that she had been drinking. Sitting-up from his sprawled position, he found himself in a rather perplexed situation. Melissa was a senior in high school and Mike knew that she probably went to parties and had a few drinks on the weekends. It did not mean that she was going to take the same path as he did. Going out on a Friday or Saturday night and drinking a few beers was what most seventeen year-olds did – even if they weren't supposed to. It didn't mean that they were alcoholics or drug addicts. Mike didn't want to overreact. On the other hand however, Mike felt an obligation to say something. This was his little sister, the center of his life. He could live with her going out and having a few drinks at a party, but wanted to make sure that was all she was doing.

Throwing her purse and denim jacket over the couch, Melissa sat down on the loveseat, across from her brother. "So mom told me you went out to meet your buddies. Did you have a good time? Was Fat Joey there? I saw him the other week at the mall and he's still pretty fat," she said laughingly.

"Yeah, it was good to see everyone." Mike looked at his sister, sitting there, wearing jeans and a black holster-top and still could not get over how much she had grown. It was hard for him to get used to. "Missy," he said in a hesitant voice, "I don't want to give you a lecture or anything…"

Melissa's facial expression immediately changed. She didn't know what was coming next, but knew it wasn't going to be fun. Nothing fun ever followed the word 'lecture', no matter how it was phrased. "A lecture about what," she shot back.

"It just looks like you've had a few drinks."

Melissa sat up in the love seat in a defensive manner. "Wait a second," she said, raising her hands. "I don't know if mom put you up to this but..."

"Whoa, whoa, hold up." Mike could tell that Melissa was feeling cornered and that was certainly not his intention. "Mom didn't put me up to anything," he said, making sure that his voice was low enough so that it would not carry upstairs to their mother's room. "You got it all wrong. The last thing I want to do is give you the third degree." Melissa appeared to ease her defenses a little. "Maybe what I said came out wrong. Listen, I don't even know if you've had anything to drink. For all I know you've been at Allison's watching TV. That's not the point."

"So what is the point?"

"All I'm tryin to say is that there's nothing wrong with going out to a party on the weekends and blowing off some steam. I don't care if you go out and have a few beers. I know that that's what everyone does. Mom doesn't have to know anything. I mean, if you don't drink at all, that's great, but if you decide to have a few drinks every now and then, it's no big deal. I just wanna make sure you're careful that's all. I want to make sure you don't jump in the car with anyone who's been drinking, or god forbid ever get behind the wheel yourself. I also just want you to know that there are some fucked-up people out there that try to get girls drunk just so they can... Well, I mean I just care about what happens to you, that's all."

Melissa eased her rigid posture and sat back in the seat. "I know," she said in a more relaxed voice. "I was just out with Allison and some other girls at this party. I only had a few..."

Mike stopped her from going further. "Listen, you don't need to tell me every little thing. I don't need to know who you're with or where you are. I know you know what you're doing and I know you'll make the right choices."

Melissa smiled as she moved over to where Mike was sitting. "You know what I think?"

"No."

"I think I'm lucky to have a brother like you."

"Just be careful," he whispered in her ears.

Chapter 3

STARTING OVER

That Monday Mike started his job at the moving company. He had made arrangements to ride to work with John, who also lived in the neighborhood. Mike would walk to the neighborhood deli where John picked him up and then dropped him off after their day was done. Work was a new experience for Mike, but he was ready to tackle it head on. He had been given various responsibilities in prison, like working in the mess hall or laundry room, but they were only for a few hours a day and were not always available. In prison, having a job was actually something that was sought after. It meant certain liberties and time away from your cell. With thousands of inmates, there were not enough jobs for everyone, so they usually went to prisoners who were there longer or had a higher standing on the social totem pole. During his later years, Mike was able to work a few days a week in the cafeteria. It was a welcomed antidote for being locked in a cell going stir crazy, but it was not the same as having a full time job on the outside.

Getting a real job was something that Mike had looked forward to for quite some time. It was a big piece to the puzzle that he needed to put together in order to start over. It was a good feeling, not only to collect a paycheck, but also to feel productive. It was sense of accomplishment; something that Mike had lacked all his life. To be able to get up in the morning and put in a hard day's work was fulfilling. For some one that never knew what that had felt like, it was almost exciting. Moving furniture was not a career and certainly not something that most people would think of as glamorous, but considering the circumstances it was not so bad. Mike was happy doing what he was doing. Maybe it was just that it was new to him, but he picked-up up each box and loaded it onto the truck with a sense of enthusiasm. Although a few of the guys he worked with were actually more muscular, they would tire out long before him. Sometimes they would laugh at his energy and pride. From when he first punched in to when he left for the day, Mike was like a man on a mission.

Of course, Mike's work ethics also went over well with his boss, Dave. Mike had promised Dave that he would not be sorry for hiring him and so far, it was a promise that was being kept. Dave was very pleased with his new employee. This however, did not mean that Mike was a brownnoser. It was gratifying to be recognized by the boss, but it was not the reason for the way he worked. Mike was not out to prove he was a better worker than anyone else or to make anyone else look bad. In fact, he always made it a point of telling Dave that the other guys on the crew worked just as hard as he did, even if they had not. Mike had learned in prison that although not everyone is always going to like you, it was important to get along with people that you were going to see everyday. Mike had learned over the years how to be a team player and it was something that didn't go unnoticed by his co-workers. There was usually a crew of three men to a job and each man was typically assigned to the same crew so not getting along could have caused problems. Fortunately though, Mike seemed to interact well with not only in his crew, but everyone else in the small company as well. If one of the guys was tired, instead of getting on his back, Mike would pick up the slack. On the other hand, Mike was not going to put himself in a situation where he was going to be taken advantage. Luckily though, that situation never presented itself. In fact the other guys on the crew would have been more than happy to help Mike if he needed it. They appreciated what he brought to the table and enjoyed not only his work ethic, but also his personality and dry sense of humor.

There were also other perks that came along with the job. Since they were in the moving business, they inevitably moved around a lot. Just about every day was a new scene, a new place. Not having to go to the same office or desk every single day was refreshing, especially for someone who had never left the same place for five years. Although most of the time was spent at people's houses loading and unloading the truck, a portion of time was spent driving from place to place. Though they only serviced New York State, they had jobs all along Long Island and sometimes even upstate.

Mike was also able to meet different people all the time. Besides the people he worked with, it was never the same faces. Each house they moved meant new people to meet. Mike made it a point to take time to talk to all of them. The first thing he would do was introduce himself and his crew. Then he tried to calm their worries about having their belongings moved. Mike knew they were not just moving pieces of furniture, but also items with sentimental value and sometimes, family heirlooms. He gave what is usually a nerve-wrecking experience a personal touch and the customers appreciated it.

Things were also going well at home. Mike was usually home from work no later than 6:00 pm and although some days he would go to the gym for an hour, there was still time to spend with his mother and sister. Though some nights Melissa went out with her friends, Mike and Betty would always eat dinner together. Everything was coming together as he had planned - as he had hoped for. They were finally a family again.

Mike also continued to see Diane. First it was just on the telephone then he invited her over for dinner. From there, they started spending more and more time together. Yet although they enjoyed each other's company, it was more of a friendship than anything else. They were attracted to each other, but neither one knew how the other felt. There was also another reason that things did not progress at first. Although they didn't talk about it, both felt that Katie's memories and what happened to her were still too fresh in Mike's mind. They both secretly felt a sense guilt that kept them from letting their relationship evolve. However, there was definitely a connection. Mike felt comfortable enough with Diane to be able to talk to her about anything and she felt the same way about him. Sometimes they would talk for hours on the phone at night until one of them could no longer stay awake. They talked about life. They talked about current events. They listened to each other's opinions and points of view. Mike talked about Melissa and how proud he was of her. Diane talked about things that were going on in her life. There was never a shortage of words or an awkward moment. Everything just seemed to flow so naturally.

Both Betty and Melissa were happy to see Mike spending time with Diane. They both had good impressions of her and above all, could see that it made him happy. In fact they thought Diane was exactly what Mike needed. She had a good job and seemed to have a good head on her shoulders. They knew what happened to Katie had been traumatic for Mike, but also knew that he had to get on with his life. Even if it was just a friendship, his mother and sister were encouraged to see that he was able to get close and be comfortable with some one else.

Of course, Mike would not have continued to spend time with Diane if she did not get along with his mother and especially Melissa. Luckily though, she enjoyed their company. She particularly enjoyed talking to Melissa. Sometimes when Diane came over the two would sit on the couch and talk about school or boys. On a few occasions, Mike and Diane took Melissa to a movie with them or out to eat.

Everything seemed to be going as planned. Mike really felt like he was finally getting on with his life. He had learned the hard way that freedom and life were not things to take for granted and made sure to remind himself of that everyday.

Mike also visited his parole officer. Since Mike was not what they considered to be a "high risk" such as a sex offender or murdered, the visits would be infrequent and the terms of his parole were not stringent. For the most part, as long as he was looking for a job and keeping out of trouble, there would be no problems.

Mike's parole officer introduced himself with a firm handshake. "How are you doing Mike? My name's Nick Johnson."

Having no reason to feel nervous, Mike responded back confidently. "How are you doing Mr. Johnson?"

"OK, but please, you can call me Nick."

He looked pretty much like Mike had expected. He was wearing a cheap suit and tie and a shirt that obviously didn't like to get ironed. Nick was a skinny man, about 5'7", with a thinly, reseeding hairline and just had that look of being a state employee. "So Michael," he said thumbing though a pile of disorganized papers on his desk. "Lets see – it says here you were released on September twelfth."

"That's right."

From the curious look on his face, it seemed as if Nick was reading Mike's rap sheet for the first time. "Your original sentence was eleven years and you were paroled after five."

"That's right," Mike responded again.

With eyeglasses hanging on the bottom of his nose, Mr. Johnson thumbed through the pages. "It looks like you entered a plea agreement with the DA."

"Yeah, my attorney said that if we went to trial and lost I could be looking at thirty-five years or even more."

Mr. Johnson shook his head. "He was right. It looks like you were able to get some of the most serious charges reduced."

His parole officer was right. One of the original charges they tried to pin on Mike was kidnapping, because Katie was under eighteen. Another one was trafficking of illegal narcotics. As part of his plea agreement the state dropped the kidnapping charge and reduced the trafficking to possession. However, after talking to inmates over the years, Mike learned that there was probably no way some of the original charges would have stood-up in court and that he should have received a better deal. In fact looking back, Mike felt shafted. Mike met one guy on the inside that was caught with two kilos of cocaine and was sentenced to the same time he was. There were guys doing less time for manslaughter. His cellmate was doing ten years for killing someone in a bar fight. Some guys were doing five years for rape and some of them even had previous records. Of course, the difference was that many of them had good attorneys. Mike, who didn't have thousands of dollars to throw at a lawyer, was represented by a public defender. Over the years, after hearing countless stories, Mike learned how the system worked. Public defense attorneys were not there to prove anyone's guilt or innocence. They were there to ensure the quickest conclusion. Their caseload was way to overwhelming to provide each defendant the personal care and commitment they needed. It was a numbers game and they just simply didn't have the time to tend to each client as a personal defense attorney would.

However the public defenders were not the only ones playing a numbers game. So were the Assistant District Attorneys. Their job was also to ensure the quickest conclusion possible for each case. Sure, they had unlimited resources, but like the public defenders, they too were overloaded and simply didn't have the time. Except for the rare sensational cases that might bring them public spotlight, the last thing they wanted to do was go to trail. It was too involved and meant spending time that they didn't have. In Mike's case, the prosecutor knew that proving his guilt in a trial on some of the charges would be difficult. In fact, the DA was probably ready to go even lower on the deal, maybe taken another year or two off. However, he also knew that Mike's attorney didn't want to go to trial either. It was a game of chicken and Mike's lawyer blinked first. At the time though, Mike did not know any better and jumped on the deal. He was scared and would have done anything his lawyer told him to do.

Mr. Johnson used his finger to guide his eyes down the page. "Hmm", he mumbled, "what's these charges that have a different date on them; driving while intoxicated, possession of marijuana..."

"That was the whole reason I went on the run in the first place," Mike calmly replied.

His parole officer, having obviously not read through Mike's file before – at least not thoroughly – had no idea what Mike was talking about. He didn't know the whole story and seemed like he didn't want to either. "Well, the Parole Board was convinced that you should be released, so I don't see any reason to go through all the charges and what happened when and why."

Mike didn't respond, but was glad to hear that he was not going to rehash the whole incident.

"My only concern is that you're adhering to the terms of your parole." With that, Mr. Johnson closed the file and leaned back in the chair. "So Michael, have you been looking for work?"

"Well actually I was able to find a job five days after I got out. It's working for a moving company. Here, I have a pay-stub," Mike said as he pulled the stub out of his jacket pocket.

Mr. Johnson looked it over and seemed rather surprised. Most of the people he dealt with didn't find jobs for months or lied about their employment. "Well Mike, I must say, I'm pretty impressed that you were able to find something so soon. Good for you. Hopefully it's a step in the right direction."

"I know it is," Mike jumped in. "I mean I'm sure you probably hear this all the time, but I really feel that I've been able to turn things around. I mean I actually feel like a different person."

Mr. Johnson looked through his sagging glasses at the twenty-four year old parolee. Mike did not look like the people with which he usually dealt. There was something about him that just seemed different. He looked confident. He was clean-shaven and didn't have that nervous look in his eyes. "So tell me Michael, what else have you been doing with your time?"

"Well, I've been spending a lot of time at home with my mother and sister. You know when I was locked-up I had a lot of time to think about things, like how much I had taken my family for granted. I realized how much my actions didn't only affect me, but hurt them. My father died when I was fifteen so I was really left to be the man in the house. I guess I didn't do too good of a job at that."

Rubbing his chin, Mr. Johnson analyzed Mike's comments. "So now you feel like you have to make up for it – all those years you spent out partying and then when you were locked-up."

Still relaxed, Mike shook his head. "Yeah. Yeah, I do. I felt really guilty that I couldn't be there for them. I still feel guilty about it. I especially feel bad about not being there for my sister."

"How old is your sister?"

"Melissa, she's seventeen. She had to go through the most difficult years without having a father figure – without having an older brother." Mike paused for a second. "It must have been real hard on her."

"You know Mike, there's a lot of girls that grow up without a father or older brother."

"I know."

Suddenly Mr. Johnson started sounding more like a psychologist than a parole officer. "Maybe it's just that you're afraid that she will make some of the same mistakes you have."

"Yeah, you know I guess that could be part of it. But believe me, she's a lot smarter than I was. She's got a good head on her shoulders."

Nick gave a rare smile. "Well that's good to hear."

"In fact, she's a real smart kid," Mike continued. "She always got good grades and I'm making sure she's going to college."

Mr. Johnson let out a passing laugh. "Well don't you think that might be her decision?"

"She knows she has to go to college to get a good job. But even if she has other plans, I don't care; she's going to college. In fact, I'm thinking about getting a second job so I can save up money to help with her tuition. She's going to a good school. My sister's not going to piss away her life like I did."

"Well Mike, that's a very noble cause," Nick replied as he removed his eyeglasses. "I know you care about your sister and I think that shows a lot of character about you, but you can't live your whole life through her. You have to think about your own future as well. There's no doubt that you made some very bad decisions along the way, but you haven't pissed your whole life away yet. I mean you are only twenty-four. That's more than young enough to start over again. Maybe you should think about taking some college classes yourself."

Mike shook his head. "Yeah, I know. I just want to make sure that I look out for my sister."

"I understand."

The two talked a little longer before Mr. Johnson shook Mike's hand and told him to keep up the good work. They both walked away from their meeting with a positive feeling. Mr. Johnson was satisfied that Mike had found a job and seemed to be staying out of trouble. He was also pleased that Mike was a departure from the typical scum with which he was used to dealing. Mike was just happy that his parole officer was satisfied.

Later that night, Mike talked to Melissa about her future. He had asked about her plans a few times already since coming home, but mostly just in passing. Like many teenagers, Melissa was still uncertain what career she wanted to pursue. She had always been interested in the stars and entertained notions about being an astronomer, but knew that there were not a lot of job opportunities for professional astronomers. Melissa also went off and on about being a teacher. , For the most part Mike didn't like the idea. It was not that he had anything against teachers. In fact, he saw them as people that should be looked up to. It was just that he had higher aspirations for his sister. He knew that most teachers didn't get paid well and above all, he wanted it so Melissa would never have to struggle. It was not necessarily that he wanted her to be rich. It was more that she would always be well taken care of. He wanted it so Melissa would never have to depend on anyone else, which ruled out the rich husband idea. Mike wanted her to become a doctor or lawyer. He wanted her to have a career where she would always be independently secure.

        As October came to a close, things continued going well for Mike. It had only been a little over a month since he had been released from prison, but it felt more like a year to him. Time seemed like it was going in slow motion – which by no means was that a bad thing. Mike was enjoying life like he never had before. His job was going well. He started to see even more of Diane. He continued doing things with Melissa – although she started spending a little more time with her friends. It was a good time and things felt like they were only going to get better.

        On Betty's birthday, October 20th, Mike treated her and Melissa to dinner at an expensive Italian restaurant in the city. Although most people think of Manhattan as New York, many people that live in Long Island hardly ever went there, the Patterson's included. For them, going into the city was like going to a different state. However, it was a special occasion. They all put on their best clothes. Mike even donned a suit and tie that he had bought especially for the occasion. Mike saved most of the money he made, but he had not celebrated his mother's birthday in over six years and wanted it to be special. He told them to order whatever they wanted. At first Betty was worried about it being too expensive, but finally gave in to Mike's persistence that she just relax and have a good time. They all had a great time.

Chapter 4

THINGS TO COME

Halloween, Mike had plans with Diane to take her nine year-old niece trick-or-treating. He met Diane at her house, but waited outside. Diane's parents did not approve of their daughter being with an ex-con. They couldn't care less about all the talk their daughter was giving them about him being a new person and turning over a new leaf. They were not impressed by the fact that he was working or that he loved his mother and sister. It bothered Diane more than it did Mike. He knew exactly where they were coming from. The fact was that he would not want his daughter hanging out with some guy that had been in prison. So he kept telling Diane not to worry about it, that it didn't really bother him. Diane said that she told her parents she was twenty-four years old and would hang out with whomever the fuck she wanted.

"Oh, is this Mary?" Mike asked as Diane walked out of the house holding her niece's hand.

"Yeah," Diane answered with a smile.

Mike bent down to Mary's level. "You must be Princess Lea."

"Yeah," she replied in a soft, shy voice.

Mike stood back up and looked at Diane. "She looks so cute. How'd you get her hair like that?"

"I'm not supposed to look cute," Her niece shot back. "Little girls are cute. Princess Lea is a woman."

"On you're right, you're right. I'm sorry."

"Mary," Diane said with a stern voice as she looked down at her niece.

"No, no, that's ok. She's right. Princess Lea is a woman – and a very important woman at that. The whole fate of the galaxy depends on her. It won't happen again your highness," Mike said with a smile. "Hey look, I think I have something for you."

From behind his back, Mike pulled out a plastic toy and handed it to Mary. "No way," she yelled as her eyes lit up. "It's a light saber. Look Aunt Diane it's a light saber. It's one of the cool ones too, that lights-up."

Diane gave Mike a look as if to say he shouldn't have. "Well what do you say Mary?"

"Thank you."

"No problem," Mike replied, happy to see that she was getting so much enjoyment out of it. "Now I know Princess Lea doesn't usually carry a light saber, but you never know if you'll need one." Mike crouched back down to Mary's level. "I hear Darth Vader might be walking around the neighborhood tonight."

"Well we'll take care of him. But how did you know what I was going to be?"

Mike rolled his eyes. "Let's just say a little bird told me."

The three then walked around the neighborhood going from door to door, passing a sea of other little trick-or-treaters along the way. As any child would on Halloween, Mary wore a permanent smile from ear to ear. Every door was a new adventure. Every time she opened the pillowcase that she used as a sack, a new treat was thrown in. It was Halloween the way it was meant to be. The temperature was mild and the sky was clear. A bright, almost-full moon even added to the spookiness of the night. Kids flooded the streets in elaborate costumes. At one point some older kids ran down the street, probably running from a house they had just egged or from some one they had sprayed with shaving cream.

It reminded Mike of when he was a child, back when his father was still alive. Like most kids, Mike used to wait all year for Halloween. After all, for a kid, it was the most festive night of the year. He remembered helping his father decorate the house by putting cobwebs and jack-o'-lanterns by the windows. They used to hang rubber bats on the tree in the front yard and a fake tombstone by the walkway. His father always seemed to have as much fun as his son. Each year they tried to come up with new ways to scare the trick-or-treaters. One year his father even put in a kit that made the doorbell sound like a woman screaming. That was a good trick, Mike thought to himself as he laughed.

There was also the mischief. For the older kids, it was not Halloween unless you engaged in some mischief. Mike was of course, no exception. At the age of ten, he started going trick-or-treating on his own. He would meet-up with the other kids from the neighborhood – some of whom he was still friends with – and egg or teepee houses. Mike remembered what a rush they used to get. Back then, that was their drug; that was how they satisfied their adrenaline. There was nothing malicious about it. It was just boys being boys. It was what you did when you became too old and bored with going door-to-door for candy.

Walking from house to house with Diane and her niece, Mike remembered what a good time he used to have. His troubles had clouded those joyful memories for so long. A lot had happened since those days, but there he was, nearly fifteen years later enjoying Halloween – enjoying life – once again.

As they walked down one of the streets, Mike noticed Melissa's best friend Allison standing in her driveway with another girl. "Hey, that's my sister's friend."

"Who," asked Diane?

"The one wearing the cow girl costume, next to the nun," he said as he began walking towards them. "Hey Allison," Mike shouted.

Allison turned to look. "Oh hey Mike, what are you doin? I like your costume."

"Very funny," He answered back. Mike was not wearing a costume. As they walked up to the two teenagers, Mike noticed how elaborate Allison's costume was: everything from the hat, to boots with spurs, to the realistic looking guns draped around her slender waist. "Where's the rodeo," Mike asked, to which she simply replied with a sarcastic smile.

Allison then turned her attention to Mary. "Ahh, who's this?"

"Oh Allison, this is Diane and this is her niece Mary. We're taking her around the neighborhood trick-or-treating."

"Well hello Mary, or should I say Princess Lea?" Mary said hello back in her usual shy voice.

Diane extended her hand towards Melissa's friend. "Hi Allison, It's nice to meet you."

"So you're the one that Mike's always talking to on the phone."

"Yeah, that's me."

Allison then introduced her friend, Ginger, who was dressed like a nun. Mike asked where was Melissa. "We're going to meet up with her later," Allison responded. "We're going to a costume party."

"Well, just be careful," Mike replied. "And don't shoot anybody with those guns of yours."

Just then a car pulled up with its muffler roaring and stereo blasting. "We gotta go Mike, our ride's here."

Mike looked at the brown Chevrolet with two derelicts in the front seat. They were older, maybe even Mike's age and had a greasy, rugged look to them. One had long hair and a leather jacket with an upside down cross sown onto the sleeve. The other had short hair and earrings, which from Mike's distance, looked like silver skulls. "That's your ride?" He asked in the voice of a concerned father.

"Don't worry, that's just their costumes," she replied jokingly. "No seriously, they know Ginger's older brother and they're just giving us a ride. They're not even going to stay at the party."

"C'mon," the driver shouted out the window with the stereo still blaring.

"Alright, hold on," Ginger hollered back.

"Well, it was nice meeting you Diane," Allison said as she shook her hand again. "It was nice meeting you too Mary."

After finishing their quick goodbyes, Allison and Ginger jumped in the car as it sped off, roaring down the residential street. Diane didn't like the look of the guys either and thought that Allison was probably lying about who they were, but didn't say anything to Mike, seeing no need to make him more paranoid than he was already.

Mike and Diane walked Mary around the neighborhood for another half hour, until she could not fit any more candy in the pillow case. Besides, she was anxious to finally get inside and start going through the candy for which she had worked so hard. When they reached the house, Diane told Mike to wait while she put Mary inside. Before doing so though, Mike told Mary what a pleasure it was meeting her and asked if she had a good time.

"I did," she excitedly replied. "I can't believe how much candy I got. And thank you for the light saber."

"Your welcome," Mike replied with a smile. He then waved goodbye as Diane led Mary into the house.

After about ten minutes, Diane walked back out. "C'mon, I'll walk you home," she said.

"Don't you have to watch Mary?"

"It's ok, my parents are home. They'll watch her for a while."

So the two began casually strolling down the block. "When's your sister gonna pick up Mary?"

"She's gonna spend the night and then my sister will pick her up in the morning. Her and her husband went to some costume party with people from his work. Hey, I want to thank you for going with me tonight."

"Ah, it was no problem. I had a good time."

Out of nowhere, Diane put her hands around Mike's shoulders and kissed him on the lips. However, almost immediately she pulled away. "I'm sorry."

"Sorry for what."

"I just don't want to rush you. I know you've been through a lot."

Mike gently grabbed both her arms. "No Diane, you don't understand, I've been wanting to kiss you for the longest time." Diane lifted her head as their lips locked together in a long passionate embrace.

The two spent the rest of the night walking around the neighborhood, holding hands and exchanging kisses. With butterflies in their stomach they told each other the feelings they had been previously kept inside. For at least a moment, all was perfect. There was nothing else besides the two of them. There was no other night besides that very night. As they finally parted ways, there was no doubting that what they had just experienced together was only a beginning.

That following Friday after work, Mike and John went to Baxter's to meet up with Brian. It was the first either of them would be able to talk to Brian since he was arrested for a DWI on Halloween night. Up to then they had only heard about it through the grapevine.

Still in their work clothes, they walked in to see Brian already at the bar drinking a beer. "Hey guys, what's up?" Brian said as he walked over to them with a half-empty pint.

"Sorry we're late man," John replied, noticing that it probably was not Brian's first beer. "We got held-up at work."

Mike gave a sarcastic smile. "He means *he* got held up at work. Me and my guys were done over an hour ago."

"Yeah, well you guys didn't have to move a house in fuckin' Patchogue," John replied while taking off his coat. "Dam man, that place is fucking out there."

Mike wasn't through giving it to his friend. "I don't know. I think our crew would have had that thing finished up by three. You guys need to eat some Wheaties or something."

"What do ya' guys bust each other's balls all day."

Mike and John looked at each other and laughed. Busting each other's chops had become a pastime at work. Since they worked on two different crews, they would always taunt each other about whose group was better. It was healthy competition that all the guys at the company were in on. The main motivation for getting a job done expediently had become not wanting to hear the other guys talk crap. It was all in the name of fun, but sometimes it could get brutal. If someone could tell that it was getting to you, they would ride you that much harder. Then God forbid if you ever broke a piece of furniture; you better have kept it to yourself, because that was something no one would ever let you live down.

After ordering a pitcher of beer, the three grabbed a table. It was a usual busy Friday after work crowd, but they always managed to get a table. It was as if they had one reserved with their names on it; and why not, they had been pumping money into the place for long enough.

It was only the third time since Mike was out that he was drinking a beer. However, like the two previous occasions, he was not drinking to get drunk. He had succumbed to the fact that although he never wanted to go back to the way he was, he probably wasn't going to live the rest of his life without ever drinking a beer again.

"So Brian man, I can't believe what happened," John said, shaking his head. "That really sucks man."

Brian gave a frustrated look. "You're telling me."

"How the fuck did they pull you over?" John asked as he poured himself a fresh one.

"They followed me out of O'Malley's. Do you believe that shit, they were waiting in the parking lot for people to come out of the bar and into their cars so they could catch them drive away."

"O'Malley's," John practically yelled. "That place is in fucking Huntington. How many times do I gotta tell you not to be drinking in driving around there! Those Huntington cops don't fuck around!"

Brian gave him a "don't-fucking-start" look. He knew John had given him that very advice on a number of occasions. "It turns out that my registration was expired. Can you believe that fucking shit?"

"Were you that drunk?" Mike asked.

Brian laughed. "Man, I was fucking hammered. I had been drinking Jack and coke and beers all night. One of the guys we were with kept on buying rounds of shots. I was fucked up. We started drinking at Patty's house at five o'clock and I already had a good buzz on by the time we got to the bar." Brian paused to take another swig of beer. "By the time I left the bar around two o'clock I was shit faced. When the cop pulled me over I practically stumbled out of the fucking car."

It wasn't a funny matter, but John and Mike couldn't help but laugh. For some reason they both had a visual of the Brian crawling out of the car. "You didn't have any weed on you did you?" John asked.

"No, but I had just finished smoking a joint in the bathroom with some bitches. That's another reason why I was so fucked up. Before that, I hadn't smoked any weed in a couple of months. I mean I don't smoke that shit all the time like I used to."

Suddenly John was getting a very different visual. "You were smoking weed in the bathroom of the bar with girls?"

"Yeah man, it was a pretty fucked up place. We should all go there sometime. I don't know, maybe it's just that it was Halloween, but it got pretty crazy over there."

Although the girls in the bathroom seemed intriguing, Mike was more interested in his friend's problems. "But this is your first offense right?"

"Yeah. I mean believe it or not I've never even been arrested before."

"That is amazing," John shot back putting in his two cents.

Brian gave a frustrated pout. "I have to appear in court next week."

"If it's your first offense, don't worry man. You'll probably just get a slap on the wrist." Mike was not just trying to make Brian feel better, he was telling the truth. In the mid 1980s, police had really not yet started the crackdown on drunk drivers the way they would in the years to come. In fact back then even for your second offense you probably were not going to spend any time in jail. "I mean they didn't cite you for anything else did they? You didn't have anything else on you?"

"No, all I got was a ticket for driving while intoxicated. But I know I'll at least get my drivers license suspended. I work in fucking Queens."

"So, you take the train to work. It'll work out," John said trying to re-assure his friend.

The three ordered another pitcher and talked some more about Brian's predicament. Brian gave them all the details, like who else was there that night and where he was going. He also told them about the lawyer that his parents hired. In the midst of their conversation, Mike noticed Melissa's boyfriend Tom walk into the bar with some other guy. Mike knew that Tom was only eighteen years old, but Baxter's was notorious for catering to an underage crowd. Yet he was still surprised to see him there. Mike leaned over the table towards John and Brian and broke-up their conversation. "Hey, that's my sister's boyfriend," he said, pointing Tom out.

"Melissa's going out with that guy?" Brian said in a tone that implied she could have done much better.

"Hey Tom!" Mike shouted across the bar. "Tom!"

Finally, after three tries, he was able to get Tom's attention. Yet for some reason, Tom didn't exactly look happy to see Mike. After whispering something to the guy he was with, Tom walked over to their table with a look on his face that a kid gets when he's been called to the principle's office. "Hey Mike," he then said in a rather drab voice.

Mike stood-up and shook his hand and pulled out a chair for him. "What are you doing here?"

"Me and my buddy just came here to meet someone, then we're going to split."

"Hey listen, I don't care if you drink a couple beers. I used to come in here all the time with my fake ID. Just don't be driving around my sister if you've been drinking." Mike then introduced him to Brian and John. "This here is Tom. He's going out with Melissa."

"Haven't you heard" Tom asked with a confused look. "Melissa dumped me."

Instantly, Mike's facial expression changed. "When did that happen?" He asked almost angrily.

"Just this last week."

"What the hell happened?" Mike knew that they had been seeing each other for over a year and was surprised that Melissa had not said anything about it.

"I guess she just wants to be with other people," Tom replied in a spiteful tone.

John and Brian leaned back in their chairs as they saw Mike's face slowly start to turn red. There seemed to be a certain insinuation about what Tom said. Mike may have liked Tom, but there was no leeway for anybody when it came to Melissa. "What does that mean," Mike barked back.

"Mike, I know you have this picture of Melissa as just this sweet, little innocent girl..."

Fortunately for Tom, John interjected before Mike had a chance to reach over the table and choke him. "Hey Mike, the kid's just upset. Wouldn't you be?" He then gave Tom a look that asked if he was crazy.

"Listen, I loved Melissa. I still do, believe me."

That seemed to diffuse the growing tension at least for the moment. Mike actually leaned back in his seat and let out a breath. Then, the waitress came over with the beer. "Here kid, have a beer." Brian filled up a mug and slid it over to Tom hoping that it would knock some more sense into him.

Tom practically downed the whole beer in one gulp, but the end result was not what Brian had hoped. Instead of becoming more sensible,

Tom became braver. "All I'm tryin' to say is that you think of Melissa as your baby sister so much that maybe you can't see what's really going on."

Mike's entire body tensed up in a combustible ball of rage. "And what exactly is going on Tom?" He asked in a seething voice as the veins in his neck slowly started to appear one by one.

"Look, don't take this the wrong way, but as good a person as Melissa is – and she is – it doesn't mean that she's immune to all the temptations that are out there."

"Listen, I know Missy's no angel. I know she goes out on the weekends and has some beers."

Tom polished off the rest of his bravery juice. "I'm not talking about going out and having a few drinks. There's no problem with that. But if you think that's all Melissa is doing…"

Mike cut Tom off before he could finish the sentence. "What are you trying to say?"

"All I know is that over the summer, Melissa started hanging out with a different crowd. I mean me and my friends like to party too, but some of the people she's hanging around with are into some bad shit."

John and Brian both shook their heads. Was there no stopping this kid? Mike had been a calm guy since being released, but they knew his blood was boiling. They could see him start to shudder like a volcano that was ready to explode. "What the hell is that supposed to mean?" Mike lashed out.

"Listen, I'll I'm saying is that she started getting a little heavier into the partying over the summer and ever since the school year began, she's just been spending more and more time with people – people that we never used to hang out with. I told her they're bad news, but she didn't want to listen. I mean, like I said, I like to party too, but I don't want anything to do with the crowd she's hanging out with. We had a big fight about. I told her that these guys were just going to try to use her. She told me that she didn't need me around anymore telling her what to do. She said that I was just trying to stop her from having fun. Now I've got to think about her hanging around those guys doing god knows what."

Mike clenched his fists. "And what would that be?" he barked at Tom. The volcano was about to explode.

Tom however, couldn't seem to keep his mouth shut. "C'mon man," he continued, "the guys I'm talking about – no girls hang out with them unless…"

That was it. Mike smashed his fists down in rage, breaking the round wooden table in half as beer flew everywhere. Like a bomb falling out of the sky, everyone in the bar stopped what they were doing and turned to look. "Unless What?" Mike yelled back as he stood up, lunging towards a now petrified Tom.

"You better get him the hell out of here," Brian said, referring to Mike. He looked down at the splintered table, glass and beer all over the floor and knew that they could not just smile about it and get on with the evening. The bar was full with a Friday after work crowd. People standing and sitting at tables next to them were doused in beer. It was a complete spectacle. None of the neighborhood bars had bouncers, but Brian knew there was a possibility that one of the bartenders already called the cops and that was the last thing that Mike needed. Brian also knew they had to get Mike away from Tom before he killed the poor kid.

"Unless fucking what!" Mike screamed again as he reached for Tom's neck.

"C'mon Mike, let's get out of here." John held onto Mike's arms with both hands, knowing however, that if Mike really wanted to get at Tom he would not be able to hold him back. "C'mon man, you don't need any trouble." With every eye in the bar peering at them, John managed to slowly pushed Mike towards the door, like a bodyguard trying to whisk a celebrity through a crowd.

As they neared the door, Brian gave Tom a firm slap on the back of the head. "What the fuck did you do that for?"

"I didn't know he was going to go ballistic," Tom replied, trying to catch his breath, still afraid that Mike was going to run back in and attack him.

Brian just gave him a look. "I don't know what the fuck is wrong with you, but you should know how Mike is about his sister."

"Hey listen, the only reason I told him was because I care about her too. Maybe he can talk some sense into her."

Standing on top of the shattered beer glasses and sea of spilt beer, Brian shook his head. "Talk some sense into her. You're lucky if he doesn't find these guys she's hanging out with and kill 'em."

Once outside, John walked Mike across the parking lot trying to calm him down. "Listen man, the guy probably doesn't know what the hell he's talking about."

Mike wasn't listening to a word his friend was saying. "John, if I find out some one's been giving my sister drugs I will find them and I will kill them. I will fuck them up so bad that their ancestors will feel it. I fucking mean it."

"Just calm down a little," he said with his hand still on the back of Mike's shoulder. "Just take a deep breath man. You're gonna fuckin give yourself a heart attack or something."

Trying to slow down his breathing, Mike turned to Brian. "I gotta go home man."

"Whoa, whoa, wait just a minute. First you gotta calm down a little before you go home." John had a vision of Mike marching through the front door and storming into Melissa's room. John knew no good was going to come out of that scenario, so he tried to persuade Mike into simmering down. "Listen man, you don't want to go there and say or do something you might regret."

Mike turned and broke free from John's hand, which was still on his back. "I'm going fucking home!"

"I'm telling you man, I'm not gonna let you go home like this."

Mike went right up into John's face. "Not gonna let me?"

"Look at you. You're ready to kick my ass and I'm your friend. I'm just trying to help you out Mike."

Suddenly, Mike realized that Brian was right and apologized for getting in his face. The two then walked around the shopping center for a while as Mike cooled down. However they made sure not too walk to close to Baxter's just in case somebody had called the police. The more they walked the more Mike returned to normal. John tried to assure him that Melissa was a smart girl and that there were two sides to every story. After about a half hour, John could see that Mike had calmed down enough to go back home. As they parted, John left him with a few more words of assurance that Melissa knew what she was doing.

Along the way home, Mike kept telling himself to remain calm when talking to his sister. He knew John had been a hundred percent correct about not saying or doing anything when you're upset. However when approaching the house, Mike found it harder to keep his cool – yet somehow managed to do it. As he walked through the door, he could see that Melissa was on her way out. After all, it was Friday night.

"Hey Mike." She said casually. However as soon as she took a good look at her brother, she knew something was wrong.

Before saying anything, Mike made sure that their mother was not in listening distance. "Melissa," he said trying to control his voice, "I have to talk to you about something."

Melissa? Mike never called his sister Melissa – it was always Missy. "Is everything ok?" she asked as her face fell pale. "Did something happen to mom?"

"No nothing happened to mom."

"She's not home yet," Melissa said frantically.

"No, nothing happened to mom. She's probably just working late. It's nothing like that. I just have to talk to you about something."

Melissa took a deep breath. "Well then what is it? I was just on my way to Allison's."

"Are you sure you're not going to meet your new friends?"

Melissa gave her brother a puzzled look. "What new friends? Listen Mike, you're acting a kinda weird, but if you really need to talk to me you can walk me to Allison's."

So that was exactly what Mike did. After waiting for Melissa to finish packing her purse and grab her jacket, the two locked-up the house and started walking. "Now what is going on? What's so important… and what'd you mean by that remark about my new friends?"

"I ran into Tom today."

Not twenty feet from their house, Melissa stopped in her tracks. Suddenly everything started to make sense. "Yeah," she said in an annoyed tone of voice "and what did *he* have to say."

"He told me that you dumped him."

Melissa folded her arms and gave Mike a look of irritation. "Did he tell you why I dumped him?"

"He told me that you started hanging out with a bunch drug addicts and he just didn't fit into the picture anymore," Mike bluntly replied.

For a moment, Melissa just stood there with a look of disbelief. "Is that what he told you?! And I suppose you believe that?" She asked as her eyes began to swell with tears. Suddenly Mike felt two inches tall. Not knowing what to say, he just stood there frozen under the spell of his sister's watery eyes. "The truth is that I dumped him because I found out that he was cheating on me with one of my friends."

Mike could feel his stomach sinking as he cursed himself for putting any merit into what Tom had said. "Are you serious?" He asked in a near whisper.

"Yes I'm serious. He was screwing around on me for months. My friends tried to tell me, but I didn't want to believe them. Then last week, I was outside this party and saw him in car with her." As soon as the last word left her mouth, Melissa burst into tears, falling into her brother's arms. "They were…"

"Shh, shh." Mike rubbed his hand down her long blonde hair. Nearly moved to tears himself, Mike felt as if some one had just reached in and ripped out his heart. However, after a few minutes, his distress turned to anger. "I'll fucking kill him," he proclaimed! "You here me. I'm going to go to his house and bust his fucking head open."

"No Mike," she replied while using her sleeve to dry the rest of her tears. "I don't want you to do anything. That's exactly why I didn't tell you. I knew you would get all crazy like this."

"But..."

"No buts. You have to promise me that you won't do anything Mike. I just want to forget about him. It's all for the best anyway."

Somehow Melissa finally made her brother promise not to hunt Tom down. Then, while still consoling her, he walked her the rest of the way to Allison's house, which was about ten blocks away.

The next day Mike returned to the scene of the crime: Baxter's. He felt terrible about the way he had acted and wanted to pay for any damages. Much calmer then the night before, Mike walked into the bar, which had a sparse Saturday afternoon crowd. Hanging his head in embarrassment Mike walked over to Nick, who owned the bar.

In most neighborhood bars on Long Island, the owners also worked behind the bar. They weren't bars that were franchises like T.G.I. Fridays or Houlihans or clubs that were owned by people that also had a dozen other businesses. They were more like mom-and-pop stores. For most of the people who owned them it was their whole life. They owned it, operated it and were there almost every day to make sure things ran smoothly; to watch over the register and make sure nobody was stealing booze. Unlike the city, where many of the bars were owned by retired cops, in Long Island most of them were owned by guys in their thirties and forties who always dreamed about opening a bar. Yet when they finally opened it they realized how difficult it was.

Nick, who owned Baxter's, was no exception. Always wanting to own his own bar, he bought Baxter's from the previous owner in the late seventies, when he was in his mid thirties. The story was that Nick was able to purchase it with money he came into from a lawsuit settlement with the city. Supposedly, while working for the New York Transit Authority, part of a new subway platform he was working on gave way and he fell on the tracks below, just missing the third rail. The settlement was for a back injury he suffered as a result of the incident. What no one could ever understand though, was that he walked just fine and was always carrying heavy things around.

Feeling embarrassed Mike walked over to Nick, who was behind the bar cleaning a glass. Stopping what he was doing, Nick walked over and met Mike half way. "Mike," he said with a disappointing look on his face.

"Listen Nick, before you say anything I just want you to know that I came here to pay for the damage last night." Mike then pulled out a stack of folded twenties from his pants pocket. "Whatever it cost just let me know. I feel like a complete asshole about what happened and I understand if you never want me to step foot in here again."

Nick looked back at Mike who was holding out the neatly folded cash. "Well, a new table is gonna cost me at least forty bucks."

"Here's sixty," he said, handing three twenties to Nick.

Nick put two of the twenties in his pocket and gave the other one back to Mike. "Forty should cover it."

"Are you sure? Really Nick, I feel terrible."

"Yeah forty is fine. Don't worry about the glasses." Nick could have easily stuck him for more, but had known Mike for a while. "Listen, I appreciate you coming in and paying for the damages." He could tell that Mike felt awful about the whole ordeal. "I've seen a lot worse things happen in here. I'm sure you have to. I guess a broken table isn't all that bad in the grand scheme of things. I mean nobody got hurt."

"Still, I feel like an ass. I can't believe what a big fuckin scene I made."

"Don't worry about acting like an ass. Everybody's entitled to act like an ass every now and then. I just don't want to see you get in any trouble. I know you just got out of the can. I don't want to preach to you, but you gotta be more careful Mike. I was talking to Brian last night after you left and he told me how you've really turned your life around. You don't want something stupid to mess everything up for you."

Mike nodded his head. "No, you're right. Believe me, you don't know how right you are. It's just that this asshole that was going out with my little sister was talking shit about her – not that that's an excuse."

"That was the guy you were trying to choke?"

Mike nodded his head. "Yeah, that was him. He said that my sister was doing drugs and hanging out with these scumbags. I just blew up. I mean that's my little sister he's talking about."

"How old is your sister?"

"Seventeen."

"So what do ya think, he was just saying that to piss you off or get back at her for something?"

Mike paused for a second. "I don't know. I talked to her about it. She said that she dumped him because he was fooling around."

"What about the drugs?"

Mike hesitated before answering. "I don't know. I really didn't push it. I mean he was just sayin shit to get back at her."

Nick stopped to greet a customer that walked into the bar. "So you don't think she's into any of that shit?"

"No. My sister's too smart to get into that shit. I mean she goes out drinking every now and then – everyone does in high school. But drugs, cocaine and shit like that – no way man. Besides, she saw where doing drugs got me. She should know how fucked up that shit is better than anybody." Mike paused for a second. "Why, you think I might be taking too much for granted?"

Nick let out a sigh. "Well I don't know your sister Mike. Hopefully you're completely right about her being too smart. It's just that sometimes we care about someone so much that we're not able to be subjective.

Sometimes we're so blinded by the way we want to see things that we don't see them for how they really are."

"That's a good point."

Nick leaned over the bar closer to Mike. "My brother – he's thirty – he was going out with this girl for five years." Nick looked around as if to make sure his brother wasn't in the bar. "Everyone tried to tell him that she was screwin around. His friends would go out to a bar and see her there hanging all over different guys."

"Ouch," Mike replied.

"I'd go over their place sometimes – they were living together - and ask where Karen was. That was her name - Karen. He tells me that she was out with her friends. I'd say 'Johnny, not for nothing, but every time I ask where this girl is you say she's out with her fuckin friends. I've heard of girl's night out, but what – you can't ever hang out with her fucking friends too? What are they too fucking good for you? What are you supposed to stay home while she whoops it up?' He didn't want to hear any of it. Then one night I was over there with some other guys playing cards. In walks this broad at three o'clock in the fuckin morning drunk as hell, with her hair all fucked-up and a rip in her dress."

"Her dress was ripped-up?" Mike asked, almost in disbelief.

Nick shook his head. "No shit. She looked liked she just got finished fucking someone in the back of a car. Me and the guys looked at each other in shock. My brother asked her what happened and she told him that she got so drunk that she fell on the dance floor and ripped her dress. You fucking believe that. I mean I couldn't believe the balls of this bitch."

"Holy shit. Did he finally dump her?"

Nick took another quick look around the bar. "You know what finally happened? He married her."

Mike's jaw dropped. "He married her? You gotta be fuckin kidding me."

"Yeah, he married her. Then a month after the wedding, he came home early from work one day because he wasn't feeling well and there she was in their own bedroom fucking her ex-boyfriend. No shit. It turns out she was fucking him all along. Do you believe that shit?"

"What did he do when he walked in and found them there?"

"He freaked out. He told the guy if was there when he got back he was going to kill him. Then he just ran out of the fucking house. He wanted to strangle them both of course, but it was just too much for him so he just ran out of the house. But you see my point is that for years all the signs were there. Every one tried to warn him, even me, his own brother. But he didn't want to listen. He didn't want to see what was going on. Why? Because he wanted so much to see this girl as some one that would never hurt him and would always be there for him. So that's all that he saw. To him, she was this perfect girl that he had put on this fucking pedestal and no one was going to take her off." Nick paused to wave to a customer that was leaving the bar. "Listen, like I said, I don't know your sister. Maybe she's never gonna touch a drug in her life. But sometimes we want to see something so bad that that's all we see. And sometimes we want so much not to believe something that we convince ourselves there's no way it could be true."

Just then, the other bartender called for Nick from across the bar. "Hey listen, I gotta take this call, but I shouldn't be long."

"Na, that's ok. I have to be going anyway." With that, Mike left the old neighborhood bar.

After coming home from Baxter's Mike made some sandwiches with Melissa and sat in front of the TV. A part of him wanted to talk to her about the whole drugs thing, but he didn't. He felt that she was too smart to be using drugs and that bringing it up would only make it seem like he was accusing her. She had already told him that she only has a few beers on the weekends. Like any good relationship, theirs was built on trust and he didn't want it to seem like he thought she was lying. Besides, their mother was home and it was a conversation that if he did have with her, would be in private.

Over the next few weeks, Mike saw little of Melissa as she started spending more time after school with her friends. However, Mike started spending more time with Diane. Their relationship continued to grow. He knew it would and was ready for the commitment. However, a part of him still felt guilty. After all, Katie still weighed very heavily on his mind. At the same time though, Mike knew that he had to move on. It had already been five years since she had died and waiting six more months or another year was not going to make any difference. He also knew he would be a fool to let some one like Diane slip away. He was lucky to have found some one like her, some one he could talk to about anything and would listen to whatever he had to say.

Some nights, while lying awake in bed, Mike would hold a picture of Katie and talk to it. He assured her that no one would ever replace her, but that Diane was some one who cared about him. It was as if he were asking for Katie's approval, but part of him knew that he was just trying to get approval from himself. After telling Katie about Diane he would lay her picture on his chest and cry, though softly enough so that no one could hear. Mike missed Katie. He missed all the times they shared. Though most of all he cried because of what happened to her. She had always been so vibrant and full of life, yet in the end, he could not help but remember her lying in a pool of blood on that motel floor so still and lifeless. He wanted so much for it all to be just a bad dream. Even if they could not be together, he wished that she were just alive. There was so much that she was never able to experience. There were so many things that she never had a chance to appreciate.

Chapter 5

THANKSGIVING

M ike had waited for this Thanksgiving for five long years. No day was tougher to be behind bars than Thanksgiving – not even Christmas. Every year that Mike choked down the gray slop they passed off as Thanksgiving dinner, he would think about his mother and sister sitting around a crisp, golden bird with home made stuffing, thick, rich gravy and sweet potatoes. He had pictured the linen tablecloth rolled out like a red carpet for a special occasion. The plates and silverware that his grandmother had passed on to his mother would make their rare appearance. He would picture them sitting around the table, laughing, filling their plates for seconds and thirds as some soft holiday music played in the background – probably Frank Sinatra. His mother loved Frank Sinatra.

Being incarcerated was unforgiving itself, but being separated from his family on Thanksgiving was especially hard to handle. However, it was those times that made Mike realize how much he really loved his family, how much he missed them and had taken them for granted. Like they say, sometimes the harshest lessons are the ones most learned. However, all that was in the past. This year, it would be real turkey instead of turkey-flavored mystery meat. This year, instead of the endless rows of inmates, it would be just his family sitting at the table. There would be no guards circling around like hungry dogs. There would be no need for him to watch over his shoulder with every bite. This year, Mike would not have to dream about being home – he was there.

Too anxious to sleep, Mike rolled into the kitchen at five in the morning, wanting to get started. He could not wait any longer. Not sure exactly how to cook everything though, he just stared into the refrigerator for a while. His mouth was already watering as he stared at the three-pound bird he had bought with his mother a few days before. Like a kid peeking at his Christmas presents, he opened up the pumpkin pie and pulled out the draw with the sweet potatoes. Just the thought of all the food out on the table was enough to make him salivate. It was going to be a feast. It was going to be a celebration. Diane was coming over for dinner. He was going to be with his mother and sister. Everything was going to be perfect.

Around seven o'clock, Betty came downstairs to find her son on the couch watching television. Still in her nightgown she walked over and greeting him with a smile. "Michael, I thought you would sleep in a little today."

"Oh, hey ma," he said not realizing that she had woken up. "Are you kidding me? I've been waiting five years for this day." Mike stood up from the couch like a man ready to take on a mission. "I already cut the celery and carrots for the stuffing, but I didn't know what else to do."

His mother laughed. "It's O.K., we have plenty of time. I know you've probably already been staring at the food in the refrigerator, but it's only seven o'clock."

"Yeah, but there's a lot of things to do."

Smiling, Betty shook her head. "I know, but at least let me get some coffee first."

Mike was not the only one glad that he was home for Thanksgiving. For the last five years, just as Mike had thought about his mother and sister at home eating Thanksgiving dinner, Betty had thought about her son miles away. She may have been at home, but her mind was always with him. The turkey was fresh and the stuffing homemade, but every bite had to be forced down. She had Melissa there by her side, but all she could think about was Michael and how awful it must have been for him, how alone he must have felt. There was no one happier that Mike would be eating Thanksgiving dinner at home than she.

By noon, the small kitchen had been turned into a full-fledged Thanksgiving operation. Mike and his mother worked side-by-side, chopping and measuring and stuffing. The clanging of pots and pans, the buzz of the blender, the sound of knives hitting against the cutting board all echoed in Mike's head like the voice of an old familiar friend. Melissa had spent the night at Allison's house and was not expected home for a couple of hours, which meant that Mike and his mother was a two-person crew. As they handed each other knives and pots they reminisced about Thanksgivings gone by. Cutting and peeling they laughed about times that brought back warm memories. They talked about the year that the gas went out while the turkey was in the oven. They laughed about the time when squirrels ate the pies that Betty had put in the backyard to cool. Mike joked about how after dinner his father would go straight to couch and fall asleep sitting up, watching TV. He'd sit there snoring, with his mouth wide open. They were all good memories.

As the afternoon progressed, they continued to talk and cook and pick on the food as it was being prepared. After all, it was the responsibility of the chefs to try out everything before it was served to everyone else. Then, as Betty was telling Mike how long the turkey has to cook for, the doorbell rang. "I'll get it," Mike volunteered.

Opening the door, he was surprised to see Diane standing there, holding a pie. "Who is it?" Betty shouted from the kitchen.

"It's Diane," he shouted back.

"Hey." Mike greeted her with a slow, but brief kiss on the lips. "I thought you weren't coming over 'til around four. Did you guys already eat over your house?"

Before Diane could answer, Betty walked over from the kitchen. "Oh hi Diane."

"Hi Mrs. Patterson," Diane replied as she gave Betty a hug and peck on the cheek.

"You look lovely."

Diane thanked her and then went on to answer Mike's original question. "No, we didn't eat yet. In fact I don't think we're gonna have Thanksgiving dinner." Her words were followed by an uncomfortable laugh."

"Why, what happened?" Mike asked as he took the pie from her.

"Well my sister and brother-in-law came over the house to eat Thanksgiving with us. But they were only there for about a half hour before my father and brother-in-law got into it like they always do. My brother-in-law Kevin – that's his name – was laid off of work a couple of weeks ago and my father started in right away about how is he going support my sister and their daughter with no income. I mean it's not the guy's fault that he got laid off. His company laid off five hundred employees."

"Oh I'm sorry to hear that," Betty replied.

Diane then continued the story. "So anyway, it turned into a screaming match. Then my sister and father started yelling at each other. It was getting pretty ugly. Finally she said that she doesn't need this you know what and starts packing up her stuff. So then my mother starts crying. Remember, at this point the turkey is already in the oven cooking. Anyway, my mother's begging my sister to stay. My father's storming around the house banging things, yelling at everybody. It was a complete disaster. I just had to get out of there at that point, so I came over early to help you guys out in the kitchen. I mean that is if you don't mind."

"No of course not dear," Betty replied, putting her hand on Diane's arm. "I'm just sorry to hear about what happened."

"Oh, no Mrs. Patterson, it's o.k." She said, not wanting Betty to be upset over it. "I didn't mean to throw my dysfunctional family stories at you as soon as I walked in. Besides, it's not even a surprise to me. My father can't stand my sister's husband and every time they come over, this is how it ends."

Diane's comments seemed to only make Betty more upset. "That's terrible," she replied. "And what about your poor mother? She cooked all that food."

"Really Mrs. Patterson, it's ok. What'll happen is my mother will probably wind up driving to my sister's house – she just lives in Lindenhurst – and bring some turkey and stuff over there."

Mike put his arm around Diane and smiled. "Well don't worry, there's plenty of food here. And there's plenty you can help us out with," he said trying to lighten up the mood. Then, like a gentleman, Mike helped her take off her jacket.

Feeling that they could use a moment alone, Betty walked back into the kitchen. As his mother left the room, Mike asked Diane if she was all right. From previous stories, Mike knew that her father blowing up was a common occurrence, but it *was* Thanksgiving. However, Diane assured him that she was ok and Mike did not press the subject any further. So after another, longer kiss, they went into the kitchen to help with the cooking.

Back in the kitchen, the mixing, chopping and measuring continued. So did the carefree atmosphere. The three of them laughed and joked as they tried not to bang into each other. If some one spilled or dropped something, they would all laugh about it. If some one put too much of an ingredient in something, it was o.k., they would work around it. They wanted everything to taste good, but it was more about just having a good time and throwing all worries to the wind.

"I can't believe how much food you guys are making for just the three of you."

"Well, you make four," Mike pointed out as he sat on a stepladder, peeling a sweet potato over a small, plastic wastebasket.

"Still" Diane replied while cutting a cucumber for the salad. "You guys have enough food here to feed an army."

Betty looked around at the kitchen. "Yeah, I guess we did go a little over board. It's just that Michael hasn't had a real Thanksgiving dinner in so long that I wanted to make sure we had all his favorites."

Mike stood up from the stepladder to give his mother a kiss on the forehead. "See that's why you're the best ma."

"Well I brought over an apple pie."

Mike shook his head in approval. "That's good, because, you know it wouldn't be American if you didn't have an apple pie." Suddenly Mike realized he was forgetting something. "And oh yeah, it wouldn't be complete without my mother's famous bread pudding. You're gonna love my mother's bread pudding."

"Oh that reminds me Michael, I need the recipe so I can get started on it."

Mike gave his mother a look of disbelief. "Ma, what are you talking about? You used to make it every Thanksgiving. You're telling me you forgot how to make it? Ma, c'mon, that's like forgetting how to spell your own name."

"Well Michael, it's been a wile since I made it. I just forget how many eggs I need to put in."

"Well, where's the recipe, I'll go get it for you."

"It's in the junk draw in the amour. It's on a blue piece of paper. There should be other recipes clipped to it."

Putting down the peeler and potato, Mike left the kitchen to go get the recipe. As he did, Betty and Diane continued to talk about how much food there was. Betty kept telling Diane that she would have to take some food home, but Diane replied that there was going to already be plenty of food left over at her house – especially that her sister and brother-in-law didn't wind up eating over. Meanwhile, Mike shouted from the other room that he could not find the recipe. Betty shouted back that if it was not there, to try looking on the shelf where all the mail was.

As Betty and Diane turned their conversation from food to junk mail, Mike suddenly appeared in the kitchen entrance holding a piece of paper. From the livid look on his face, Diane could tell that it was not the recipe. "What's this?" he asked in an irate tone of voice.

"What is it?" his mother asked, although already having a good idea of what it was.

"It's a letter from Melissa's school," Mike snapped back. The smile and jovial demeanor he flaunted just moments before were now gone. "It says that she's been cutting classes and her grades are dropping."

At first Betty just stood there, not sure what to say. Mike had taken her completely off guard. "I know. It came a couple of days ago," she finally answered, in a hesitant voice.

"It came a couple of days ago? I guess you weren't going to tell me about it."

"Calm down Michael. I was going to talk to you about it over the weekend. I just didn't want to ruin your first Thanksgiving back home." Silently, Betty cursed herself for not putting the letter in a more inconspicuous place.

Caught in the middle, Diane looked at Mike, who was still standing in the entranceway holding the letter in the air. She knew that Mike was a fanatic when it came to Melissa, but had never seen him so angry. "Maybe it's better if I leave," she said in a sheepish voice.

"No it's all right honey, please don't go," Betty replied.

"No, don't go," Mike added, realizing that he may have come off a little too strong. "I don't want to ruin Thanksgiving dinner," he said in a more subdued voice. "It's just that you know how important it is for Melissa to do well in school. How is she going to get into a good college with failing grades?"

"I understand Michael. I know you want your sister to do well in school, but I hope when you talk to her about it you don't get too excited. If you just start yelling, she's not going to listen."

Mike walked into the kitchen and stood in front of the refrigerator. "I know that. You know I don't yell at her. Maybe that's the problem." Mike's voice turned from anger to one of disappointment. "I don't know how many ways I can tell her how important a good education is."

"I know," Betty mother replied with disappointment of her own. "I don't know what's gotten into her. She's always been a straight 'A' student and was never in trouble before," she said to Diane, who had sat back down by the kitchen table. "I really thought that once Michael came home she would straighten-up. Melissa thinks the world of Michael."

"Wait a second. How long has this been going on?" Mike asked.

At first Betty was hesitant to tell him anything, figuring he would just get more upset, but then finally answered. "Well the second half of her junior year, her grades started dropping a little, but she still got mostly B's on her report card with a couple of C's. It's just that before, she would always get A's – maybe a B here and there." Almost not wanting to tell Mike directly, she directed her comments to Diane, who was feeling a rather uncomfortable in the middle of the family squabble. "Over the summer though she started spending all of her time with that Allison girl. There's just something about her I'm not too crazy about."

"I can't believe what I'm hearing," Mike with a raised voice while throwing his arms into the air.

"Well Michael, I mean it was never serious before, until I got that letter from the school. So there was nothing really to tell you. I knew you would talk to her once you came home anyway."

"Nothing serious?" The frustration poured out of his body as he leaned back on the counter with both hands. "Didn't she learn anything from me? I mean she's seen what happened to me. She knows where I've been for the last five years. I've told her, that path leads nowhere."

Hesitantly, Diane jumped in. "I'm not trying to minimize anything Mike, but maybe you're over reacting. I mean it's not like she got arrested or kicked out of school or anything like that. Maybe you should just talk to her about the letter and see what's going on."

"It's just that Melissa is Mike's whole world." Betty bit her tongue, realizing what she had said – more importantly whom she had said it to.

Mike also realized what his mother had implied: that he didn't care about anyone (i.e. Diane) but his sister. "Listen," Mike said in a softer, more rational voice, "maybe you're right. I'll just talk to her about it tomorrow."

After folding the letter up and putting it into his pocket, they all went back to what they were doing before the incident. Although Mike was still upset, he tried not to talk about Melissa. It *was* his first Thanksgiving dinner at home in over five years. Diane was there. Mike didn't want to ruin the moment for himself or anyone else.

Around four o'clock, everything was finished cooking except for one of the pies and the bread pudding. They had planned to eat at 4:30, a time that they had set earlier in the week, but Melissa was still not home. When Betty called Allison's at 3:30, her mother said that Melissa had left a little while ago. However Allison's house was only about a twelve-minute walk, so it was obvious that she had gone somewhere else. As 4:30 rolled up there was still no Melissa. Mike fought hard to conceal his growing frustration. He even suggested waiting another fifteen minutes before putting the food out on the table.

Finally, around 5:15, while everyone had just sat down at the dining room table, Melissa came in the door. "Oh you guys are already sitting down to eat?" she said as she casually started walking upstairs to put her overnight bag away. "I thought you said we were going to eat at five thirty."

"We said four thirty," Betty replied, stopping Melissa at the base of the stairs. "We said it several times."

"Sorry, I thought you said five thirty. What do you want me to tell you? I'll be right back down."

Before she could though, she was stopped by her brother, who had come out of the dinning room. "Where were you?"

"I was at Allison's. You know that."

Melissa realized hat she probably wasn't going to make it all the way upstairs without answering a few more questions. "God, what is this an inquisition or something? Oh, hi Diane. I didn't see you over there." Diane uncomfortably reciprocated. "I… I had to stop at Michelle's," Melissa continued. "I had to return a jacket I borrowed from her when we went out last night."

"It's Thanksgiving. She couldn't wait 'till tomorrow?" Her mother asked.

"She was going to her uncle's later and she wanted to wear it. What can I say?"

Betty gave her daughter an undeniable look of disappointment. "Well why don't you go upstairs and clean-up. We haven't started eating anything yet."

With that, Melissa started back up the stairs. Mike quickly followed behind. He had left so abruptly that neither Betty nor Diane had a chance to try to stop him. As Melissa threw her bag on her bed, Mike walked into the room. Melissa, who had left the door open, figuring that she was just going to put her stuff away and head back down, was surprised to see him standing there. "Listen Mike, I'm sorry I'm late. I thought mom said five thirty."

Mike closed the door behind him and walked over to his sister. Her hair was unusually a mess and her eyes had bags under them. Then, once face to face with her, he could smell a distinct odor. "What's that?" he asked while sniffing aloud.

"What's what?" Melissa turned her head and started to walk over to the dresser, away from her brother.

"I smell pot," he replied in a voice soft enough that it would not travel beyond the room.

Melissa turned to him with a surprised look on her face. "What are you talking about?" she shot back in a heavily defensive tone.

"I think I've smoked enough weed in my time to know what it smells like," he replied, sounding more surprised than angry. "You've been smoking pot."

"Dam it Mike, are you gonna start this shit now? What's the matter with you today?"

Mike walked over to where his sister was standing. "What's the matter with me? What's the matter with you? I found this letter from your school today," he said pulling it out of his pants pocket, "that mom tried to hide from me. Now you come home looking like you've been partying all night and smelling like weed. What's going on with you?" Pausing for a second, Mike let out a deep breath. "Do you wanna end up like me? 'Cause let me tell you something kid, it's a hard road. Just cause I've straighten up my act and things seem to be going good for me now – don't let that fool you. I may have done five years, but I consider myself lucky. A lot of people don't make it back from that road."

"Listen Mike, just because I skipped a few classes and I don't have all A's, doesn't mean I'm going to end up in jail. I'm not you." Melissa realized her words had come out wrong. "All I'm trying to say," She said in a calmer tone of voice, "is that just because bad things happened to you and people you know, doesn't mean they're gonna happen to me. Look, I realize that you're just trying to look out for me, but you can't make me live in a plastic bubble. You have to let me live my own life and trust me. I know you're worried about me, but I'm not going to do anything stupid. I Know I have to pick my grades up and I will – I always do. Believe me, I'm not gonna let anything screw-up my future."

Mike looked at his younger sister and realized that she was not that young anymore. Whether he liked it or not, she had grown-up and was no longer that little girl that would listen to his every word. He could provide her with the map, but could not steer her down the road. The path she chose would be her decision alone. It frightened him. It frustrated him. But all he could do now was guide her and hope that she had more sense than he did. In the end though, she was right – her life was in her own hands.

"Missy, whether you believe me or not, I'm not just trying to give you a hard time or have you make up for all the mistakes that I made when I was younger. I know you're not me. I know you're not Katie. And it's not that I don't trust you, because I do. It's just that I've seen things that you haven't seen. I know things that you don't. You know that old saying: 'I wish I knew then what I know now'? Well, all I'm trying to do is let you know all the stuff that you may not be able to realize for yourself yet. Not because, you're not smart, but because you just haven't had to go through the experiences."

Melissa put her hands on her brother's shoulders. "Mike, I understand and I appreciate it – I really do – but I'm not doing anything that's going to jeopardize my future. Yes, I take a couple of hits off a joint every now and then," she reluctantly admitted, "but that's as heavy as I get. I'm not tryin to say…"

Mike turned his head and stepped away, not wanting her puppy-dog eyes to influence anything he may have wanted to say. "Missy, I just want you to know that you don't have to be a cocaine addict or deal drugs to have something bad happen to you. Sometimes you can just be at the wrong place at the wrong time. Sometimes it's not even you, but the people you're with. Maybe you only had a couple of beers but the person that's driving you around is wasted and you wind up getting into an accident. You can get killed. It happens all the time."

"Mike believe me, I make sure never to get in a car with some one that's been drinking too much. I'm not stupid."

"It's not just that," Mike went on. "One guy in our cellblock was doing two years because the cops raided the house he was staying at and found ten sheets of acid. It wasn't even his, it was his roommate's who was a dealer, but under the law if they find any drugs in the house they arrest everyone in the house. One guy, his brother was at this house just buying a bag of weed when guys in masks broke in to steal all the drugs and wound up shooting and killing everyone in the house. His brother was only sixteen. Then we had guys in there that were doing time for putting drugs in girls' drinks and raping them while they were passed out."

"That's disgusting!"

"It sure is, but my point is that these girls weren't into anything bad. They thought they were just going to a party to have a few drinks. I mean some of these girls were as young as fourteen." Mike turned back to look at his sister and softly grabbed a hold of her arms. "Listen Melissa, god forbid anything happened to you…I don't know what I would do. But it's not just about me. You have so much promise. You have the chance to really do things with your life." With one hand, Mike gently combed through her long, straight blonde hair. "I want more for you then to just get some mediocre job where you have to worry about how much money is in your saving's account. I have high hopes for you Missy and so should you. Don't you understand - there are no limits to what you can accomplish."

Melissa stared back at him. "Listen Mike, I know you only want the best for me and believe me, so do I."

After a hug the two ventured back downstairs. Neither Diane nor Betty asked what they had talked about. They were just glad that both of them came back down and weren't arguing. Before finally digging into the feast laid out before them, Betty said grace. As everyone bowed their heads and clasped their hands, Betty gave thanks for the elaborate meal that they were about to eat, for finally bringing Mike back home and that they were able to be a family once again.

As they all indulged in the smorgasbord of Thanksgiving delights, they passed harmless conversations around the table, tucking away any tension, like dust being swept under a rug. Regardless of the letter from the school, regardless of everything, it was still Thanksgiving. It was still the first time in years that they were able to share it together. In saying grace, Betty assured everyone that they had much to be thankful for and despite any problems or bumps in the road no one at the table had any reason to think otherwise. Betty had both of her children back home. Diane was sharing Thanksgiving with the person she cared about most. Mike could not help but to remember where he had been just a Thanksgiving ago. He felt thankful to be home, that he was able to find a job and had found someone like Diane.

Chapter 6

A CHANCE ENCOUNTER

A week after Thanksgiving, Mike decided to start Christmas shopping. Borrowing his mother's car on a Saturday afternoon, he went to the mall to get it all done in one shot. He really only had to buy gifts for his mother, sister and Diane. Maybe he would get a little something for Brian and John, but that would be easy. He would just get them an album or personalized beer stein. Mike knew he was going to get Melissa a new stereo for her room and had thought about getting Diane a necklace, but had no idea what to get his mother. So he decided to walk around the mall and see if anything caught his eyes. Mike wanted his mother's gift to be special, but no matter how much time he spent thinking about it he just couldn't think of that perfect gift. In fact his mind was drawing a complete blank.

Walking through the mall only a few weeks before Christmas was the first time that Mike was not so glad to be back in society. It was a complete and utter madhouse. People were shoving each other. Old ladies were mowing down people with their overstuffed shopping bags. At nearly every store, lines for the cash register were out the door. Kids were screaming as their parents dragged them through the maze of mayhem. Children were running loose, running and screaming, oblivious to all the other people in the mall. Announcements were being made on the mall's intercom that no one could ever understand. Jingle Bells reverberated throughout the corridors at concert volume. The combined noise of the music with thousands of people trying to all talk at once was deafening. It was a complete nightmare. Mike wanted no part of it, but knew that it would only get worse the closer it came to Christmas. Just grin and bear it he told himself. It was a necessary evil that had to be done.

Finally, after looking at all the stereos twice for Melissa and every piece of jewelry in every store for Diane, Mike had two gifts to show for all his aggravation. It wasn't easy, but he was half way there. Now it was time to concentrate on his mother. However, while wading through the soup of people and hysteria Mike found his concentration on finding the perfect gift hopelessly diminishing. With each shopping bag that pumped into him, each high heel shoe that stepped on his foot, his standards lowered. Frustrated he now looked, not looking for the perfect gift, but for anything he could buy and get the hell out. Mike loved his mother, but being in that mall was too much to handle.

After about two hours Mike found himself in Macy's. With a shopping bag in one hand and a box with Melissa's stereo in the other, he fought his way through the thick streams of people that clogged up every available passageway. Somehow he had come up with the idea of getting his mother a gift certificate for a facial and hair appointment. At first he wasn't too sure about the idea because she was not someone who would get a facial or pamper herself. On the other hand, that's what made it the perfect gift. Relieved about finally figuring out what to get, Mike walked over to the escalator to look at the store map. However, it seemed more confusing than helpful.

As he looked around for a salesperson to point him in the right direction, standing no more than two feet away was Katie's mother. For

Mike, it was like seeing a ghost. Mutually surprised by the chance encounter, Katie's mother dropped her one shopping bag as its contents spilled out onto the crowded floor. Suddenly, a deadly silence filled the air where the noise and clamor had been just a second ago. Everything stopped in an instant as the two faced each other, only feet apart.

Speechless, Mike stood there watching her eyes quickly fill with rage. The initial shock had worn off and there was no mistaking the anger that was streaming through her body. "Murderer!" she shouted as everyone in the store stopped what they were doing and looked over. Taken off guard Mike stood there paralyzed. "You killed my little girl!" she yelled, waving her index finger in his face. Appalled, the crowd of people that surrounded them gasped – then started whispering into one another's ears. "They told me you were out. Look at you! Look at you!" Only inches away, Mike could feel the spit from her words and the sharpness of her eyes.

"Mrs....Mrs. Fuller" he stuttered.

However, his words bounced right of her. "My Katie's gone forever," she roared. "I'll never see my little girl again and for what! It's your fault! Katie would still be alive if it wasn't for you." The large crowd that had surrounded them was now getting even bigger and the whispers louder. Mike could feel a hundred pairs of eyes piercing through him. "You took my Katie away from me!"

Now covered in cold sweat, Mike felt as if he had been sucked into hell. However it was not because she was calling him a murderer, but rather because he realized how much anguish and devastation he had caused. It was not her fury that devastated him; it was her pain. Mike could feel her pain more than anything else and realized that there was nothing he could say or do to ease it.

"I hope you're happy with yourself!" She yelled as the friend she was with finally whisked her away. "I hope you have a nice life," were the last words Mike heard as she disappeared into the still staring crowd.

Although all eyes were still upon him, Mike remained frozen. His entire body had gone numb, not even noticing the packages which he was still gripping. All he could feel was a cold, sinking sensation; the same sinking feeling he felt when he heard the sound of that gunshot, five years earlier. A wound that he thought had begun to heal had been ripped open and bled freely onto his new skin. But it was not his blood alone. It was also the blood of Katie and all those who she had been taken from. As people stood there pointing Mike could feel the hot, bright lights of judgment shining down as the guilt poured from his body in the form of cold sweat. His own pain was acceptable punishment, but the pain he inflicted on others was insurmountable.

Finally, with security guards coming to see what was going on, Mike tried to leave the scene. But it was not easy. His legs felt like jell-o and his heart was pounding so hard it was about to jump out of his chest. With every step he nearly blacked-out, yet somehow made it to the nearest exit. In a dreamlike daze, Mike opened the door and pushed his way into the parking lot. Somehow he found his way back to the car and threw the packages in the trunk. Then, for what seemed like an hour, he just stood there with the trunk opened, still in shock. He could not get Katie's mother's face out of his mind. It was as if she was still there screaming "murderer". As his stomach turned and twisted Mike fell helplessly to his knees and threw-up, right there in the middle of the crowded parking lot.

After there was nothing left to vomit, Mike hesitantly climbed into the driver's seat. Wiping away the sweat from his forehead, he fumbled to get the keys in the ignition. Finally, after several attempts, the key slid in and the car came alive. Throwing it into reverse, Mike backed out of the parking space and fought to keep his composure enough to be able to drive.

Fortunately for Mike, neither Melissa nor his mother was home. The last thing he wanted to do was talk to anyone. After throwing the gifts in his closet, Mike sat on the bed and tried to bring his breathing back to normal. However the face of Katie's mother was still there. "Murderer" and "I hope you're happy" still rang through his head. It was not long before tears helplessly began to join the sweat that streaked down his face. He wanted to crawl up in a ball and cry for days, but knew that it was only a matter of time before someone came home. With one look anyone would know that something was terribly wrong and Mike had neither the will nor want to explain it. So after brushing his teeth he ventured outside into the cold December air.

There was no destination. There was no place to seek refuge from the ghosts of the past that howled as loudly as the gusts of winter wind blowing through the hollow trees. Under the thick dull sky he walked alone through the neighborhood that perhaps knew him better than he knew himself. Mike wished he could go back to a time when he walked the same streets as a child – but there was no going back. There was no washing away the years. Mike had spent endless days trying to make a better future for himself, but what good was it if the past was always there, gnawing at his every thought. It had attached itself to him like a ball and chain that would never unlock. And why should it have been any other way, he told himself. Why should he be free of the past when others would suffer its stranglehold everyday of their lives? Why should he get a second chance? In the end there was no making things right. It was why parents always tell their children that the choices they make early on may affect them the rest of their lives.

Mike's mind ran rampant as he strayed from the neighborhood streets into the surrounding woods. There, Mike would not have to worry about some one he knew driving or walking by. He could be alone. In no particular direction his boots shuffled atop dried, fallen leaves and twigs. Tall trees, their branches brittle and bare, blocked out the rest of the world. Just yards away from busy streets in some places, the woods provided a much needed isolation; a much needed separation. There, Mike's thoughts blew freely in the winter wind as if sending a message in a bottle that would never reach a destination. Mike no longer felt sick, but rather eerily calm. His heart had stopped palpitating and his hands no longer shook. The sweat that minutes ago ran profusely down his brow had dissipated into the chill of the afternoon air.

Paying no attention to where he was going, Mike had unintentionally walked to the next town over, Massapequa Park. Not wanting to walk too far, he decided to leave the woods and walk along the road. Through all the commotion the afternoon had unnoticeably ticked away and the already gray skies were darkening. For the first time Mike looked at his watch and noticed that it was 4:45pm. However, he did not feel like going home just yet. He wanted more time by himself, yet was getting tired of just walking around aimlessly. So he decided to head for one of the neighborhood bars that were near the train station.

Feeling like he had walked to a different state, Mike randomly walked into one of the several bars that were all on the same block. It could have been Baxter's, minus the familiar faces. All the neighborhood pubs looked the same. The only thing different from one to the next was the people. Wasting no time, Mike pulled-up a bar stool in the corner where no one else was sitting and laid down a twenty-dollar bill. Mike had a few beers every now and then since being released, but had yet to really get drunk. That was about to change.

In between thoughts and catching a glance at the television that hung from the ceiling, Mike sat alone drinking a beer. Not feeling the effects fast enough though, he soon switched to rum and cokes. After about an hour the alcohol started to kick in. Having no one to talk to, however, was getting old. Mike chatted with the bartender when he passed by, but it was getting to the point where he needed some one with which to drink. Perhaps it was the booze, but suddenly Mike loaned for some company. So with drink in hand, Mike walked over to the pay phone and called-up Brian. Why not Diane? He knew Diane would have felt sorry for him and would have tried to get him to leave the bar. Mike felt comfortable talking to Diane about anything, but didn't want to lay another Katie episode on her. She was always there to listen, but he didn't want to abuse the privilege. Besides, at that moment, what Mike needed was a drinking buddy.

Brian happened to be home and grabbed the next train over, which was only one stop.

After about twenty minutes, Brian showed up. Greeting his friend with a handshake, Mike asked what he was drinking. "I'll have a Budweiser," Brian replied as Mike ordered one up. "So you wouldn't tell me on the phone. What the hell are you doing here?" Brian asked as he unzipped his leather jacket and put it on the back of the barstool. "And how the hell did you get here?"

Mike took a swig of his rum and coke. "Well bro, I've been trying to figure that out for twenty-four years."

Brian laughed. "Man how many drinks have you already had?"

"Not enough." Mike replied with a smirk.

Brian took a swig of his own drink, which the bartender had just brought over. He knew there was a reason that Mike was sitting alone in a strange bar getting drunk. At Brian's suggestion, the two grabbed their coats and drinks and moved over to one of the empty booths. "Hey, I thought you were going Christmas shopping today?"

"Yeah, I did." Mike paused while debating whether or not to open up the floodgates. "You know who I saw there?"

"Who?" Brian asked, thinking it would be one of their long lost friends.

"Katie's mother."

Suddenly Brian started getting a picture of where this was all heading "Mrs. Fuller? Did she see you?"

"Oh yeah," Mike replied before finishing the rest of his drink in one big swig.

"Did she say anything to you?"

"She called me a murderer," Mike replied nonchalantly.

Brian spit out his beer. He certainly wasn't expecting anything like that. "What? Are you fucking serious, she called you a murderer?"

"Well actually she yelled it at me in the middle of Macy's."

"Are you fuckin serious?"

Mike motioned the waitress over for another round. "Yeah, I'm serious. You should have seen all the people's faces, standing there in disbelief as she yelled that I was the reason her daughter was dead. Her friend had to practically restrain her from attacking me."

Brian could not believe what he was hearing. No wonder Mike was at the bar getting smashed by himself. "Man, I can't believe that. I mean what the hell is wrong with her?"

"Nothing. Nothing is wrong with her. If I were in her shoes I would have done the same thing – probably worse. I probably would have kicked my ass."

Just then the waitress brought over a fresh round of drinks. "I don't know man. I mean I can obviously understand why she's so upset, but Katie took her own life right? I mean you would have never done anything to hurt her."

Mike sucked down half the rum and coke that the waitress had just brought over in one swig. "C'mon, who are you kidding? Katie would have never been in that situation if it wasn't for me."

"I think you're being too hard on yourself now," Brian replied. "Not for nothin' Mike, but nobody made Katie go with you. She went with you because she wanted to. Besides, what makes you think that she wouldn't have done the same thing if she stayed right at home." Brian paused for a moment to take a drink of beer and gather his thoughts. "Listen, Katie's no longer here – God rest her soul - because of all the drugs – the cocaine and all the pills she used to pop. I mean that shit will fuck anyone up. But you know as well as I that Katie was going to do them with or with out you. "

Mike just shook his heavy head. "I'm not so sure about that."

Brian may not have been there those last few days, but he was around both of them in the weeks before they left. "Listen bro, you weren't in your right mind anymore than she was. I mean let me tell you, there for a while I couldn't even hang out you. I mean I was fucked up myself then, but you were gone and so was Katie. The bottom line is that it was the drugs that killed her, not you. Everyone knew how much you loved her. I mean you wouldn't even look at another fucking girl." Brian exhaled a breath and leaned back in the chair. "Listen, I know you man. Katie was your whole life.

You never would have let anything happen to her. Your only crime was being too fucked up on drugs yourself to realize what was going on."

"Oh, is that all?" Mike shot back sarcastically.

"You know what I mean."

Mike sat up straight and put down his drink. "That's bullshit man! I mean that's like saying that the guy that got into a car after drinking all night and mowed down a family isn't too blame because he was too drunk to know what he was doing."

"You didn't mow down anybody."

"No? Well what about the guy's friend, who knew he was too drunk to drive, but let him get behind the wheel anyway? No, I may have not pulled the trigger, but I sat by and watched as she destroyed herself and did absolutely nothing to stop it. I knew how fucked-up she was. I knew she needed help. But what did I fucking do about it – nothing!" Mike paused to take another swig of his drink. "I watched her deteriorate right there in front of my eyes. You know what I told her? I told her that we would get one-way tickets to California and everything would be ok. Everything would be ok?! That's like someone letting their friend drive drunk but telling them to drive slowly. I mean I knew she needed real help. Did I think that we were going to get out to California and she was just going to stop doing drugs and we were going to live some fairy-tale life?"

Feeling their voices were carrying, Brian leaned over the table and talked in a lower tone. "You may know now that it wasn't realistic, but that's what you thought at the time."

"That's not the point Brian. She may have wanted to go with me, but it was my choice to go to California. It was my choice to run away. I wanted her to come because I was thinking of myself. I didn't want to be alone. I didn't want to lose her. None of this would have ever happened, if I hadn't been so afraid losing her."

Brian shook his head. "That only proves how much you loved her."

"That only proves how selfish I was. I wanted her with me because it made me feel good."

Brian leaned back in the chair again; frustrated that Mike was so hell-bent on guilt-tripping himself to death. "Listen bro," he said in a calm tone, "you can sit here and drown in your guilt all you want. You can come up with a million reasons why what happened is your fault, but the fact is all you would be doing is just destroying another life – yours. No matter what happened, or why it happened, there is no going back and changing it. You've spent five years in the slammer. Now you're out and you're turning your life around. There's no more drugs. You have a good, steady job. You're back home with your family. You have a beautiful and levelheaded girl like Diane who cares about you. Despite all that's happened and what you might think, believe it or not you're actually quite lucky in many ways."

Mike polished off his drink and let out a sigh. "But why should I be lucky? Why should I be able to move on and get a second chance? I mean I looked at Mrs. Fuller today – she'll never have her daughter back. Why should I just be able to pick up and move on? We can't run away from the decisions we've made. We can't go back and change the paths we've taken. Our actions have consequences; some of which we'll never be able to escape from. That's the point I try to drive home to Melissa."

"Missy? What's she got to do with any of this?" Brian asked in a confused tone.

"Nothing. You know, she's just been having some trouble in school and when I went to talk to her about it I knew she had been smoking weed."

"Is that what this is all about – Melissa?"

Mike waved the waitress over for yet another round. "What are you talking about? This is about how I ran into Mrs. Fuller in the mall," Mike said as his speech started to slur.

"No, it's more than that – whether you know it or not. You're worried about your sister. You think Missy's into something besides just weed?"

"I don't know man," Mike replied in a frustrated, but subdued voice. "She says she just has some beers on the weekends and smokes a few joints every now and then, but I'm not so sure." Maybe the alcohol was acting like a truth serum, but for the first time Mike had conceded that

Melissa might be in deeper than she was letting on. "When I first came home I would spend hours hanging out with her, just bullshitting. Now, I hardly see her anymore."

Brian knew how close Mike was to his sister. "Well I mean you've been working and spending time with Diane. Also, you gotta remember that Melissa is seventeen years old. I mean that's what kids do her age – they hang out. They don't spend a lot of time at home. You know that." Brian stopped for a second as the waitress brought another round of drinks to the table. "This isn't about that night at Baxter's when you went off on that guy is it? You think that guy was telling the truth?"

Mike brushed his hand though his hair. "I don't know. I mean maybe that's just a part of it, but you put that together with skipping classes and never being at home. I mean I understand that she has friends, but she's with them more than she's home. For the past couple of weeks she's spent just about every weekend at her friend Allison's."

"You don't think she'll level with you?"

"I'm her brother and she loves me, but if some one asked us when we were seventeen about the shit we were into, what would we tell them? We lied through our fucking teeth about what we were up to."

Brian rubbed his chin. "You got a point man. Have you tried snooping around in her room? Maybe that way you'll be able to find out if she's really into something or if you're just being paranoid."

"No. I mean I want to find out what's really going on, but I just can't bring myself to look through all of her personal shit. I mean she would never trust me again. Besides, I've been in prison for five years. I have very strong opinions about a person's right to privacy."

Brian put his head in his hand, thinking of a way Mike could get to the bottom of what was going on. Not only was Mike a friend, but Brian also had grown-up with Melissa. She was like a cousin to him and he didn't want to see anything bad happen to her anymore than did Mike. "Hey, I got it. Why don't you talk to some of the people she hangs out with to see what's going on? Your sister may be able to bullshit you, but they won't."

"What, like go interrogate her friends?"

"No. Just when one of her friends comes by the house and is waiting for Melissa to get ready, sit 'em down and strike up a conversation. You've been around the block. You know how to ask certain questions without raising suspicion. Maybe even offer them a drink."

Mike laughed at the notion. "Yeah, maybe I'll have them come inside and slap down a fifth of tequila on the table. Maybe that way they'll get so bombed that they'll tell me everything they know."

"Hey man, I'm just trying to help by giving you some ideas here."

"I know man. I appreciate it – I do. It's just that I don't know what the fuck to do." Brian could hear the frustration in Mike's voice.

The two friends stayed at the bar another two hours before finally leaving. It was Saturday night and Brian was supposed to meet up with some of the crew and go out to a club in the city. He invited Mike, who was tempted, but knew that if he had anymore to drink he wouldn't be able to walk. After four rum and cokes Mike had switched back to beer in an attempt to not get too drunk. He had even eaten a burger and fires, which helped a little, but the damage had already been done. Mike was completely shit-faced. His face flush and eyes half shut, he stumbled out of the bar with Brian, mumbling words that made no sense. What had started as a few beers to relax turned into a three and a half hour session of bliss. It was 8:30 and Mike was lit like a forest fire.

The two life-long friends caught the next train back to Massapequa, which was only a five-minute ride. However it was about a fifteen-minute walk from the train station back to their respective houses. Brian was anxious to get back so he could change and meet up with the gang. For Mike however, the long walk was more than welcomed. The train ride, albeit short, made his stomach feel a little queasy and everything was just a few notches away from starting to spin. The cold, fresh December air was exactly what Mike needed. The more he walked, the better he felt. Nonetheless, he was still smashed and wasn't sure exactly where he was walking. His mother knew he sometimes met up with some of the guys and maybe even had a beer or two, but he had not yet come home wasted. If at all possible, Mike wanted to keep that streak alive. Stopping by Diane's was an option, but he didn't want her to see him that drunk either. Mike felt like a paranoid kid, afraid to let anyone know he had been drinking. Strangely though, wrestling with the decision of where to go distracted him from realizing how drunk he really was.

Finally deciding on going home, Mike opened the front door as stealth as possible, trying to sneak past his mother who was on the couch watching television. However she had noticed him walk in and immediately wanted to strike up a conversation about how his Christmas shopping went. As soon as Mike walked over, she realized that he was drunk. He had tried to put on his best sober face, but it did not work. Mike assured his mother that he was all right and had just lost track of time. Purposely leaving out the part about running into Katie's mother, he explained that he met Brian after finishing shopping and the two went out for some drinks. To make his mother feel better he told her how Brian was going to meet up with the guys and go out to the city, but that he had decided to come home. Worried at first, Betty was glad that at least he didn't go out to the city and continue to drink. She also found solace in the fact that Mike had been responsible enough to bring the car home before going to the bar. So she decided not to make a big deal out of it.

Diane, however, was not so understanding – at least not at first. She had left several messages for Mike, so he went upstairs and gave her a call. Right away she let him have it. Mike had forgotten that he was supposed to call her after his shopping was done. Diane said how worried she had been. Telling her that he had just met Brian for a few drinks did not help the situation. It wasn't the fact that he was with Brian or that he had been drinking; it was that he didn't call to tell her. Diane was not the possessive type, but they had plans to see a movie that night – plans that Mike had obviously forgotten all about. Mike had never blown her off before and always called if he was running late or if something had come up. Perhaps Diane was being paranoid herself, but asked if there was something he wasn't telling her. Not wanting to lie, Mike explained the whole story about running into Katie's mother. Not only did Diane feel guilty for snapping at him, but she also felt terrible about what happened. In fact she wanted to hang-up the phone right away and go over to comfort him, but Mike assured her that it was not necessary. However she came over anyway. In the end, she felt she had to be there for him. And regardless of what Mike said, he wanted there too.

When Diane came over, they went straight up to Mike's room and lied on the bed and talked for what seemed like hours. In fact they talked until finally falling asleep in each other's arms. Then, in the middle of the night they both woke up groggy and in a daze, still in one another's arms. Yet instead of Diane going home they made love into the early morning. Without exchanging any words, they began to undress each other, each knowing what the other was thinking. Trying not to wake up Mike's mother, they buried themselves beneath the covers. When they finally finished, Diane was too exhausted to worry about going home. All she wanted to do was go back to sleep in Mike's arms.

They awoke again around 10:30 am, still naked and holding onto each other. After exchanging glances and smiles in remembrance of the night that had passed, they realized the awkward situation. At first, Mike wondered how he was going to get Diane out of the house without his mother knowing. Then it dawned on him – he was a grown adult. It was his mother's house and he certainly didn't want to be disrespectful, but he *was* twenty-four years old. Mike finally convinced Diane, who was embarrassed to walk out of the room, that their story would be they lost track of time and just wound up passing out. Surely there was nothing wrong with that, he told her. After all, they had been together for over a month. It was different than sneaking some girl into his room that he had met that night – that would be disrespectful. Still embarrassed, Diane finally gave in, realizing that there really was no other option. Mike was more worried about what Diane was going to tell her father when she got home. He knew even though Diane was twenty-four he treated her as if she was sixteen. Diane's plan was to tell her parents that she wound up falling asleep at her friend Rachel's house. She said that Rachel was out of town so it would work and promised a worried Mike that it was no big deal.

After Diane left, Mike spent the rest of the day nursing his intense hangover. It had been a while since he had felt so shitty. With pains from head to toe, Mike wondered how the hell he used to go out and get smashed every night. For the whole afternoon, he laid on the couch watching football, fading in and out of sleep. Luckily his mother had to run errands for much of the day and Melissa was out with her friends, because Mike did not feel like talking to anybody – about anything. Occasionally he would try to force down some water or hobble to the kitchen for a snack. Nothing came easy though, even just lying on the couch seemed like a feat. Mike was convinced that if he had to actually get up and do something that day, he probably would die.

Chapter 7

A DANGEROUS PATH

For Mike, going to work that Monday was not a fun experience. Still feeling the effects of his hangover and still emotionally drained from running into Katie's mother, Mike dragged his feet the entire day. Usually in high gear whenever it came to work, each box, each piece of furniture felt like it was 200 pounds and his entire body ached. Also, the clock seemed to standing still. What even made it worse was that Mike had always joined in the playful teasing whenever anyone else came in with a hangover. Now it was their turn to reciprocate the favor.

"Hey what's the matter Mikey," joked Carl, one of the guys on his crew. "What'd you go out last night? You look a little pale."

"Na," replied Mike, straining himself just to talk. "It's from Saturday night."

That's when the other guy on the crew, Kevin, jumped in. "Saturday night! Man, what are you a pussy? You're telling me you're still hungover from two days ago."

"Fuck you Kevin." Mike knew they were only joking just as he always joked with them, but he was in no mood. He tried to brush it off knowing that the worse they saw that it got to him the harder they would press, but he just couldn't seem to put on a game face.

"Hey Mikey," said Carl, who was 6'4" and even more muscular than Mike, "we're gonna go to the Ann Street Pub out in Farmingdale after work. You wanna come? C'mon, a few shots of Jack Daniels will fix you right up."

Just the sound of it made Mike want to vomit. "Na, that's all right. You guys go and knock your self's out."

"Hey Mike, after we're done loading the truck, we have to deliver this shit to they're new apartment in Queens and it's on the third floor."

"Yeah, man that's going to be a bitch," Kevin added. "Those freight elevators in queens are as small as my closet. Most of the stuff we're gonna have to lug up the stairs. You ready for that Mikey?" They both watched Mike cringe at the thought. Of course they were only pulling his leg. The three of them always busted each other's chops. It was just guys being guys. It wasn't anything personal.

Somehow Mike managed to make it through the rest of the day, even with Carl and Kevin riding his back the whole way. It wasn't easy, but knowing how hard he was going to get on them the next time they came to work with a bad hangover made it almost worthwhile. For the time though, all he wanted to do was go home, get something to eat and sit in front of the television. In fact, doing nothing ever sounded so appealing.

However, as soon as Mike walked though the door his mother informed him that Melissa's school had called her at work. Melissa had been caught with three other girls, smoking pot in the girl's bathroom. Lucky for her, in 1985, most schools still handled such incidents by themselves and rarely called the police. Nevertheless, Melissa was suspended for a week and the principal wanted Betty to come in the next day for a talk.

Mike was furious. Fortunately for Melissa, she was not home at the time, probably realizing that the school was going to call. "I'm going there tomorrow," he shouted as his face cringed with anger.

"Going where Michael?"

"I'm going to that school and get to the bottom of this," he replied sternly while talking with his hands. "I'm going to talk to the principal and find out what the hells' going on."

Betty put her shaking hand on her forehead. "Michael, they asked for me to go – her mother. Besides, look at you. If you go there I know what's going to happen. You're going to go off on a tirade just like you are now. That's why I was reluctant to even tell you at first."

"I don't care! I'm going to that school." Pacing in a circle around the living room, Mike tried to compose himself. He would have to calm down if he was going to talk his mother into letting him go to the school. "Listen," he said in a more subdued, but still agitated voice, "I know they asked for you to go, but I'll just tell them that you couldn't get out of work."

"Oh, sure, how does that make me look? My daughter's about to get kicked out of high school and I won't even take the afternoon off work to go to the school."

Mike then tried to plead his case from a different angle. "Ma, just listen to me, is Mrs. Fitzpatrick still the principal?" Betty shook her head. "O.K. I know Mrs. Fitzpatrick."

"That's even more of a reason why you shouldn't go," she replied in an unusually aggravated tone. "Do you forget the rapport you had with Mrs. Fitzpatrick and the rest of your teachers? It wasn't exactly a loving relationship Michael. In fact you probably gave most of them ulcers."

"Very funny ma. Listen, we both know that if Melissa's going to listen to anybody, it's going to be me."

Betty shook her head. "I hope so Michael. I mean I hope you can talk some sense into her."

Mike realized what his mother must have been thinking: that everything she went through with him she was going to have to go through with Melissa – and wondered how much more trauma one woman could endure.

Somehow, Mike managed to talk his mother into letting him go to the school. When Melissa finally came home that night, neither Mike nor his Mrs. Patterson said anything about the school calling. They both felt that there was no use discussing it before Mike had a chance to talk to her principal. That did not mean however, that it wasn't hard for either of them to bite down on their tongues – especially Mike.

The next morning Mike called into work sick, knowing that his co-workers were going to bust his chops, thinking that he was still nursing a hangover. But what they thought was the furthest thing from his mind. All he was concerned about was Melissa. Melissa had left the house that morning like she always did, holding her backpack full of books, unaware that Mike and her mother knew that she had been suspended. Where she was really going was anybody's guess. Mike knew wherever it was though, she would be up to no good. At first he wanted to stop her from walking out the door, but resisted, still feeling that it was better to talk to the principal first.

Before Mike left the house, he made sure to look his best, putting on a pair of black dress slacks and a sweater over a button-down collared shirt. It was important to for him to make a good impression on Mrs. Fitzpatrick, not only for Melissa's sake, but also his own. The last time she saw him was in faded jeans and a Black Sabbath t-shirt, with hair halfway down his back and bloodshot eyes. He was sure that Mrs. Fitzpatrick knew what had happened to him – doing time in prison – but was determined to show her the responsible young adult he had become.

Mike drove his mother to work and headed for Melissa's school. As Mike approached his old high school, a strange and unexpected sensation overcame him. It was the past once again staring back at him. Although it has been less than ten years since he had last walked through the halls of the school, it seemed a lifetime ago. Mike found it ironic that six years ago he was the one always in trouble. He was the one that didn't want to listen to all the rhetoric of how the decisions he was making were going to affect the rest of his life. Now there he was, making the same trip for Melissa that his mother made for him many times before. As Mike parked the car in the visitor's lot he could not help but turn back the years. Looking around he remembered cutting classes and having someone pick him up in that very same parking lot. He remembered how groups of them used to sneak across the street to houses that were being built at the time. They would sit inside their unfinished frames sometimes all afternoon getting stoned and trading stories about girls and music. He remembered how the handball courts, adjacent to the parking lot, used to be filled with kids smoking pot and selling drugs. He reminisced how every afternoon after the last dismissal bell rang, there would be a fight out in the parking lot. It was an eerie sensation for him to once again walk through those halls. Some things seemed exactly like they did years ago, yet others were so different.

The front office looked the same, but none of the faces were familiar. That was of course until he arrived at Principal Fitzpatrick's office. In a way Mike could not believe that she was still the principal of the school. Then again, he could not imagine anyone else at the helm. Feeling a sudden sense of nervousness, Mike told the unfamiliar secretary that he was there for Mrs. Fitzpatrick. When the secretary asked for a name, Mike explained that he was a former student and wanted to see if Mrs. Fitzpatrick would remember him.

The middle-aged secretary, whose nameplate simply read Mrs. Caroll, pressed a button on the square metal intercom. "Mrs. Fitzpatrick, there's some one here to see you."

"Who is it?" the familiar voice asked over the small speaker.

"He didn't want to give his name. He says he's a former student and wanted to see if you remember him." Mrs. Caroll, her finger still on the intercom, took another look at Mike. "If you want me to get his name…"

"No that's ok, I'll be out it a minute."

Sitting on a metal chair outside the office, Mike waited impatiently, wondering if she would recognize him right away. He looked different, but then again, Mrs. Fitzpatrick used to see him on an almost daily basis. In fact he was probably in her office more than her secretary. As a student, Mike had always hated Mrs. Fitzpatrick with a passion, but in hindsight understood that she was just doing her job and that *he* had been the one with the problem. In fact, Mike knew that if he had listened to her then, things probably would have turned out a lot different – for the better.

Alas, the moment arrived, as Mrs. Fitzpatrick opened the office door and stepped out into the small waiting area. Immediately Mike stood at attention with an anxious smile. The short, slender, gray haired principal looked at him with great curiosity as if trying to solve a riddle. Then, after about ten seconds she put her wrinkled hand over her opened mouth. "Michael Patterson, is that you?"

Mike's smile grew, like a child meeting Santa Clause. "Mrs. Fitzpatrick, yeah it's me. It's Michael."

"My gosh, you look so different. Look at you, I can't get over it."

Mike blushed, but was elated inside. "I cut my hair."

"Yeah, I can see," she replied, still looking him over in amazement. "You also grew some muscles," she said pointing to his arms. "And got a new wardrobe. Well, come in."

Looking all round, Mike followed his old principal into the familiar office. "Wow, seems like old times being in here doesn't it? It almost feels like I should be in trouble or something."

Mrs. Fitzpatrick laughed as she motioned Mike to have a seat. "Yeah, I guess you were in here quite a few times huh?"

"I'll tell you Mrs. Fitzpatrick, I wish I would've listened to you all those times. I wish I knew then what I know now."

"Well you know what they say: hindsight is always 20/20."

"Isn't that the truth?" Mike replied, glad to be having a civilized conversation with the woman he used to call the "Old Devil". "I just want to apologize up front for all the hard times I gave you. I must have been a real pain in the behind."

Mrs. Fitzpatrick smiled. "Don't worry about it Michael. It comes with the job. Besides, that's all in the past now. So tell me, how are you doing?"

Mike gave her a condensed five-minute version of how he had turned his life around. "Well Michael, I'm certainly pleased that things are going well for you now, but I must say that I am a bit surprised to see you. I was actually expecting your mother."

Mike cleared his throat, remembering the real reason for the meeting. It was good to see Mrs. Fitzpatrick and let her know how he was doing, but this reunion was not about him. Despite his own need for closure, this trip was about Melissa. "Well I'll be honest with you Mrs. Fitzpatrick, I convinced my mother that I should come see you instead of her."

"I understand that you're probably concerned about your sister, which is admirable, but the thing is Michael, it's really important that your mother be here."

Mike pulled his seat up and leaned over the cluttered desk. "I understand and the only reason she's not here is because of my persistence – and it wasn't easy talking her out of coming. But believe me; if Melissa's going to listen to anybody, it's going to be me."

"Have you tried talking to her before?"

"I've talked to her about drugs and about getting a good education, but maybe I wasn't stern enough. You see I didn't really know the scope of her troubles until I found out that she was suspended." Mike paused. "I don't know. I mean I hope she'll listen to me. If not, I don't know what's gonna happen."

Mrs. Fitzpatrick could see the frustration in Mike's face and hear the concern in his voice. "Well Michael, I hope she'll listen to you too."

"So tell me, other than what I already know, how bad is it?"

Mrs. Fitzpatrick hesitated before answering. "It's bad Michael. I'm afraid Melissa is heading down a very dangerous path."

Letting out a sigh of distress, Mike combed his hand through his hair. "Well obviously what she was suspended for is very serious – and that's bad enough – but are there other things that I should know about?"

In a concerned tone Mrs. Fitzpatrick briefed him on Melissa's situation. "Well, I guess starting in the second semester of last year your sister's grades started to slip. She also starting missing a few classes, but it still wasn't anything too serious. Yet I guess it was just a sign of things to come. I don't know what happened over the summer, but since the start of the school year, her grades have been taking a downward spiral – I mean Melissa used to be a straight 'A' student."

"I know," Mike frustratingly replied.

"Her teachers tell me that she hasn't turned in any of her homework the last few weeks," Mrs. Fitzpatrick continued, "and she's been cutting more and more classes. A couple of weeks ago one of the security staff caught her and another girl trying to skip out of school. When they were stopped, they were about to get into a car with a couple of boys that looked to be in their twenties. She's been hanging around a crowd that two years ago she would have never associated with. And this last incident, it's very serious Michael. Your sister was caught with two other girls smoking marijuana in the girl's restroom and when we brought them to front office, we found an empty vile in one of the girl's pockets."

Mike's face turned pale. "An empty vile?"

"It was empty, but it had a white, powdery film on it. They're just lucky that it wasn't full, otherwise we would have had no other choice but to call the police."

Mike could not believe what he was hearing: an empty vile, the police. It was worse than he had even thought. "Was one of the girls Allison McCall?"

"Yes –her partner in crime – but she wasn't the one with the vile."

"I don't know Mrs. Fitzpatrick. I really thought that when I came home things would be different. I never imagined this."

It was hard for Mike's former nemesis to see him in such disarray. "Well Michael, I realize that you are a good person to talk to Melissa because of your experiences and hopefully she'll listen to you, but if she doesn't, there *is* professional help you know. I can recommend some very good counselors that specialize in drug treatment. There are also places that are specifically designed for this sort of thing."

"Wait a second," Mike objected. "Are you talking about some sort of rehab?"

Mrs. Fitzpatrick could tell by the tone that Mike did not like the sound of it. Even so, she tried to plead her case. "They're called treatment centers and there's a reason they're called that. I know it may seem a bit dramatic, put if she really does have a problem these places…"

"Whoa, Mrs. Fitzpatrick," he interrupted again. "With all due respect, it's clear that Melissa has some serious straightening-up to do, but she's not some kind of junkie. I mean those places are for people who can't function without doing drugs. They're for people that are addicted to cocaine and heroine and whacked-out on PCP. I mean I've seen some of the people that are in these rehabs." Mike paused to gather his thoughts making sure to remain calm and respectful. "Make no mistake about it Mrs. Fitzpatrick, I'm in no way condoning my sister's behavior. In fact I'm more upset about this than anyone. And you're right, she is heading down a dangerous path, but she's not some addict. She's not at the point of needing to go to some rehab. Believe me, I would know. All she needs is some serious talking to and trust me, I'm not going to let her B.S. me this time."

When Mike finally left the office it was with mixed emotions. It had been good to see Mrs. Fitzpatrick after all those years, but wished it could have been under different circumstances.

Mike told Mrs. Fitzpatrick that he would talk to Melissa and that would be enough, but inside he was not sure. The fact was that Mike was unprepared for what was happening. It was nearly impossible for him to see Melissa as anything but his young, innocent baby sister who would one day grow-up to be a doctor or some executive. Her future had always appeared so limitless and the possibility that it was in jeopardy was something that Mike could not accept. How could this have happened, he asked himself as his frustration turned to anger, then to the fear, then back to frustration. He knew something had to be done.

Barely concentrating on the road, Mike headed home as his thoughts continued to bounce back and forth. One minute he would go back to thinking that all Melissa needed was a good talking to, but then wondered what if she didn't listen. After all, she had not listened before. One minute he tried to convince himself that she was just going through a phase; many teenagers experiment with drugs and turn out to be fine. There were many famous people who did a lot worse than smoke some pot and get suspended from school. Maybe he was just overreacting because of what *he* had gone through? But what if it was not just a phase? What if she was on a course to end up like all those kids that you never hear about, because they never made anything of their lives? What if she ended up in jail or even worse? Then Mike started thinking about the guys she was hanging out with. What was she doing with them? It was all so overwhelming.

After arriving home Mike walked into the kitchen to get a glass of water and wound up standing in front of the refrigerator, staring aimlessly in a daze. He wanted to do something, but did not know what to do. It was an utter feeling of helplessness. For what seemed like an hour – but was probably more like ten minutes – Mike stood there frustrated, wondering what it was he could do. Then finally, out of the chaos of his scrambled thoughts, Brian's voice appeared in his head: "Have you tried snooping around in her room?" At the time it was suggested, Mike shot down the idea. He had never invaded his sister's privacy, even when they were little kids growing up. It was a matter of trust and respect, which was part of the foundation that allowed them to build such a close relationship. Nevertheless, Mike now knew that it had to be done. Besides, Melissa had already broken that trust.

After taking off his coat and sweater Mike reluctantly climbed the stairs up to his sister's room. Swinging the door open, he was overcome by a sense of guilt, but knew it was something that had to be done. Standing there in the middle of the room, with the overpowering silence of the house playing on his mind, Mike zeroed in on the wooden dresser and decided to start there. As he opened the small, wood jewelry box on the dresser top the guilt grew, but still he pressed on. Finding nothing but jewelry and a picture of Melissa with Allison, Mike moved onto the top draw. It was not easy to shuffle through his sister's most intimate apparel, but knew that the underwear draw was one of the most common places that people used to hide things in. Carefully he searched and felt through the neatly folded stacks. Then, almost ready to move onto the next one, his hands felt something at the bottom of the draw. Mike could not believe his eyes as he pulled out a box of condemns. He then noticed the box was opened and some of the individual wrappers gone.

Mike continued to search the room for hours. He had learned in prison the clever and inconspicuous places that people could hide contraband – and that was in a 10x10 cell. There were literally hundreds of places where Melissa could have stashed something in her room – especially a small baggy or pipe. Mike had the whole afternoon though and was determined to find anything that may have been hidden. He searched beneath the mattress, in the night table, in the pockets of the clothes that were hanging up in the closet, behind the posters to see if anything was taped to the back of them. Then, while going through the shoes that were in her closet, Mike pulled out a small white piece of paper folded into the shape of an envelope. Mike knew immediately what it was. Anyone that knew anything about drugs knew how to fold a piece of paper into a coke seal. It was cheaper and less cumbersome than a vile and you didn't have to go out and purchase little tiny zip-lock baggies. All you needed was any piece of paper from a notebook or magazine and after you were done snorting the contents, you could lick the paper and just throw it away. Mike opened it, revealing two small glistening rocks of cocaine, probably weighing a total of a half-gram. Mike knew specifically that it was cocaine and not something else because he had seen and done enough of it. Sitting Indian-style halfway in the small closet, Mike held the opened piece of paper in his shaking hands, staring at its snow-white contents. The last time Mike had held cocaine – or even seen it – was the night Katie committed suicide. Captivated by being so close to it, Mike wondered how such an innocent, white substance could reap so much devastation.

Mike had grown-up in the disco era when cocaine was glamorized as some sort of social wonder drug. At the swank Manhattan clubs, people snorted it as casually as they would sip a glass of wine. In the late seventies the news proclaimed it a drug for the upper-class and as such it reached an almost acceptable status. After all, most of the people in the clubs blowing lines would get up on Monday and go to work in their posh high rise office buildings. They were stockbrokers and advertising executives and CEOs. Those who knew no better looked upon it as some sort of weekend escape that let normal people put on a different mask. However Mike *did* know better. He knew that dismissing cocaine as a harmless byproduct of the disco clubs was dangerous ignorance. Mike was unfortunate enough to see first hand the darker, more prevalent side of the "wonder" drug. He knew of the truth. He had seen the lives cocaine had left destroyed in its all-consuming wake. For every story of harmless experimentation, there were five more of people becoming addicted. For every story of an addict being able to quit and turn his life around, there were ten more of those who would never make it. Mike knew that the stranglehold cocaine had on so many of its unsuspecting victims was far from an exaggeration. People staring out windows and thinking their phones were tapped; people hearing voices; selling all their belongings for another fix; being admitted to the emergency room; having to smoke and shoot it up because their noses were clogged with dried blood – they were true and Mike had witnessed them all first hand. He knew about all the things that they never showed on the news or taught in school and it terrified him to know that Melissa had journeyed into that unforgiving world. He did not know how far in she had gone – if she would be one of the lucky ones or become another victim – but the door had been opened and she was in there somewhere. His job was now to find and bring her back. The only hope though, was that she had not ventured too far for him to grasp.

By the time Mike was finished searching through Melissa's room, he had found the condoms, the envelope with the cocaine in it, a marijuana pipe, a razor blade and glass straw, both with cocaine residue on them. What bothered him the most – maybe even more than the cocaine itself – was the glass straw; a three-inch hollowed out glass tube. The casual cocaine user would just use a rolled-up dollar bill to snort a line. The fact that Melissa had her own glass straw meant that she was probably doing it more than just on the weekends at parties.

Leaving her bedroom door open, Mike went to his own room and lay listlessly on the mattress, wondering how he could have been so blind. He of all people should have been able to see the warning signs. Alone in the unsettling silence of the house, he cursed himself for not realizing what was going on right beneath his nose. However, the forewarnings were there, Mike had just chosen not to see them. He had been blind only because he had blinded himself. Melissa had always represented everything that was pure and innocent in the world and for her to have been corrupted by life's evils meant that the last bit of innocence that he believed still existed in the world was gone. For five long years while incarcerated, watching men stab each other for a cigarette and commit other unspeakable acts, Mike would think of his little sister and realize that there was still good and virtue in the world. To succumb to the fact that she was as fallible and tempted as everyone else would change everything. She was the hope still safe in Pandora's Box and now that too was gone.

Suddenly the sound of the front door opening shattered the silence of the house. Immediately Mike sat up on his bed and looked at the clock. It was 4:15pm. His mother didn't get home until after five, which meant it had to be Melissa.

"Mom, are you home?" Melissa's voice carried from downstairs.

Mike yelled back down. "No, it's me."

"Why's mom's car in the driveway?" she shouted, still downstairs.

"Mom's getting a ride home from one of her friends." Awaiting the inevitable confrontation that was soon to come, Mike's heart began to palpitate. "Can you come upstairs? I have to talk to you about something."

"Can't you come downstairs?"

"Just come upstairs!"

Nervous about confronting Melissa, Mike fretfully walked back into her room and waited. His stomach tightened as the footsteps of her climbing up the stairs echoed in his head. The closer the footsteps became, the more his stomach knotted; the more his hands shook. It seemed like it was taking her forever to walk up that one flight of stairs, as if someone had put everything into slow motion. Standing in the middle of the room holding the cocaine, pipe and straw Mike scurried to think of exactly what to say. Then, as the footsteps sounded like they were just right down the hall, Mike nervously put his hands behind his back.

"What are you doing home?" Even though Mike had heard Melissa coming all the way up the stairs, her entrance still startled him. "And what are you doing in my room?"

"I didn't go to work today because I was at your school talking to Mrs. Fitzpatrick."

Instantly, Melissa's facial expression morphed into the guilty look of some one that had just been caught red handed. For a second, neither Melissa nor Mike knew what to say. A tension had built around the room like a wall and no one was going to escape without knocking it down. At first, Melissa's mouth opened to speak, but no words came out. Then she tried a second time. "What were you talking to Mrs. Fitzpatrick about?"

"About you being suspended for smoking weed in the school bathroom," Mike snapped back.

Melissa appeared outraged that she had been busted. She stood there in the doorway scurrying for words to say. She couldn't deny being suspended or getting caught in the bathroom. There was no blaming it on somebody else. There was no plausible excuse. There was no way to bullshit her way out of it and that was what infuriated her the most. "Does mom know?"

"Of course she knows," Mike replied with his hands still behind his back. "The school called her at work yesterday."

"So the two of you knew about it yesterday and didn't say anything?!!"

"I wanted to talk to Mrs. Fitzpatrick first, before I talked to you."

"Why?" Melissa shot back at her brother in a tone she had never used towards him before. "What business of it is yours?"

"It's my business because you're my sister and I care about you!"

It was clear from the hostile look on her face that Melissa was not going to try to sweet talk her brother this time. This was a conversation that was not going to end in an understanding and a hug. "Oh, all of a sudden you come home and you feel the need to play everybody's guardian angel."

Mike was taken aback by his sister's remark. "What's that supposed to mean?" He asked as his adrenaline started to pump even harder.

"It means that since when did you become holier than thou. I mean it's not like you were never suspended from school. Hell, I kind of remember you dropping out of school."

"This isn't about me Melissa!"

Again, Mike could see his sister struggling to find words to throw back. "I told you before Mike that you can't run my life."

"You also told me to trust you," he replied, finally bringing his hands forward, revealing the coke seal and other paraphernalia.

Melissa's jaw instantly dropped to the ground. "You went through my room," she shouted as she raised both hands. "I can't believe you fucking went through my room!" Melissa had never cursed at her brother before.

"Listen Melissa, I didn't want to, but…"

"You didn't want to!" she yelled with flying spit as she drew closer to her shaking brother. "I can't fucking believe this! And you have the balls to talk to me about trust!"

Mike had never heard his sister talk like that before and had never witnessed her in such utter rage. For a second he thought that she might pick up a lamp or picture frame and throw it at him. "Melissa, don't you know what this stuff will do to you?"

"Oh I see," she yelled back, "all of a sudden you've become the righteous one! There was certainly nothing wrong with it when you were doing it. Or I guess there are different rules for you, huh! I guess only the great Mike Patterson can get high and get in trouble at school and get arrested!" Melissa was screaming so loud that Mike was waiting for the windows to shatter – either that or for her head to explode.

"I told you before, this isn't about me." Mike tried to keep telling himself that Melissa did not mean the things she was saying – that she was just mad at being caught – but her words were sharper and cut deeper than any sword. "That's right, I did all those things! That's exactly why I know what I'm talking about. I know what this shit can do to you."

Catching Mike completely off guard, Melissa tried to snatch the cocaine from his hand, but was unsuccessful. "What the fuck are you doin! That's my shit!" She screamed.

"What am I doing??!! What are you doing??!! Are you fucking crazy? Look at yourself! You've completely lost control! I can't believe it."

Melissa had become so infuriated she was starting to cry. "Just leave me the fuck alone! What the fuck do you want from me?"

"I want you to get some help Melissa. I mean look at you – you're doing cocaine, you're getting yourself kicked right out of school, you have a box of condemns in your draw…"

"You went through my underwear draw?" she growled, as her eyes pierced into her brother like two pointed arrows. "What, did that turn you on?"

"What?"

"You heard me! You probably got off on it!"

At that point, Mike was not sure exactly how to respond. All he knew was that the fiery figure in front of him could not have been his sister. He could not accept the fact that she was actually saying these things to him. However her onslaught was not yet over. "Just because you ruined Katie's life doesn't mean you have to make up for it by trying to control everyone else's! I mean where were you for the last five years? Even better, where have you been for the last eight years?" Mike just stood there speechless, dying inside. "Where were you when I needed you? You haven't been around for most of my life. Now you want to save me just so you can make yourself feel better about your own fuck-ups? Well it's not going to work, Mr.

Born Again. The last thing I need is to be saved by some one who couldn't even save them self. Hell, you couldn't even save Katie. So I don't need you in my business! I'll do what I want and fuck who I want!"

With that, Melissa stormed out of the room and down the hall. Mike wanted to follow her, but was frozen. It was as if Melissa had ripped out his heart and taken it with her. He felt like crying, he felt like passing out, he felt like giving chase, but all he could do was stand there in a trance as her lingering words continued to stab deep into his soul. He fought to unglue his feet from the floor and conjure up enough strength to run after her, knowing that if she left the house there was no telling when she would be back again. Then, finally somehow instinct took over as he ran blindly through the hall and down the stairs.

When Mike reached the base of the stairs, he caught something through the corner of his eyes: it was his mother sitting on the couch with her head in her hands, crying. She must have come home while they were upstairs. How much she heard, Mike did not know, but it was obvious that she had heard enough. Paralyzed again, Mike stopped at the foot of the stairs and watched her there, crouched over and sobbing helplessly. Yet he knew he still had to chase after Melissa. So trying to block out the haunting sound of his mother's muffled cries, Mike continued the pursuit. However, by the time he finally made it to the front door, Melissa was gone. With his heart pounding fast enough to cause a heart attack, he ran out to the sidewalk and looked down the street both ways, but she was nowhere in sight. Still determined, he started to run down the street calling her name, but realized that she probably had a three to five minute head start on him. Finally giving up he stopped half way down the block as neighbors peered from their windows to see what all the commotion was about.

Mike walked slowly back to the house as if he was a death row inmate being led to the gas chamber. Part of him wanted to run back and console his mother, but the other part wanted to just runaway. Mike did not want to believe what he had just seen, what Melissa had said to him or what he had found in her room. He didn't want to believe any of it and wished that it was all some cruel, bad dream. The whole world was crumbling before his eyes and it was taking with it everyone he cared about. Not even in prison did Mike feel so wounded, so uncertain, so afraid.

Eventually, Mike walked back to the house and comforted his mother. He felt that he could talk to her about anything, share any emotions, but he was wrong. He could not express to her the pain he was feeling. He could not even put it into words. Mike did not ask his mother how much she had heard and she did not say. They sat on the couch together only talking about where Melissa might have gone and when she might be coming back. Mike mentioned nothing about the things he had found in her room.

That evening Mike called the few friends of Melissa's to which they had the phone numbers. But it was to no avail; either they hadn't seen her or were lying. Mike had no idea where his sister was, nor knew when he would see her again.

Later that night Diane called and immediately picked up the distraught tone in Mike's voice. When she asked him what was wrong, Mike divulged the whole story: about Melissa being suspended, about finding the cocaine in her room and her storming out of the house. However he left out Melissa's scornful words. It was still too painful for him to repeat. Diane tried to console Mike, telling him that everything would work out, but inside she was not so sure. Diane was angry with Melissa for putting Mike and their mother through such turmoil, but was also worried about her. She was afraid of what might happen, how deep she would dig her hole. Yet Diane did not share her apprehension with Mike, knowing that he was distressed enough.

Not surprisingly, Mike was unable to get any sleep that night. For hours he tossed and turned in the bed as wide-awake as if it was the afternoon. So many thoughts and worries raced through his twenty-four year old mind, each one of them more burning then the next. If he even tried closing his eyes, the thoughts formed into images, making things even worse. Not since his first months in prison did anything weigh so heavy on his conscious. Mike thought about Melissa out there somewhere. Was she safe, he wondered? Was she outside somewhere in the bitter cold? Who was she with? What was she doing? When would she come home? He thought about his mother, with the picture of her crying on the couch still embedded in his mind. What was *she* thinking? Was she lying in her bed crying, wondering if Melissa would end up behind bars just like him – or even worse? He wondered how he could console her. What could he say to set her mind at ease – was there anything at all? He questioned how much more his mother could take and was overcome with a helpless guilt for what *he* had put her through. Perhaps most of all though, Mike thought about what Melissa had said that afternoon. Her words sustained in his head as if she was right there in the room still yelling them. People always say things they don't mean when they're mad, but they had to come from somewhere. Mike felt an overwhelming sense of guilt. No matter how hard he tried to change his life around, there was no making up for the past. Mike couldn't go back and be there for Melissa's first day in high school. He couldn't go back and be there when she first started dating or getting into trouble. There was no going back to be with her all the years he was absent from her life.

The next morning Mike called into work sick again. He had only slept for two hours and felt miserable, but the real reason was the hope that Melissa would come home that morning. However, she never did.

Waiting until after school, Mike made another round of calls to Melissa's friends, this time asking for the phone numbers of other people with whom Melissa might be staying. In all, Mike made over a dozen calls, but to no avail. If anyone knew where Melissa was they weren't saying. It was frustrating, but he didn't know what else to do, short of breaking down doors and physically searching people's houses.

When his mother came home from work, they sat at the kitchen table for nearly two hours trying to figure out where she could be, how they could make her come home and most of all how they could get her help.

After giving it much thought, Mike finally told his mother about the cocaine he had found in Melissa's room. It turned out that she had already known about it from overhearing most of the confrontation the day before. Like Melissa's principal, Betty thought that rehab was the answer. Surprisingly, Mike still felt that he could reach out to his sister.

When Mike arrived at work the next morning he was stopped by his boss Dave, who asked how he was feeling. Dave was not trying to see if Mike was lying about being sick the past two days. Rather, it was out of genuine concern. Not wanting to lie to his face, Mike confessed. "Listen Dave, I'm gonna level with you. I wasn't really sick the last few days. My sister Melissa got herself suspended from school Monday for smoking pot in the girl's bathroom so I took the day off to go talk to her principal."

At first Dave looked a disappointed. "Mike, you could've just told me that in the first place."

"I know Dave and I'm sorry. It's just that she's got me so crazy I can't even think straight. I know that that's not an excuse, but I'm just at my wits end. After I got back from the school I searched her bedroom and found a seal with coke in it." Still without much sleep and emotionally drained, Mike paused to catch his breath. "Then when she came home we had this big altercation. She blew up and pretty much called me the anti-Christ. Then she stormed out of the house and didn't come back. I tried calling some of her friends, but nobody knows where she is – or at least they're not telling me. That's why I didn't come in yesterday. I thought she would come home during the day. I mean after all, she didn't even take any shit with her."

At that point, Carl walked by and patted Mike on the back. "Hey, how you feelin' big guy?"

"OK," Mike replied in a worn out voice.

"Well I'll see you at the truck," Carl said, seeing that Mike and Dave were in the middle of a conversation.

"Sure thing," Mike replied as Carl walked away.

The conversation then turned back to Melissa. "Did you have any idea that she was into that?" Dave asked in a concerned voice.

"No man, that's the thing. All of this is completely out of left field. I mean I thought that she maybe put down a few beers on the weekends, maybe took a puff off a joint now and then, but that's it. You don't understand Dave. If you would have told me my sister was doing blow – that would have been like telling me the pope is Jewish."

Dave felt bad for Mike. "Do you think she's really into it or it's just something she tried a few times?"

"I don't know," he replied in frustration. "About three weeks ago I ran into her ex-boyfriend who said she had started hanging out with this real bad crowd and kind of implied that she was into that kind of stuff, but I thought he was full of shit at the time. When I asked my sister about it she told me that he made it up 'cause he was pissed off that she had dumped him."

Dave knew that Mike was afraid of his sister winding up making the same mistakes as him. "Well what are you going to do about it?" Mike bowed his head towards the floor. "I don't know? Both her principal and my mother think she should be put in some rehab." Mike paused and rubbed the back of his neck. "But I don't know, that sounds pretty harsh. I mean I don't know if she's at that point yet? Besides, you did time," he said pointing at Dave. "You know what it's like being locked-up. I don't want to have to put my sister through that. I mean shit, she's only seventeen."

Dave let out a deep breath. "Well I'm not trying to tell you what to do, but I don't think you can go comparing rehab to prison. I don't think you can compare anything to being in prison. You should know that."

"I guess you're right."

"Look, I'm not trying to put my nose in your business, but if your sister is in over her head you know she's not just gonna stop on her own. You know that's not the way it works." Dave sounded more like a mentor than a boss and Mike listened to him as such. Mike understood that Dave had been there and knew what he was talking about. "These rehabs these days, it's not like just being locked up in some room for twenty-four hours a day. They have regular high school classes and other activities and some of the counselors are ex-addicts so they're not just talking out of their ass. And it's not like prison where you're in there with a bunch of murderers and rapists where you have to watch your back every second. I don't know Mike…"

Before Dave could finish the sentence, some one called for him from across the garage. After telling the person that he would be right there, Dave put his hand on Mike's shoulder. "Listen, you know I have a business to run, but I understand the tough predicament you're in. Besides, you always come to work on time and bust your ass. Hell, you're the best worker I got," he said low enough so none of the other employees would hear. "So if you need to take another day or two off to take care of things, just let me know."

For the first time in days Mike actually cracked a smile. "Thanks Dave, I appreciate it, but I should be ok. And I'm sorry for leaving you strapped the last two days."

"Well it's not like you don't have any sick days coming to you. And don't forget, for what it's worth, the shop's going to be closed all Christmas week."

With that, Dave patted Mike on the back and wished him good luck. Mike knew he was fortunate to have Dave as a boss, not only because he was easy to work for, but also because they could relate to each other. They could understand where each other were coming from and it was one thing to listen, it was another to understand.

Understandably, it was difficult for Mike to concentrate at work that day. More than a few times he nearly dropped a box or piece of furniture. His body was exhausted and his mind was someplace else. It wasn't long before Mike let Carl and Kevin in on his sister's situation and why he hadn't been at work the last two days. It wasn't that he wanted everyone to know about his business, but they could see that something was wrong and he just did not want to lie to them. The three worked side-by-side together five days a week, eight hours a day for nearly three months. They had become a team and as such had formed a certain bond.

Both Kevin and Carl sympathized with their buddy's situation, but shared different views. Kevin told Mike that Melissa was just doing what most kids her age did and that she would eventually come out of it on her own. Carl, on the other hand, thought that moving would be the best answer. He said the only way Melissa was going to straighten up would be if she were separated from her friends. Carl told Mike that even if Melissa went to rehab, once released she would be surrounded with all the same people she used to hang out with and the temptations would be too great. That's why rehabs didn't work in most cases, he argued.

By Friday, more than two days had passed without any word from Melissa or her whereabouts. However, all that was about to change. Mike had just come home from work and was getting ready to canvass some of the local bars and hang outs when the phone rang. It was the police. Melissa was a passenger in a car, whose driver was stopped for drunk driving. Yet that was just the beginning. One of the other passengers had outstanding warrants and was taken into custody. Melissa was not under arrest, but because she was technically still a minor, the Sergeant said that she could only be released to a parent or guardian. Betty, who was already home from work, could tell from overhearing Mike on the phone that something was wrong. When he told her what it was, she went into a complete panic. Throwing her hands around in the air, she started going through the entire gamut of emotions, from anger to concern to discontent. "How could she do this? What the hell is wrong with your sister?" she yelled. "Oh my god, we have to go get her Michael. She must be so scared." Then she would go back to anger. "Maybe we should leave her there. Maybe that's exactly what she needs." Then came the disappointment. "Oh Michael, how could she do this to herself. Doesn't she realize that she's going to throw her whole future away?"

In a reversal of roles, Mike became the calm and collective one. In a very business-like fashion he grabbed his coat, gloves and car keys. Mike was distraught, but was focused on getting Melissa home. He knew that there was probably more to the story than what the sergeant had said over the phone. He didn't know what it was, but that didn't stop paranoid theories from racing through his mind. Mike did not buy the reason that was given for holding Melissa in custody. Were they just waiting for his mother to get there to arrest her? Were they trying to get her to roll over on somebody or become a snitch?

Less than ten minutes after receiving the call, they were on their way to the police station. Too nervous to drive, Betty sat in the passenger seat continuing to rant and rave about her daughter and the dead end road that she was heading down. Mike, who was focused on nothing but getting to Melissa, did not say anything as he weaved in and out of traffic.

From the moment they pulled into the parking lot of the station house a queasy sensation started gnawing at Mike's focus and it had nothing to do with Melissa. Although Mike blamed all his past troubles on no one but himself, he still held certain skepticism and paranoia towards the police. Being surrounded by all those patrolmen and detectives brought back many memories that he would rather not have revisited. Regardless of the reasons for their troubles, no who gets arrested or spends time behind bars has warm and fuzzy feelings for any part of the criminal justice system. It was not that Mike had an animosity towards the cops or even thought about them at all. After all, he was a law-abiding citizen now and had no reason to be arrested. It was just that he had assumed that he would never have to deal with them again. He had thought that he would never again have to see the inside of a police station. Now there he was, walking into one voluntarily.

As Betty informed the Desk Sergeant why they were there, Mike swore that every cop that walked by looked him over with suspicion. An unforeseen anxiety grabbed hold of his gut as not so pleasant flashbacks came to life. Even though Mike knew he was not in any kind of trouble, a small part of him still wondered if a door was going to lock behind him. He could not help it. With cold sweat starting to cover his hands, Mike inconspicuously glanced at the handcuffs dangling from the belts of officers who passed by. At one point Mike grabbed hold of his wrist remembering exactly how they felt. It was almost as if he could feel their cold, hard steel tightly clamping down on his skin. Standing by the front desk, waiting impatiently for some one to come and bring them to Melissa, Mike just wanted to get her and get the hell out of there. For him, being at that station was like a person who was afraid of the water being put on a raft in the middle of the ocean.

Finally a uniformed officer came and escorted them through a door and subsequent maze of desks to the sergeant that had called the house. "Sergeant Fitzsimmons, these people are here for the girl who was picked up with Mr. Dolsky and his friend."

The partially bald, husky Sergeant stood-up from his cluttered desk and extended his hand to Betty. "You must be Mrs. Patterson," he said in a congested voice as he shook her trembling hand. "And you must be her brother Mike, who I talked to on the phone."

"Yes," replied Mike as he gave the sergeant a sweaty handshake.

"Where is my baby?" Betty asked frantically.

"She's right over there, Mrs. Patterson", he said pointing to a bench on the other side of the room. Sitting there with a blank, emotionless stare was Melissa.

Betty put her hands over her mouth and gasped. Melissa looked terrible. Even from across the room Betty could see the heavy bags under her eyes and yellow tint to her skin. She was wearing dirty jeans and an oversized sweater that obviously did not belong to her. "Where's her leather jacket," Betty asked as she waved to get her daughter's attention.

"She wasn't wearing a jacket when she was picked up," the Sergeant replied matter-of-factly.

"But she had it on her when she left the house. Michael that was her favorite jacket. I bought it for her on her last birthday."

Mike grabbed hold of his mother's shaking hand. "It's ok ma. We'll worry about the jacket later." Still holding onto her hand, Mike looked over to where Melissa was sitting. He knew that she saw him, but she didn't look up. Instead, her eyes remained fixated on the floor. Mike had never seen his sister look so disheveled. Her hair, which was usually so glossy and free-flowing, looked like it had knots in it. Her eyes were heavy and her always soft and flawless skin appeared brittle and dry. Mike even noticed a small patch of acne under her lip. It was the first time he had ever seen any kind of blemish on her face. In fact Mike remembered Melissa saying once that her friends were always jealous because she never broke out.

"Please, sit down," Sergeant Fitzsimmons politely asked, pointing to the chair by the side of his desk. "There are some papers I need you sign." He then grabbed another chair for Mike to sit on.

They sat there as the middle-aged sergeant searched on his desk for the forms, shuffling through files and moving a cup of coffee that was close to falling off the edge. "My son said that Melissa was a passenger in a car that you pulled over for drunk driving."

Sergeant Fitzsimmons stopped rummaging through the papers and turned to Betty. "Well Mrs. Patterson, I'm afraid that's only the beginning of it."

"What do you mean?"

Mike leaned forward, also curious to know the whole story. Being in the police station may have brought back bad memories, but he knew that it was his only chance to hear what really happened. Mike knew that Melissa would give some bullshit version of what transpired.

With his hands clasped together, Sergeant Fitzsimmons leaned back, addressing both Betty and Mike. "Officers Donaldson and Spitz were driving down Sunrise Boulevard when they noticed a vehicle driving erratically. It was crossing in and out of lanes, practically running into other cars driving by." Betty let out a loud gasp, thinking of how close her daughter came to getting into an accident. "After pulling the car over, Officer Donaldson determined that the driver was apparently drunk," the sergeant continued. "He put in his report that the driver could barely stand-up. After administering the field sobriety test, the driver was placed under arrest for driving while intoxicated and searched. It was at that time that the one of the officers found a vile containing crack cocaine in his possession."

"Crack!" Betty yelled out so the whole precinct could hear.

"Yes, I'm afraid so," he replied, erasing any chance that they had just heard it wrong.

Mike clenched his hand into a fist and pounded it on his leg. "I can't believe this."

"Well I'm afraid it gets even worse," the Sergeant proclaimed, keeping his business-like demeanor. "Both the driver and other male passenger had outstanding warrants on them. They're both accused of breaking into a string of houses in Babylon over the summer. They were arrested in September, but posted bail and never showed up for their next court date."

Fighting back tears, Betty turned to Mike. "How did she get caught up with people like this?"

Sergeant Fitzsimmons handed her a box of tissues. "Well your daughter's story is that she was just hitchhiking and they picked her up. However the driver told one of the officers that they had met her the night before at a party."

Mike had heard enough. It was right then and there that he knew Melissa had to go to rehab. There was no other way. He knew that as bad as things were, they would only get worse unless drastic measures were taken. Mike feared that the next phone call might be Melissa saying she was in jail, or even worse, the hospital calling to say that she had overdosed. Turning to look at his sister who was still staring towards the ground, Mike wanted to cry. It was unimaginable to him how far deep she had fallen. There were no more excuses he could make for her and had given up on any splinter of hope that she was somehow just going through a phase and would grow out of it on her own. Mike's blinders had finally been removed, letting him see things for the ugly truth that they were. Melissa had wandered far down that dangerous path to a point where some never return from.

Still gazing at her from across the bustling police station, Mike suddenly felt a hand around his arm. "Michael. Michael." Snapping out of his thoughts, Mike realized that his mother had been trying to get his attention. "I was telling Sergeant Fitzsimmons that we hadn't heard from Melissa since Tuesday and that you tried calling all of her friends."

Mike just shook his head affirmatively with a glazed look on his face. His mother's words started to blend in with all the other white noise of the crowded room as the hot flash that had run though his body turned to a cold numbness. He wanted to leave and to erase it all from his head.

Sitting there was becoming too much for Mike to bear. The constant clicking of a dozen typewriter keys being hit all at the same time and sounds of people yelling and laughing began to overload his already worn senses. As his mother and Sergeant Fitzsimmons continued their dialogue, their words floating into the air and combining with all the other conversations going on at the same time, Mike looked in a daze around the room. From the corner of his eyes, he saw an officer sitting down what appeared to be a hooker onto the bench next to Melissa. It was an image that instantly burned itself into his mind – his baby sister sitting there in a crowded police station next to a prostitute. A part of him could not help but to wonder if someone saw them sitting there would they think that they were two prostitutes brought in together.

On the ride home, Melissa continued her silence, staring aimlessly out the rear passenger window. Again, Betty asked Mike to drive, though he could barely concentrate on the road. If the atmosphere in the car was tense on the way there, it was now explosive.

"How the hell can you get yourself mixed up with such derelicts?" Betty yelled. "Wanted for breaking into houses?! What the hell is wrong with you?!"

"Ma, it's all right. Just calm down," Mike pleaded as he tried to pay attention to the other cars. Mike was as upset as his mother, but just could not take anymore. His entire mind and body were shot.

Still, Betty continued. "Crack, Melissa? Don't you watch the news? Don't you know how many people die from doing that? Jesus Christ, what are you trying to kill yourself?"

"It wasn't mine," Melissa replied lethargically, finally breaking her silence.

"Well what am I supposed to believe, huh? Tell me," her mother yelled back. "You're picked-up with two..."

Before she could finish, Mike interjected. "All right," he hollered. "Please lets just everyone calm down for a second before I crash the damn car!"

When they arrived back home Melissa ran straight for her room. Neither Mike nor Betty followed. Instead, they adjourned to the kitchen, where Mike told his mother that they had to put Melissa in some kind of treatment center and right away. From there, they discussed the details. Mike could write a book on prison, but neither of them knew anything about rehab. How would they find the right one they asked each other? How would they admit her? Do they just bring her to the front door? Was there a waiting list? Were there even any rehabs on Long Island? They were all important questions that needed to be answered – but time was not on their side. Time was not on Melissa's side.

While Melissa stayed locked in her room, probably sleeping for the first time in days, Mike and Betty spent the rest of the evening on the phone calling treatment centers that they had found in the yellow pages. Luckily their hours were not nine to five. Both Mike and his mother knew that they could not wait until Monday to find a place. They knew there was a good chance that Melissa would take off again that weekend and there was no telling how long she would be gone for this time or what danger she might get into. They could not lock her in a room for two days to ensure that she would not run off. The time for action had come. Whatever the cost, whatever had to be done, they had to have a place to bring her the next morning. Otherwise, the next time Melissa left the house she might not come back.

Chapter 8

GETTING HELP

Around noon the next day, Betty went into Melissa's room and woke her up. It was not easy and when Melissa finally came to, it looked like she could have slept for another ten hours. "Just let me sleep a little more," she begged in a weary moan while burying her head beneath a pillow.

"No, come on," Betty replied in a loud, but non-confrontational voice. "Come on," she said again, clapping her hands. "You have to get up."

"Why," Melissa whined from underneath the pillow.

"We have to go."

Melissa grudgingly took the pillow off her head and sat up in the bed. With her legs still buried under the blanket, she pushed the tangled hair out of her face. "Go where?"

Betty explained that the police wanted to question her some more about the two guys with whom she picked up. Melissa assured her mother that she already told the police everything, but Betty was persistent. She told Melissa that if she did not cooperate in the investigation, she could be charged with obstruction of justice. Melissa thought the police were trying to intimidate her mother, but was not about to call their bluff. The last thing she wanted to do was go back to the police station and answer more questions, but if it was either that or being arrested, there really was no choice. Infuriated to have to do anything besides lay in bed and sleep, Melissa threw the rest of the covers off her and reluctantly headed for the bathroom.

By the time Melissa came downstairs, Betty and Mike were standing by the front door with their coats already on. After a comment about still not understanding why she had to answer more questions, Melissa grabbed an old ski jacket from the hallway closet. The three then walked out of the house, into the cold, arid air of the December afternoon. Melissa, who still had not said one word to Mike, climbed into the back seat of the car and began staring out the window as she had the day before.

As they headed on their way, no one spoke a word. It felt as if they were going to a funeral, not exchanging any conversation, not even looking at each other. Finally, about five minutes into the drive, Mike turned on the radio to cut through the uncomfortable silence. Not long after that Melissa popped out of her cocoon long enough to say that they were going the wrong way.

"We're not going to the same station," Betty replied. "They want us to go to the precinct house in Maspeth. That's where one of the officer's is working out of today."

It sounded plausible enough not to arouse any suspicion from Melissa. All she knew was that Maspeth was about a thirty-minute drive, giving her time to doze in the car. So that's exactly what she did.

When Melissa opened her eyes again, she realized they were in a parking lot. "This is a police station?" she asked, while shaking off her daze. Suddenly she noticed that there were no police cars or officers walking around. She also noticed that neither her mother nor brother was answering. "Where are we?" she asked in a more apprehensive voice as she sat up in the seat. Still, no one answered. Melissa was now wide-awake but still uncertain of where they were. Her anxiety was starting to mushroom. As she looked around for answers, Mike pulled the car up to the side of the drab, brick building that looked almost like a hospital. There she saw three men by a sliding glass door that looked as if they were waiting for them. "Mom," she said, now with unmistakable fear in her voice, "what's going on?" Still, her mother would not answer. "Mom," she said again while leaning over into the front seat. Then, as Mike opened the car door and was met by one of the men, she saw a sign by the entranceway: The North Shore Treatment Facility. In an instant everything came together. "You lied to me! The whole thing about the police wanting to ask me more questions was just a scam!"

"It's for your own good honey," Betty replied.

"For my own good," Melissa, shot back. "How can you do this to me?!"

As Melissa opened the back door and climbed out of the car she was met by the man that had greeted Mike. "We'll explain everything to you when we get inside," he said in a in a dry, monotone voice.

"Who the hell are you?"

"My name is Mr. Johnson," he replied as the other, much bigger man came over to form a wall between Melissa and the parking lot. "Like I said, I'll explain everything to you once we get inside."

"I'm not going anywhere!" Her words, although defiant, were filled with fear.

Suddenly the man who called himself Mr. Johnson stopped being so polite. "Listen Melissa, you can walk in on your own or we can carry you in.

Melissa looked back across the car at her mother and brother. "Mom," she cried out in a frantic plea for help.

"Just go with them honey… please." Betty could see the fright in her daughter's face, but knew that it had to be done.

Mike, who had his back to Melissa, could not even watch. As the man with Mr. Johnson grabbed Melissa by the arm, her sharp cries for help pierced right through Mike's head. "Mike," she cried out at one point as the men lead her away. Still Mike could not bring himself to look. A part of him wanted to rescue her. A part of him wanted to attack the men that led her off, but he knew, like his mother, that it had to be done.

With Melissa finally whisked away Betty and Mike followed Mr. Johnson into his office. There, he went over in detail all the rules of the center and there seemed to be many. In fact, Mr. Johnson handed them both a thick book of rules and regulations. Betty bombarded him with question after question, making sure she fully understood what was going to happen to Melissa. At first Mike also asked some questions, but soon drifted back to the image of his sister being dragged away.

Once back home, Mike called Diane, needing to vent and more importantly, needing to get out of the house. He knew just sitting there would drive him mad. So, after making sure his mother would be ok by herself, Mike went to meet Diane – having already given her the abridged version of everything that happened. After walking to Diane's house they drove to a bar/restaurant that she had recommended, which was a few towns over in Lindenhurst. Mike had never heard of it but didn't really care where they went, as long as it wasn't Baxter's. Mike just did not feel like running into anyone else. He just wanted to go somewhere where he could it down with Diane for a while and talk without being distracted.

Fortunately the place was not crowded and they were able to grab a secluded booth in the corner. As soon as they sat down, Diane called over a waitress and asked for two menus. "That's all right, you can only bring one menu," Mike said to the waitress. "I'm not really hungry," he then said to Diane.

"When was the last time you ate anything?"

Mike thought about it for a second. "Yesterday afternoon."

Diane looked back at the waitress. "You can bring us two menus. Thank you." Diane then leaned across the rectangular table. "I can't believe you haven't eaten anything since yesterday afternoon."

Mike let out a deep breath. "I'll tell you, I didn't even realize it until just now. It's just been so crazy. The last two days have been like a blur."

Diane took hold of Mike's hand. It hurt her to see him so worn and distraught. He looked like a man at the end of his rope and she could understand why. It was not even two weeks ago that he ran into Katie's mother. Now he had to go through all of this with Melissa. Diane knew he was strong, but everybody had their breaking point and Mike looked like he was about to reach his – if he had not reached it already. "You know you did the right Mike," she said in a soothing voice, still holding onto his hand.

"I know. It doesn't make it any easier though." Before Mike could continue, the waitress came back with the menus. While she was there, Mike ordered a beer and Diane a coke.

"You should have seen her there, Diane. I'll never forget the look on her face when she realized where she was. She tried to come off so tough and defiant, but I could tell how scared she was." Mike's eyes looked right through Diane as if he was picturing the whole incident all over again. "Finally I had to turn away. I couldn't look anymore. There's no way I could've watched those guys drag her away."

Diane could hear the sheer destitution in his voice. "They had to drag her away?"

"Well I think they just grabbed her by the arm and she finally went with them. Thank god, because I don't know what I would have done if she started running and they had to tackle her. I don't even want to think about that."

Diane was captivated by how much internal struggle there was in Mike's eyes. "Well the important thing is that she's there now and she'll finally be able to get some help."

"Still, a part of me can't believe that I did that to her."

Diane shook her head in frustration. "Melissa did it to herself and you know that," she replied as her soothing voice turned stern. "The only thing you did to her was help her."

"I know I did the right thing and you're right, the important thing is that she's going to get some help now. But you have to understand, she's still my baby sister and lying to her today and having her locked up... A part of me somehow feels like I led her to the lions. It's hard to understand, but I guess for me it's different. I mean I was locked up for five years. I know what it's like, it's awful. I can still remember when I was led away. That's something you don't forget."

"I don't think you can compare rehab to prison," she said in voice soft enough so no one at the other tables could hear. "Besides, I kind of remember you telling me on a couple of occasions that being locked up was probably the best thing that ever happened to you. In fact I remember you saying that it probably saved your life."

Before Mike could respond, the waitress came back with their drinks, diffusing the seriousness of the moment. While she waited, they quickly looked over the menu and ordered their food. From there, they continued to talk about Melissa, but in a more relaxed manner. Diane asked about how long Melissa would be there. She also asked how his mother was holding up. At one point Mike asked what was going on in Diane's life. How was her job at the bank going? Did she have any blowouts with her father lately? Mike had been so consumed with what was going on with his sister, he felt guilty that all they ever talked about lately was Melissa's problems. He didn't think it was fair that only one of them should be able to vent while the other always listened and sympathized. Maybe his problems were more pressing at the time, but he wanted their relationship to be a two way street. He wanted to be there for Diane just as she was always there for him. However, true to her form, Diane shrugged off Mike's questions and was only concerned with being there for him.

Over a couple of bar burgers, the conversation turned more mundane. "I can't believe how good this burger is," Mike declared.

"I told you they had good burgers here."

For the first time in days, Mike smiled. "Yeah and they're huge too," he replied with the enthusiasm of a child talking about a favorite toy. "I'll tell you, this place was a good choice. I think this might be one of the best burgers I've ever had. And just for the record, these fries are pretty damn good too."

Diane was happy to see Mike smiling. It had been a long time coming. Even if it turned out to be a fleeting moment, she was glad that he was finally able to relax and joke around a little. "So when are you and your mother going to visit Missy," she asked, hoping the question wouldn't sling him back into depression.

"Oh I didn't tell you," he replied, putting down the half-eaten burger. "She isn't allowed any visitors for the first two weeks. She isn't even allowed any phone calls," he said in a calm tone.

"Why is that?"

Mike finished chomping down some fries before answering. "It's standard procedure. They say it's mainly for two reasons. The first is that if we go to see her, in say a couple of days, she'll probably start crying and pleading and we might feel so bad that we'll go along with it. You know, the whole 'please, I promise if you get me out of here I'll straighten up' thing." Diane didn't say anything, but could see Mike falling for that one, hook line and sinker. "The second reason, is that she needs at least two weeks just to detach herself from the everything and get used to her new surroundings, which I can understand. I mean when I was first locked-up, it took me about three months just to realize where I was and how I got there. You just kinda need to detox from everything before you can start thinking clearly."

As they continued to eat their over-sized burgers, the conversation drifted to other things. Mike talked about being off of work for eight days starting the day before Christmas Eve. Every year the moving company he worked for closed for the week of Christmas. Apparently, not many people are in need of movers during that time. Since the time off was paid, in order not to lose too much money the company didn't give out bonuses, but Mike wasn't complaining. Although he enjoyed working, he could use the time off.

By the time they left the bar, it was dark out. With nowhere else to be and not feeling like going home, they walked to the car and talked about where to go. However talking lead to kissing, then to groping and although they still were not sure where to go, it was clear what they both wanted to do. So like a couple of high school kids, Diane drove until they found an empty parking lot in an isolated part of town where they made love in the back seat. A part of it felt silly. After all, they were both in their twenties. Yet a part of it felt seductive and even romantic. Maybe it was the excitement that they might get caught or that they were doing something naughty or taboo. For nearly an hour they were in that back seat, though it might as well have been a suite at the Waldorf Astoria.

After expending themselves, they climbed back into the front seat, and gazed out the windshield at the starlit night. Diane rested her head on Mike's shoulder, as he draped his arms around her like a coat. They had turned on the heater, but while it warmed up, the coldness of the December night still crept into the car. It was one of those serene moments that a person looks back on later in life with nostalgia. Sure, Mike had been going through a difficult time, but sometimes it is when things are at their ugliest that we most appreciate beauty.

"I want to thank you," Mike said in a subtle voice that seemed to blend into the tranquility of the moment.

Wrapped in his womb-like embrace, Diane lifted her head and smiled. "You don't have to thank me. It was my pleasure."

Mike smiled back. "I'm not talking about sex silly. I mean thank you for being here for me."

Not sure quite why, Diane found herself wanting to cry. She did know however, that it was not out of sadness. "You don't have to thank me for that either. I'm here for you because I want to be, just like you would be for me. That's what people do when they care about each other."

"I know," Mike replied in a fading voice. "But I just want you to know how much I appreciate it. I really do. A lot of other people would have been scared off with all the problems that are going on right now. And I know I haven't been myself..."

Diane stopped Mike before he could say anymore. "I'm not a lot of people. And nothing's going to scare me off. And don't worry, everything will work out."

Mike wanted to tell Diane that he loved her, something that despite all their time together, they had not yet said to each other. He wanted to tell her right then, but stopped himself. It was not that he thought Diane wouldn't reciprocate. In fact he knew she would. It was that he did not want it to appear that he was just saying it out of need. Mike loved Diane not because she was just some one that was there for him. It wasn't just because she acted like some sort of crutch he could lean on. Mike loved her because of who she was and wanted to make sure she understood that.

The following week was much calmer than the previous one. Although Mike and his mother could not see or talk to Melissa, they called the treatment center every other day just to make sure she was all right. It was difficult for both of them not to have any contact with her, but knowing that she was getting help made it palatable.

Monday, Mrs. Patterson went to Melissa's school to inform them where she was and make the necessary arrangements. The treatment center had said that they worked with various high schools to let patients finish their classes while being treated. The schools would send over assignments and tests and the center also had teachers on hand. Fortunately, Mrs. Fitzpatrick was more than willing to work something out and to Betty's delight, said that they had worked with The North Shore Center in the past. The principal was just happy to see that Melissa was finally getting help.

Mike spent most of the week occupied with work, trying to get back to his normal, productive self. Although much still weighed heavy on his mind, he was able to get back to concentrating on work without worrying about dropping boxes or feeling like passing out. Mike enjoyed working and the camaraderie he had with the other guys on the job. He liked joking around with them and breaking each other's chops. Mike also started going back to the gym after work. There, he was able to get his aggressions out and take his mind off of everything for a while. He was also glad to get back into a workout routine after neglecting it for the last two weeks.

Compared to the chaos of the week before everything seemed so calm and slow moving. There were no emergencies. Every time the phone rang, Mike and Betty were not afraid to pick it up. There was no wondering where Melissa was or what she was doing. The week crept along without any hitches and the tension that had permeated the house had lifted, leaving a much-needed sense of peace. It was as if Betty and Mike were able to finally catch their breath. Both of them knew that the road to recovery had just begun, but it really seemed like everything was going to work out.

Not lost however, were Mike's worries about his sister. Even though she was somewhere getting help, he still stayed up at nights wondering about how he had missed all the warning signs, how she could have become mixed up in so much trouble. He also wondered if rehab was going to save her. Mike was glad she was off the streets and out of harms way for the time being, but there were still many questions that needed to be answered.

Mike also could not help thinking about how close it was to Christmas. No one was certain for sure how much time Melissa would have to spend in rehab, but it was obvious that she would not be out in time for Christmas. Mike remembered how alone he felt all those years in prison and felt awful that Melissa would have to suffer that same fate. He knew better than anyone how abandoned she would feel and could hear her voice in his head: "How could you and mom do this to me? How could you leave me in here during Christmas? Mike, you of all people, how could you do this?" It was also not just any Christmas. It was supposed to be their first Christmas together as a family in over five years. Mike had been looking forward to this Christmas for so long. Not a week went by when he didn't think about it, picturing it in his mind. It was supposed to be the year when they could finally sit around the tree together, opening presents like they used to. They were supposed to have Christmas dinner together and say a prayer about how fortunate they were to be a family again. He had pictured Melissa coming down the stairs early that morning with a glowing smile on her face like she had when they were kids. She and Mike would tell jokes around the tree and reminisce about Christmases long past, as their mother proudly looked on. That is the Christmas Mike had envisioned. It was supposed to be perfect. Now, none of that was possible. Neither Mike, Melissa nor their mother would be able to celebrate Christmas as they had hoped – as they had dreamed about for the past five odd years. There would be no celebrations at all. Their perfect plans would have to wait at least another year.

However, as hard as it was knowing that Melissa would not be home, Mike knew that the big picture was what mattered the most. In the grand scheme of things, one Christmas seemed a reasonable sacrifice compared to the risks of what might have happened had Melissa spent one more day without getting help. She had been rapidly spiraling out of control and the consequences of her next actions could have been far more dire than not being able to be home for the holidays. There would be other Christmases God willing and Mike was willing to trade a little pain today for a lot of pain tomorrow.

That weekend Mike and Diane took Diane's niece to a movie. Mike had not seen Mary since Halloween, but the two picked up right where they left off. She told him that she still played with the light saber he had bought her and the two started talking about Star Wars again. Coming from a small family, Mike did not have any nieces or nephews or cousins. Maybe it was because Mary was so well behaved, but he loved spending time with her. He enjoyed her innocence and refreshing wit. Diane, who enjoyed being around children herself, also took pleasure in the way Mike interacted with Mary. Not only because it was her niece, but also because he seemed so happy around her. Diane loved watching the way he joked with her and the way she stared back at him with wide eyes and smile.

After the movie, they took Mary to get her picture taken with Santa Clause. Diane knew that her sister and brother-in-law had already taken her, but couldn't say no. She also knew there was no way Mike was going to pass up the opportunity. The mall was crowded and it was a long line, but none of that seemed to matter. As they waited there smiling, trading tales about Santa Clause and the North Pole, it was as if all of Mike's troubles were a million miles away. Afterwards they went to Friendly's for ice cream. It felt just like they were a family. For Mary it was just a good time – a typical day of being young. For Mike, it was therapeutic. Diane –she was just happy to see Mike smiling for a change.

Sunday night, Mike met Kevin for a few drinks at Baxter's. Since neither of them had to get up for work the next morning – they were off for Christmas week – they figured they'd meet up for a few brewskies and to shoot the shit. Mike filled his friend in on the whole Melissa saga. Kevin seemed to have a hard as time believing what happened to Melissa as Mike. He tried his best though, to be supportive and tell Mike that everything would work out. Later on Linda showed up with two of her friends. The five of them grabbed a table and talked over some drinks. Linda asked Mike how things were going with Diane, explaining what a perfect match they were. Kevin was busy trying to pick up on both of Linda's friends. Then after a few rounds, they played some games of pool. It was a nice relaxing time. Kevin and the girls were doing rounds of shots, but Mike stuck to his beer. He had a good buzz going, but wanted to pace himself, still remembering how miserable he felt the day after getting drunk with Brian.

Chapter 9

MISSY, WHERE ARE YOU?

T wo days before Christmas, any hopes that everything would somehow work out smoothly, came crashing down. Walking home from the gym, Mike noticed his mother's car in the driveway. Immediately Mike knew something was wrong, because it was 11:00a.m. Stopping in his tracks a flash of anxiety riddled through his body. At first he tried to tell himself that maybe it was not anything serious. Maybe she just wasn't feeling well or had forgotten something from the house. However, those thoughts quickly faded, leaving him fearing the worst as his imagination started to run rampant. Half of him wanted to rush to the house and find out what was wrong. The other half was too scared to find out. Mike could not stand out there forever, though, contemplating what to do. So with his heart racing faster with each step, he hesitantly walked to the house. Opening the front door, all that could be heard was silence – which worried him even more. Yelling out for his mother, she walked out of the living room and dropped the news on him like a bomb: Melissa had escaped from the rehab.

Taken completely off guard, Mike processed the news for a moment to make sure he heard it right. "What the hell do you mean she escaped?" he asked in a puzzled tone of voice.

"They called me at work."

Before Betty could say anymore, Mike cut her off. "How the hell does someone escape from rehab?!" He yelled as his confusion turned to rage.

"They said when they went to check on her this morning, she wasn't in her bed."

"This is fucking unbelievable," he shouted, using such profanity around his mother for the first time. "I mean do they have any idea where she is? I mean how the hell are they going to find her – send out a goddamn search party?" Mike pounded his fist on a nearby table, nearly breaking it. "I can't frigin believe this!"

Betty could take no more and broke into tears. "I don't know Michael? Why are you yelling at me? It's not my fault."

"Ma, I'm sorry," he said softly, putting his hands on her shoulders. Mike knew his mother already felt terrible enough about what happened. The last thing he wanted to do was make her even more upset. "I didn't mean to take it out on you, I'm sorry. I... I just can't believe she escaped. I mean I can't even believe I'm saying it."

Never one to show her weaknesses, Betty used her hand to quickly wipe away her tears. "I know, me either."

Mike threw his hands up in frustration. "I mean what are we gonna do? Where the hell can she be? She doesn't even have a coat. I mean its forty degrees out there. What is she wearing, the pajamas that the rehab gave her?"

"I don't know Michael. I called all of her friends, but none of them knew where she was or had heard from her." Betty paused to try and gather her thoughts. "What are we going to do Michael?"

Suddenly a light bulb went off over Mike's head. He knew who might be able to help. "Ma, I'm gonna need to borrow the car. You're not going back to work are you?"

"Well no, but where are you going? I don't want you to do anything stupid?"

"What am I gonna do that's stupid?" He replied in a surprisingly subdued voice. "I'm just gonna try to find out where she could be?"

Betty seemed reluctant, but was willing to try anything. Before leaving, Mike went upstairs to Melissa's room and grabbed her purse, which was still lying on the night table next to the bed. Instantly he found what he was looking for: her phone and address book. Mike was going to solicit help from an unlikely source: Melissa's ex-boyfriend, Tom. The last time Mike saw Tom was at Baxter's, when he had to be stopped from choking him. However Mike hoped that Tom cared about Melissa enough to put aside what happened that night.

Focused, Mike drove to Tom's house, which the address for was luckily in Melissa's book. Mike knew he would not be at school because it was Christmas break. However, Tom's mother answered the door and said her son was not at home. She had never met Mike before and at first was reluctant to divulge her son's whereabouts. But after Mike explained about Melissa she became sympathetic and said he was at work.

Armed with the information Mike headed for Fiestas, a Mexican restaurant where Tom was a waiter. Mike was a man on a mission and was going to find Melissa at any cost. Although he had been worried the last time she disappeared, this time was even worse. Before, there was still a sense that everything would somehow work out. Now the light at the end of the tunnel was darkening and there was a very real possibility that things would have a more tragic ending.

After taking a few deep breathes, Mike walked into the restaurant, which was busy with a lunch crowd. "Excuse me," he said in a polite, but stern voice to the hostess, "I'm looking for Tom Jamison."

As the hostess called for Tom, Mike waited impatiently, pacing by the front entrance. Every second felt like an eternity. Then, as he was about to ask the hostess what was taking so long, Tom walked up. "Mike?"

Mike could see both surprise and apprehension in Tom's face. "I need to talk to you Tom."

"Well I'm kinda busy," he replied in a tentative voice. "We still have the lunch crowd going on."

As Mike stepped closer, Tom took a step back. Mike knew the memory of what happened at Baxter's was still fresh in Tom's head and could sense his uneasiness. "Listen Tom," he said in a relaxed voice, "it's important. It's about Melissa. Is there anyway you can step outside just for a minute?"

Tom's hesitation quickly morphed into concern. "Yeah sure," he replied, fearing that something terrible had happened.

After running in the back to tell the manager he had to step out for an emergency, Tom followed Mike into the parking lot. "Did something happen to Melissa?"

Mike realized by the fear in his voice how much Tom actually cared about his sister. However, before going into what happened, there was something that had to be cleared up. "Listen, first off I want to apologize for what happened at Baxter's that night. I really acted like an asshole. I know now that you were just trying to get me to help Melissa." Mike paused to let out a deep breath that drifted in a white cloud into the cold December air. "To be honest, if I would have only listened to you that night things probably would have turned out different."

Tom appreciated Mike's apology, but knew that it was not the reason he was there. "Mike, did something happen to Melissa?" he asked again with even more concern in his voice. "You're starting to scare me."

"Melissa broke out of rehab," Mike finally blurted out.

"Rehab? I didn't even know she was in rehab." Obviously there was a lot Tom didn't know.

Mike shook his head in distress. "Yeah, we put her in there about a week ago after she ran away from home and got arrested."

Tom looked even more dumbfounded. "Arrested? What was she arrested for?" Mike gave him a condensed version of everything that had happened up to that point.

"Please," Mike pleaded. "Listen, I know I that I should have listened to you before, but if anything happens to my sister I don't know what I'll do."

Tom could hear the sheer desperation in Mike's voice and could see the unmistakable fear in his face. "Listen Mike, forget about what happened at Baxter's. The only thing that matters now is finding Melissa."

Mike let out a half-smile and nodded. "Thank you."

"I guess you already tried calling Allison."

"My mother did, but she didn't get anywhere."

After moving out of the way of a car that was trying to park, Tom rubbed his hands together, finally noticing the cold. "That's all right, she probably wouldn't tell you anything anyway. That girl's nothing but trouble. It's when Melissa started to hang out with her, that everything took a turn for the worst."

Mike put his hand on Tom's back and started to walk him back to the restaurant. "Let me ask you something Tom and give it to me straight, how deep is my sister into drugs and how long has she been doing them?"

At first Tom was hesitant to tell the truth. After all, the last time he tried that Mike turned into a raving lunatic. Yet Tom knew this time was different, so after exhaling a deep he began the story. "Well I guess like with most people, it started out kinda innocently. I mean ever since I've known her, which is about two years, she smoked an occasional joint and got drunk on the weekends. I mean who doesn't in high school. But it was always harmless. It never seemed to interfere with her schoolwork. She still always found time to hand in her assignments and pass her tests. Hell, she used to ace all her tests. Then one day last year, when my parents were out of town, she came over and pulled out this vile of coke. I mean I had done blow before, but never with Melissa. It's funny," he said as he gazed up towards the cloudy sky. "I always thought that she'd be the last person to do blow. In fact I remember a few times her saying how fucked-up the people were that did that shit. That's why I never even told her that I had done it before. I thought that if she found out she might dump me over it." As his words faded into the brittle air, the irony was hard to escape. "But yet there she was, with this vile of coke, asking if I wanted to do some. When I asked her where she got it from, she said Allison." Saying nothing, Mike just stood there and listened. It was not easy to hear, but he had to know. "So we snorted it up," Tom continued, shunning eye contact with Mike. "I mean I was surprised that she wanted to do it, but we had been drinking and..." Tom's voice suddenly crackled with a hesitant guilt. "At the time I guess I thought it was pretty cool."

Part of Mike wanted to smack Tom over the head, but he appreciated the honesty. After all, he knew the truth would not be lined with roses. "But that couldn't have been the first time she tried it."

"No. I'm sure she had tried it a few times before with Allison, but that was the first time she tried it with me. So anyway, I did it with her a few more times – if we were at a party and someone happened to offer some lines. But then over the summer things started to change. With no school, instead of her doing a few toots on the weekend at a party, she'd come over in the middle of the afternoon while my parents were at work and start chopping up lines. Most of the time she'd be in my room doing it herself while I was downstairs watching TV. I mean like I said, if some one happened to offer me a line at a party, I might do it, but that was it. It wasn't something that I wanted to do everyday."

"So why'd you let her do it," Mike snapped unable to restrain himself any longer.

Tom shook his head in distress. "Because I was fucking stupid. I guess I figured that if she wasn't doing it at my place she'd just be at home doing it or god knows where else."

"Where'd she get the money to afford it?"

"Who the hell knows," Tom casually replied. "Of course I wondered the same thing, but when I asked she'd either brush me off or blow up and start yelling that I was trying to smother her. 'What are you my father,' she'd yell. 'Do you have to know every little thing I do? How can we have a relationship if you don't trust me?'" They were words that sounded all too familiar to Mike. "I was afraid of losing her. That was my biggest fear. If only I hadn't been so selfish maybe I could have helped her."

Mike placed his hand on Tom's shoulder. "It's all right. Believe it or not, I can relate."

"Anyway," Tom continued, "during the middle of the summer, she started hanging out with a different crowd. She wanted space, so I figured some nights I would go out with my friends and let her go out with hers. Only the people she would go out with… Well, lets just say they weren't the kind of people that you would have over for dinner. I remember one night in particular. We were having one of our 'separate nights out' and I just happened to run into her at this house party. I was drinking with my buddies, having a good time when we went to go find a room to smoke a joint in. We open up this door and there's Melissa with Allison and these two older guys, freebasing."

"Melissa was freebasing?" It was as if Tom had taken a metal pipe and hit Mike over the head with it. Despite all the revelations of the last few weeks, Mike picturing his sister smoking cocaine was incomprehensible. He wanted the truth and now it was right there in front of him like a locomotive coming his way.

Tom could see Mike's anguish, knowing that he had put a picture in Mike's mind that he may never be able to get out. However Tom also knew that Mike had to know the truth, no matter how ugly it was. "Yeah, I'm afraid so. Believe me, we had a big blow out. I grabbed one of the guys and threw him against the wall. Both of the guys were bigger than me, but I didn't care. I mean I was in rage. I just snapped. But Melissa stormed out and I ran after her."

"What happened then?" Mike grudgingly asked.

"She started running through the house screaming at me to leave her alone. That's when a group of guys grabbed me, but luckily my friends jumped in." Tom shook his head in disgust. "Do you believe that? She was actually going to let me get my ass kicked. I mean that's not Melissa. That's not the girl I was going out with. Anyway, two days later she came over crying and said how sorry she was. She said that it was the first time she had ever freebased and that it would be the last. In fact she said she was going to stop doing blow all together. She said it scared her, to see how she treated me. I wanted to believe her, but knew she was probably lying. Yet, even after what she had done; after nearly having a group of thugs beat me up, I was still afraid of losing her."

"So what finally did it?"

"Well believe it or not, for a while it seemed like she really did stop using. I don't know if she was just really good hiding it from me, but things changed. In fact when the new school year started she almost stopped partying all together. She seemed focused on her grades again. I was happy. I was starting to think that maybe it had just been a summer thing and she was ready to move on with her life."

"So what happened?"

Tom let out a sigh. "One day, this last October, we were at this party and some guy we knew offered us a line. I said no thanks and thought Melissa would do the same, but she didn't. She accepted it. I said 'what are you doing?' but she just told me that I was being a stiff and not to worry so much." Tom shook his head towards the ground. "I'd been drinking and figured that maybe one line was no big deal, so even though I still didn't do one, I watched her do it."

"But it didn't stop there did it," Mike pressed on.

For the first time during their conversation, Tom looked Mike straight in the eyes. "No," he replied in a cold, straightforward voice. "In less than a week she was back hanging around the same dead-end crowd she started hanging with during the summer. She was cutting classes and I know she started in with the blow again. I tried to stop her," he pleaded to Mike, raising his hands in frustration. "I told her that shit was just going to fuck her up and the people she was hanging around weren't going to be there when the shit hit the fan. I told her that they would drag her down!" After taking a few seconds to compose himself, Tom continued in a more subtle tone. "That's when she broke it off with me. She told me I was just trying to control her life and that I didn't want her to have any friends."

Standing there listening to the same thing that Tom had said nearly two moths earlier at Baxter's, Mike kicked himself in the ass, wondering if things would have turned out differently had he only listened to Tom the first time.

"Listen Mike, I have to get back to work before I get in trouble. But believe me, we will find Melissa. As soon as I get home I'll start making phone calls. I'll talk to everyone I know. We will find her."

As Tom turned away to walk back into the restaurant, Mike placed his hand on his shoulder. "Tom," Mike said as Tom turned around. "Thank you." Tom just nodded and went on his way back to work.

Once back home, Mike went through Melissa's phone book and called every name – some people for a second time. However it was still to no avail. Just like the last time Melissa disappeared, her friends either didn't know anything or were lying. Mike had planned to canvass the local bars and hangouts that night to see if he could get some kind of a lead, but it was still only the afternoon and would be hours before it would be any use going to check them out. Mike did not want to just sit around and wait, but there was little he could do. He had already called all of her friends. He had already talked to Tom. There was nothing else to do for the time being. It was a powerless feeling. Sitting there, watching the clock was driving him mad. It was as if time was toying with him in his weakest of moments. A thousand times he looked at the clock, waiting for it to grudgingly move, but the more he looked, the slower it ticked.

Around six o'clock Diane called, unaware of what had happened. When Mike explained, her initial response was a nearly minute long silence. Like Mike, she had been taken completely off guard by the news. "I'm gonna hit some of the local bars and hangouts in a little while to see if anyone knows anything," Mike said in an exhausted voice. "If I'm lucky enough, maybe she'll be at one."

"I'll go with you," Diane responded, eager as always to be there in his time of need.

"It's all right, you don't have to."

However Diane felt that she did; not only to comfort Mike, but also to make sure he did not do anything stupid. She knew how Mike could fly off the handle when it came to Melissa and wanted to make sure that there were no incidents that might later be regretted. "No it's ok Mike. I want to go with you."

Mike was too frustrated to argue. "OK then, how about in an hour?"

"OK, but I'll pick you up and I'm driving. I want to go with you, but I don't feel like getting into an accident because you were too pissed off to concentrate on the road."

About twenty minutes after hanging up the phone, Mike could no longer take being in the house watching the clock, so he decided to wait outside in the front until Diane showed up. Wrapped in a leather jacket and gloves, Mike sat on the same front stoop that he used to sit on as a child waiting for his father to come home from work. It all seemed a lifetime ago, Mike thought to himself, as he wondered how everything became so fucked-up. Sitting there under the calm of the night sky, Mike remembered how easy and pure everything once seemed. It was hard to imagine that it was all once milk and honey – but it was. The biggest concerns were how late his parents were going to let him stay up and what toys he was getting for Christmas.

Mike looked around at the surrounding houses with their bright, colored lights and their decorative ornaments of Santa's, reindeer and nativity scenes and thought back to the time when he used to help his father decorate their house. Back then it felt like a chore. His father would always wind up getting frustrated and yell at the lights. Sometimes they were out there for hours, trying to make everything as perfect as his father pictured it. However, when they were finally finished, they always did look perfect. His father would bring his mother and Melissa out for the big ceremony. As they stood there in the front yard, freezing, Mr. Patterson would go back inside to flip the switch and in an instant, the entire house would glow. Mike remembered the lights being so bright and plentiful that they seemed to illuminate the whole night sky. His mother would always say the same thing: that they looked even better than the year before. Mike would make the same comment about how he did most of the work. Then, as his mother and Melissa went back inside to warm up, Mike and his father would stay in the front yard, admiring what they had created together. Mike would do anything to put up those lights with his father one last time. He wished he could turn around and see Melissa standing there, still only six years old, with her over-sized mittens and red, button nose. Their mother would be there clapping, with a smile on her face. Even back then it felt like a special time, Mike remembered. After all, it was a sign that Christmas was right around the corner and Christmas was always the happiest time of year.

There was also another reason that Mike wanted to have one last chance to put up the lights with his father. There were so many questions he wanted to ask him. There was so much advice that his father never had chance to give him. There were so many lessons that never had a chance to be taught. All of Mike's memories of his father were that of a strong man, that could weather any situation. There were no problems that he could not solve, no questions that he could not help answer. Mike was convinced that his father would never have let things get so messed-up if he was still alive.

Almost forgetting what he was doing waiting outside in the first place, Mike was awoken from his thoughts as Diane pulled up to the house. Slowly, Mike brushed of the past and went to deal with the problems of the present. Going to open the passenger side door, Mike turned around to look at the house, almost as if he was going to see those bright, colored lights, shining proudly with Missy and his parents standing under their glow.

"You looked like you were pretty deep in thought there," Diane commented as Mike got into the car. "What were you thinking about?"

"Oh, nothing," Mike simply replied.

Mike and Diane spent hours driving around, going to different bars talking to people. They stopped at the mall parking lot where teenagers usually hung out and smoke pot. They went to the local bowling alley. They went to the park and to the handball courts. Some of the people knew Melissa. For those that didn't, Mike had brought a picture of her, showing it around like a missing person's flyer. Unfortunately, although most people promised they would call if they saw or heard anything, Mike was getting nowhere. Some people offered suggestions as to where she might have been hanging out, but every lead they followed turned out to be another dead end. The more the night dragged on the more discouraging it became.

By the sixth place Mike was ready to start lining up people against the wall and beat the truth out of them. Perhaps frustration was getting the best of him, but he was convinced that people were lying about not knowing where Melissa was staying. Sure, some people had never even heard of her before, but some of them had to know something more than they were saying. Mike refused to believe that no one knew anything. This wasn't Manhattan. This was the suburbs of Long Island where you couldn't get arrested for jaywalking without everyone knowing about it. Add to that the fact that it was a teenager's duty to know everything that was going on with one another. They were gossiping machines that jockeyed to be the first ones to report on some one else's business. With each "sorry man, I don't have any idea", Mike lost another ounce of patients. Diane tried to make him look on the bright side by saying at least they were getting the word out, but that did little to appease him.

When Diane finally dropped Mike off at one thirty in the morning, he was surprised to see his mother still up. "Hey ma, I didn't think you'd still be up." He said wearily as he walked over and gave her a kiss on the forehead.

"I couldn't sleep," she said in as exhausted voice.

Mike looked at his mother, dressed in her nightgown, with bloodshot eyes and a drained face. He felt terrible for her.

"Tom called for you earlier tonight."

Immediately Mike's half-shut eyes opened wide, hoping that it was good news. "What did he want?"

"He said there's going to be a big Christmas Eve party at some kid's house tomorrow night. He couldn't find out if Melissa was going to be there, but said there might be a chance. He said he'd call you in the morning to give you the details."

Getting little sleep himself that night, Mike called Tom bright and early the next morning to ask where the party was and what time he should go there. Tom told him the location, but said he was going along. At first Mike was reluctant, but finally realized that he could use Tom's help. So Mike made arrangements to pick Tom up at 8:00pm.

Like clockwork, Mike arrived at Tom's house at eight on the dot. Diane had also wanted to come, but Mike somehow convinced her that he would be all right and not do anything stupid. However, Diane made him promise to call as soon as he got home.

It took them less than fifteen minutes to drive to the party. When they drove-up, there was no mistaking which house was having the party. Even from the car, they could hear music blasting inside, which grew louder every time the front door opened to let in another kid with a twelve-pack or bottle of booze under his arm. Some kids however, decided to just hang out in the front yard, drinking and trying to pick-up on the girls that walked by. One guy was even taking a piss right in the front by a bush that was strung with Christmas lights. Mike made a comment that it would be a bad way to get electrocuted. Empty beer bottles and plastic keg cups already littered the ground like a tale-tale trail of breadcrumbs that led down the street right to the front door. It was a party all right.

In a different time Mike would have been more than enthusiastic to join the festivities. He would have been the first one at the door with a six-pack in one hand, a bottle of Jack in the other and a joint hanging out of his mouth. In fact, even in the seriousness of the moment a small part of him felt like he was missing out. It was only natural. Mike may have had many regrets about his past, but there was no denying that there were also some fond memories. There were certain things he looked back on, like doing coke that made his stomach turn. However, he could not help but miss a good old fashion house party. Nevertheless, the nostalgia was quickly subdued by the realization of why they were there.

The party was already so happening that Mike had to park four blocks away. But the more people there were to talk to, the better chance that some one knew where Melissa was, or better yet, she might even be there herself. Focused on the task at hand, Mike and Tom walked towards the party like two detectives going to track down a lead. As they converged with other groups of partygoers making the same walk, they looked at each face to see if Melissa was among them. Mike even stopped a few times to wait for people walking down the block to come closer. He was not only looking for his sister, but also Allison. There was no doubt in Mike's mind that if Allison wasn't with Melissa, she at least knew where she was. As they approached the house, the entire sidewalk and part of the street was filled with people. Most of them apparently didn't want to wait to get inside, walking down the block swigging beers and passing joints around. Some kids were hanging around in groups by each other's cars. Mike was worried that it was only a matter of time before one of the neighbors called the cops and the party would be broken-up before they could find anything out about Melissa.

As they followed a group of people in the house, they were immediately greeted by Iron Maiden blasting on the stereo and the overpowering odor of marijuana. It was a bash all right. The place was crammed with already drunk, rowdy partygoers. There was people everywhere; sitting on the counters and floors and standing in the hallways.

Mike and Tom did not get five feet in the door when a drunk, longhaired kid wearing a Santa's hat greeted them with a half-empty bottle of whiskey in his hand. "Hey guys," he slurred as he put his hand on Mike's shoulder, "welcome to the party!" It wasn't his house, nor did he probably even know the owner, but felt it was his drunken obligation to welcome all newcomers. Mike thanked him with a smile and walked into the living room, which appeared to be split into two groups.

The first group was huddled around the stereo, banging their heads back and forth to the music that thundered at obscene levels. It was a small group of five guys and two girls. Of course, each one of them had a drink in their hand. Another group of partiers sat on the couch, passing around a four-foot long Graphix bong. On the coffee table in front of them was a bag of weed and an open bottle of Jim Beam. "Man, some one sold you shit weed," one of them shouted over the blaring music. "You wanna smoke some good shit?"

"Yeah man," responded a long-haired teen with a Judas Priest t-shirt and eye as red as a fire truck.

Mike stood by the edge of the couch and watched the other kid pull out a small bag from his pants' pocket. "My brother in California sent me this shit man."

"Oh no not that shit," one of the girl's who was sitting on the couch responded. "We smoked a small joint of that the other day and I was stoned off my ass for hours. I'm tellin' you, that shit's fucked-up. A couple of bong hits of that will probably kill you."

"She's right," the kid with the Judas Priest shirt, yelled. "This shit will knock you off your ass." He then began to load the bowl as the others looked on with drooling anticipation. "This shit is so moist that you can throw it against the wall and it'll stick. My brother said he got two ounces of the shit and it didn't have a single seed in it."

Finally Tom butted in. "Hey what's going on Joe," he said to the kid loading the weed.

"Hey Tommy," he replied with a shit-faced smile. "How the fuck are you?"

Tom gave him a nod. "I'm all right. I've just been working a lot."

"Hey man, why don't you stick around and have a hit of this shit. I got it from my brother Mike in California. It's fucking primo shit."

"Thanks man, maybe later," Tom shouted over the music. "Hey, you haven't seen Melissa around have you?"

Joe shook his head as he passed the loaded bong across the table. "No, sorry man. I haven't seen her in a while."

"What about Russell or any of those guys?"

Joe brushed back the hair from his face and sneered at Tom. "Those assholes? What do you want with them? Whatdya wanna buy smoke coke or something."

"No man, I..."

Right then, a huge, thick cloud of smoke blew in their faces as the kid that had just taken a bong hit erupted in a coughing fit. "Oh man," he shouted in between painful coughs, "You weren't kidding. That's some good fucking shit!"

Immediately everyone in the group broke out laughing. "Hey man, you better be careful not to cough out a lung," one of them yelled.

Joe laughed along with them. "Man, how big of a hit did you take? You're gonna be fucked-up beyond belief." He then turned his attention back to Tom. "I saw them earlier. I think they may be upstairs."

Tom thanked him and then waded through the crowds of people with Mike. People were everywhere and the stairs were no exceptions. Practically every step had someone sitting on it. At the base of the stairs, a guy and girl were groping each other as if they were in the bedroom. Halfway up, some kid asked if they wanted to buy any acid. It was a typical house party.

Finally, they made it upstairs. "Hey man, I know you," some guy standing in the hall said, pointing to Tom.

"Hey yeah," one of the girls added. "We were in World History class together," she mumbled with an inebriated look on her face. "You're Tom."

"Yeah," Tom replied, trying not to look too hard at her bursting cleavage with Mike right there. It was not easy though. Tom might have still been in love with Melissa, but he wasn't blind and this girl was a walking wet dream. Her blonde wavy hair went half way down to her rock solid ass and her eyes, blue as a clear summer sky, could probably shoot a laser beam straight into a guy's heart. And what she was wearing – well, she might as well have had flashing lights on her tits with a sign saying 'now open for business'. Tom knew he was there for serious business, but that didn't stop him from smiling back. "You're Brandi." Summoning restraint, Tom finally pulled his eyes away from her breasts. "Hey, have you seen Russell or Frankie up here?"

"Who?"

"Yeah, Russell's up here," the guy with her jumped in. He then took a big swig of beer, which partially dripped down his chin. "They're in the back room to the left, but I don't think they want anyone going in there. I think they're…"

Before the guy had a chance to finish his sentence, Mike grabbed Tom by the arm and marched down the hall to the back room. Mike didn't know who Russell was, but it was obvious that he might know something about Melissa.

The door was locked and Tom could tell that Mike was about to kick it down. "Wait a second," he said, trying to calm the situation. Knowing that Mike was going to get into that room one way or another, Tom gave three good knocks on the door.

"Go away," yelled a voice from within the room.

Before Mike could bust down the door, Tom intervened, knocking again. "It's me Tommy. It's really important."

"Who," shouted back a different voice?

"Listen man, just let us in," Mike yelled through the door. "We need to talk to Russell. There's only two of us."

Suddenly, as if Mike had given a secret password, the door opened. Standing on the other side was a skinny figure with long greasy-hair who motioned them to step inside. As they did, the door closed behind them.

It appeared to be the master bedroom of the house, which for the moment had been turned into a private party room. There were empty beer bottles on every surface and a thick cloud of pot smoke hanging stagnantly in the air. On the bed was a girl, probably around sixteen, sitting there smoking a joint. Next to her on the nightstand was a bottle of Vodka, a bag of weed and a pack of rolling papers. On the other side of the room a guy and girl were crouched over a wooden dresser, busy doing lines. Next to the small, portable glass mirror they were snorting off of was a triple beam scale with several small rocks of cocaine on it. Too absorbed in what they were doing, they did not even turn around when Mike and Tom entered the room. Standing in the middle of the room, with a bottle of beer in hand was Russell. Mike did not need to be introduced; "Russell" was tattooed in calligraphy on his left arm, along with various other art. In fact, tattoos covered most of his arms and shoulders. Wearing no shirt – obviously to show off his tattooed, but scrawny frame – Mike noticed a big, green pot-leaf painted on his stomach, right above his belly button. It was immediately evident that Russell was an intelligent, productive member of society. With slicked-back, black greasy hair and two upside down crosses dangling from his ears, he looked like someone that never grew out of being the neighborhood bully.

Mike could tell right away that Russell thought he was some kind of big dog and maybe around the neighborhood he was. However, Mike had seen dozens of Russells in prison quickly become someone's bitch. Russell may have been able to intimidate high school kids who didn't know any better, but not Mike. He had seen the *real* big dogs. He had lived amongst murderers, gang members and 300 pound monsters that could curl a small car. To Mike, Russell was just a small-time punk who was about to be in over his head if he did or said anything stupid.

Before saying anything, Russell looked over Tom and Mike – mostly Mike. Even through a leather jacket, he could see Mike's muscular physique. Mike also permeated a powerful, self-confident glow to which Russell was not accustomed. He was more used to standing in front of insecure teenagers that cowered in awe at his collogue of tattoos and rough, unshaven face. He was used to being able to intimidate people just by giving them a mean look. However, he knew right away that this was not the case with Mike. Still, he tried to put up a front. "I know you," he growled, pointing at Tom. "But who are you?"

Almost reveling in the moment, Mike stepped closer to Russell, with a stone, cold look on his face. "That's not important," Mike replied in a deep, stern voice.

Sensing Mike's offensive tone and posture, Tom jumped in. "Russell, this is…" he began to mediate in a nervous tone.

However, before Tom could get any further, Mike motioned him to shut-up. It was clear that Mike was going to take it from here. "Do you know where Melissa Patterson is?"

"Are you a cop or something?" Russell asked as the couple doing lines by the dresser finally popped their heads up.

Mike let out a laugh, breaking the tension in the room for at least the moment. "No, I'm not a cop. I'm just a friend."

When Mike first came in with Tom, Russell didn't know what to think. Now, Russell figured that they were merely there to find some one and just assumed answer the question and have them leave as quickly as possible so that he could get back to having a good time. However, that did not necessarily equate into giving a truthful answer. "No man, I haven't seen her around in weeks."

"You sure?" Mike asked again, knowing that Russell was probably bullshitting.

Russell shrugged his tattooed covered shoulders. "Yeah man, sorry."

"It's too bad to," replied the guy by the dresser as he hurriedly chopped-up another line on the mirror.

With testosterone quickly building-up again, Mike walked over to where he and the girl were standing. "Why's that?" Mike asked.

Still cutting up a line he turned to look Mike. "Because she sucks a mean fucking dick."

Instantly, Mike grabbed the back of his head and slammed it full force into the mirror. As the mirror cracked, so did his nose, spewing pools of thick, red blood down the dresser. "What the fuck did you say?" Mike yelled, as he picked up the guy's lacerated face. Streams of crimson poured profusely down his shirt and all over the drawers and carpet. "What the fuck did you say?" Mike yelled again.

Still holding the guy's head in one hand, Mike turned his attention to Russell, before he had a chance to shake off the initial shock and come to his friend's aide. "Don't even fucking think about it," he barked at Russell. The third guy, who had let them in, was still standing by the door, frozen.

If Russell didn't know how to react before, he certainly didn't know now. Mike obviously meant business, but Russell couldn't just leave his friend there bleeding helplessly. He had to do something, if not for his friend, than at least for his own reputation. After all, there were three of them and he could call for more reserves from outside. So after letting out a deep breath, Russell looked down at the utility knife that he always kept on his belt.

"You even think about taking out that butter knife and I will stick it right through the top of your fuckin skull." It was as if Mike knew Russell's next move before he even did.

"He's not kidding," Tom warned. "The guy's been in prison for the last five years." Tom would have been happy to get rid of Russell, but didn't want to be a witness to his murder.

Russell cautiously removed his hand from the sheath as his bad boy façade quickly came tumbling down. There may have been three of them and Mike may have been unarmed, but Russell could see that crazy glare in

Mike's eyes. Russell had been in his share of fights before and might have had a reputation as a bad ass, but knew when he was out of his league. He could tell that Mike wasn't fucking around and didn't want to wind up like his friend – or even worse.

"Do you know who you're fucking with," Russell's friend replied, choking on the blood bubbling out of his mouth. "You're a fucking dead man!"

Figuring that he didn't learn the first time, Mike again smashed his already bloodied face into the dresser. As his friend let out a torturous, but muffled scream, Russell finally grabbed Mike to pull him away. It didn't work. With one hand, Mike grabbed Russell's throat and forced him against the wall, putting a hole in it. As his fingers applied pressure, Russell gasped for precious air, trying to use both hands to remove Mike's one. However, it appeared futile as Russell couldn't budge even one of the finger's on Mike's death grip. Russell's other friend, still standing by the door was too afraid to come to his aide, as were the two girls. "I'm only going to ask you this one more time," Mike said in a low, but forceful voice. "Where is Melissa?"

Still trying to jar Mike's hand, Russell moved his mouth as if to talk, but no words could escape. Slowly, Mike released his stranglehold. Immediately, Russell fell to the ground gasping for air.

As Russell fought to catch his breath, Tom looked around the room to make sure no one was thinking about leaving. The situation was bad, but at least it was contained. The party was loud enough that no one outside the room heard the commotion, or at least paid it any mind. There was no telling what would happen if one of the girls or Russell's other friend ran outside for help. It was obvious that Mike didn't care if Russell had twenty friends with him, but Tom didn't share the sentiment. The situation was already out of control and all Tom wanted to do was get the hell out of there as quickly as possible.

Still kneeling on the floor, only feet away from his bloodied friend, Russell was finally able to get enough air to speak. "All right man," he managed to spit out, still short of breath. "I haven't seen her in about a month." Russell could see Mike tense up even more than he already was. "Wait...wait" he pleaded, extending his hand in a defensive posture. "I haven't seen her, but she called me just yesterday, out of the blue?"

"Is she coming here tonight?"

Russell rubbed his throat, still trying to catch his breath. "No. I told her about it, but she said she had to stay low for a while – but wouldn't say why. I guess now I know why, with crazy motherfuckers like you looking for her. What does she owe you money or something?" Russell could see that Mike wasn't amused. "Anyway, she said she was hanging out with this dude in the city."

"Where in the city?"

"He...he has a place in the east village," he stuttered, before giving Mike the full address.

Mike kneeled down to Russell's level and looked directly into his eyes, with a cold, foreboding stare. "Does this dude have a name?"

"It's Jack," Russell grudgingly replied. "I don't know his last name, but they call him Duffy. But you didn't get that information from me. He's as fucking crazy as you!"

"Don't worry, I won't tell him where I got his name from. But Russell," Mike said in cold, threatening voice, "if I find out that you're lying to me, or god forbid that you tipped dear ol' Duffy off, I will find you, sneak into your room and kill you in your fucking sleep."

Anyone could have said it, but there was no doubt in Russell's mind that Mike meant it. "Don't worry man."

Mike then stood up and turned his attention to Russell's friend, who was now standing in the arms of his girl. In a slow, controlled manner, Mike grabbed his hair, prying him from the girl's arms, which were covered – along with the rest of her - in blood. "And you," Mike whispered into his ears, "if you ever threaten me again, I will find you too. And believe me, next time there will be a hell of a lot more blood." No longer feeling invincible, the guy was finally smart – or scared – enough to keep his mouth shut.

Then, without saying another word, Mike walked passed Russell's other friend and calmly walked out the door. Not so calmly, Tom followed. Without incident the two made their way through the crowd, back downstairs and out the front door. Perhaps out of fear, neither Russell nor his cronies sought help from anyone else in the party.

At first Tom could not believe what had happened. Pinning some kid against the wall to shake out an answer was one thing, but busting up faces and choking cocaine dealers was something entirely different. No one messed with Russell. The stories about him beating up and going after people were endless. At first, Tom couldn't believe that Mike did that to him and his friend. Tom's hands were still trembling over what had happened, but he knew that Mike was not even thinking twice about it. In fact Tom knew that Mike was capable of much more. He realized that Mike really would stop at nothing – absolutely nothing – to find Melissa. That's when Tom, although he also wanted to find Melissa, knew he was in over his head. In fact, he would not be joining any more of Mike's expeditions.

Chapter 10

MERRY CHRISTMAS

The next morning Mike woke up on the living room couch, where he had fallen asleep watching television. Prying open his weary eyes, he saw his mother, standing over him like a heavenly silhouette. "Merry Christmas," she said with a smile on her face.

Still half asleep, Mike rubbed his eyes and sat up. "Merry Christmas ma," he replied with a smile of his own. In that fleeting moment they had put all their heartache and worry aside. It was as if they had stepped into the eye of the storm, a brief content moment of tranquility away from the world that was crumbling down around them. Melissa still weighed heavy in their hearts and on their minds, but it was Christmas and they at least had each other. It was the first time in six years that Betty was able to wake-up Christmas morning and give her son a kiss. It was the first Christmas in many years that she was able to look at him – to hold him – and know that he was going to be all right. She had waited long for that moment and although she would have done anything to have Melissa there as well, she was not going to let it pass by. While giving her son a hug, Betty was overcome by the healing hands of hope. She knew Melissa was in trouble, but standing there in front of Michael on Christmas morning, she could not help but feel that somehow everything was going to work out. A religious woman, it was almost as if God had given her an unforeseen sign. After nights of staying awake, thinking about the worst-case scenarios, there in that moment, her mind was mysteriously set at ease. Betty did not know how, but felt that Melissa would come home and finally get the help she needed.

Mike too, was happy to finally be home with his mother on Christmas morning, but did not share in the same feeling of hope. His contentment was much more short-lived. While his mother fought to stay in the calm eye of the storm, Mike was quickly sucked back into its perilous winds. For him, being home on Christmas was only half the picture. The other half was that they were all supposed to be together as a family. That Melissa was not there and the predicament she was in tore at his heart. Mike cared more about Melissa than he did his own life and would have done anything to trade places with her.

Not long after Mike awoke, Diane called to wish him a merry Christmas. She knew Mike was devastated about Melissa, but all she could do was be supportive and keep saying that everything was going to work out. Even to herself she started sounding like a broken record, but there was nothing else to say. Diane could not tell him how she really felt: that maybe everything was not going to be ok. After all, without hope there was nothing.

After breakfast Mike and his mother opened the few gifts that they had gotten for each other. Mike did not even want to bother, but Betty said it had been too long since they were able to open each other's gifts. So like a child forcing down medicine, Mike went through the motions. Then, suddenly, the phone rang. Instantly they stopped what they were doing and looked at each other. Sometimes, nothing is more terrifying than the sound of the phone ringing. It was the frightening uncertainty of what news awaited on the other end. Although there was a possibility that it could be Melissa, it was easy to fear the worse. As it rang out a second time through the otherwise silent house they both hesitated to see who would pick it up. Then finally, Betty flinched. It turned out to be Allison's mother. Allison had not come home the night before and although it was not uncommon for her to spend the night at a friend's house without telling her parents, she had taken a suitcase of clothes and other belongings. Allison had run away from home and it did not take a genius to realize that wherever she was, she was with Melissa.

Armed with this new revelation, Mike set out that afternoon for the city to the address Russell had supplied. Diane had begged to go along, but Mike insisted that she stay home with her family. After all, it was Christmas. Yet there was also another reason. Mike may not have been easily intimidated, but that did not mean there wasn't going to be trouble. Russell and his pretentious cronies was one thing, but there was no telling what he would find in the city. It was already clear that Melissa hung out with some very dangerous characters. Mike may have been willing to take any risk for his sister, but was not about to put Diane in any jeopardy.

Both the Long Island Railroad and subway were empty. Most people were at home with their families unwrapping gifts and preparing for Christmas dinner. It was an hour and a half ride, most of which Mike spent mentally preparing for what he might encounter. He never really hung out in Manhattan, but knew that the part he was going to was a rough neighborhood. In fact in 1985 there were a lot of rough neighborhoods in the city. Manhattan was still recovering from the bankrupt cesspool it had become in the seventies. Crime and poverty ran rampant and almost a decade would pass before it would return to the great city and tourist capital it had been so many years before. The mid eighties was also the time when the crack epidemic was just starting to sweep across the nation. Gangs were popping-up everywhere and it seemed not a day went by that at least one person didn't get shot. It was a dangerous place, not for the faint of heart. Mike wasn't scared, but knew he had to be on guard. He may have known how to fight, but he was not superman. He was going to where people played for keeps and answers would not be as easy to come by as the previous night. The city was a far cry from Long Island. Still, Mike was prepared to go to hell and fight the devil himself in order to find Melissa.

After getting off the subway, Mike walked around for a while lost, before finally finding the address. Then, acting like he had been there a hundred times before, Mike walked passed two guys sitting on the stoop sharing a bottle and into the front door. As he walked up to the second floor, he passed a homeless woman sitting on one of the steps, begging for change. The whole place reeked like the subway; like piss and body odor. It was much like he thought it would be. The stairs creaked with each step and the ceiling looked like it could come down at any time. A filthy mold covered the seams where the walls and ceiling met. The place looked like it should have been condemned a long time ago and leveled to the ground. Walking past some more shady characters in the halls Mike's determination to find Melissa grew. He could not stand the thought of her there. No, this was no place for a seventeen year-old girl.

Finally arriving at the apartment, Mike stood outside for about three minutes, listening through the door to see if he could hear Melissa or Allison's voice. All he could hear though was the faint sounds of a television set. After a deep breath he gave two firm knocks. A few seconds passed and no reply, so he gave three more, this time even harder, knocks.

"Who is it?" growled a man's coarse voice.

Mike hesitated as his heart thumped with adrenaline. "Russell sent me?" he replied in an authoritative voice.

"Who?"

"I'm looking for Duffy."

After an uncomfortable pause, the four locks on the door started to open. Still chained, the door slowly cracked open just enough for a man's unshaven face to peer out. "What do you want?"

"Russell said you might have something for me," Mike replied, not knowing what else to say.

They must have been the magic words, because the man unchained the door and motioned Mike to come in. Now Mike was able to get a look inside the dingy apartment and a better look at the man he believed to be Duffy. He looked Caucasian, but his skin was leathery and worn. He was the same height as Mike, but not as built. In fact he looked quite malnourished. It also looked like Mike had woken him up; either that or he had not slept in days. Wearing only faded, black leather pants, he gazed over Mike with a paranoid look. "Russell," he said scratching his chin as if going through names in his head. "You mean the guy with all the tattoos? You ain't Five-O or anything are you?"

"No, I ain't the cops," Mike replied, seeing that Duffy was starting to get edgy. "I'm looking for a girl named Melissa." With curious eyes, Mike glanced over the studio apartment to make sure no one else there.

Duffy slowly started to walk away from Mike, towards the couch. "Melissa? Who the hell's Melissa? I think you got the wrong place buddy."

Sensing a growing friction, Mike followed Duffy, keeping within arms reach. If prison had taught him anything, it was how to be alert. He also learned to tell when someone was lying. "No," Mike said in a more forceful voice, "I think I've got the right place and I think you know exactly who I'm talking about."

With his back still to Mike, Duffy began to lean down towards a wrinkled-up shirt that was lying on the couch. "I think you better leave now," he said nervously while reaching for something underneath the shirt. It was a gun.

Fortunately Mike was one step ahead of him. Before Duffy could even get a full grip on the gun, Mike snatched it out of his hand. With his heart now racing into overdrive, Mike slammed Duffy's scrawny frame up against the wall and jammed the .9mm into his mouth, breaking a few teeth along the way. Like anybody else, Mike didn't particularly like when people pointed guns at him. It was almost a miracle that Mike didn't pull the trigger either out of rage or even by accident. "Now listen to me motherfucker," he roared at a now petrified Duffy. "I'm only going to tell you this once, you understand?" Shaking like a leaf in a thunderstorm, Duffy carefully nodded his head. "I'm going to take this gun out of your mouth and you're going to tell me where Melissa is. If you don't I will blow a fucking whole in your head and correct me if I'm wrong, but I doubt anyone will miss you."

Cautiously Duffy nodded again and Mike slowly pulled the cold, steel barrel out of his bloodied mouth. Immediately, Duffy fell to the ground in pain, spitting out a few teeth that he luckily didn't choke on. Suddenly a yellow, pungent puddle started to form around his feet. Mike took one step back so his shoes would not be soaked in Duffy's piss. Then, in an effort to make sure that there weren't any more tricks waiting, Mike reared back and kicked him right in the chin.

Flying back, Duffy landed straight on his back and started crying. "Why the hell did you do that for?"

"I don't like when someone tries to shoot me," Mike growled, with the gun still in his hand. "Now tell me where Melissa is."

Still shaking, Duffy sat up on the floor with blood pouring from his face. "Ok, ok," he mumbled, trying to straighten his jaw back. "I had only met her a couple of times before through Russell. Russell comes up here sometimes to buy some blow." With broken teeth and a busted jaw, Mike had to listen hard in order to understand what Duffy was saying. "Anyway, she calls me up the other day out of the blue. I don't even know how the fuck she got my phone number. She tells me she needs a place to hide for a couple of days."

"So she was here?"

Duffy shook his head. "She shows up two days ago with no bag or anything. She didn't even have a jacket with her. She tells me that she broke out of some rehab. Do you believe that?" Suddenly, Duffy's had a rare revelation. "Hey is that why you're looking for her. What are you like her brother or something?"

"Just finish the fucking story!"

Duffy paused to spit out some more blood. "Anyway, she was only here for the day. She didn't even stay that night."

"Where'd she go?"

"I don't know. She said she had to meet her friend. I think her name was Allison. I told her that they should both come back, but she said they were going to be heading out of state. Besides... I don't think she particularly liked my company... not that I did anything to her!"

So many pictures and thoughts were flashing through Mike's head that he had to fight to stay focused. "Out of state where?"

"I swear, she wouldn't tell me."

Without saying another word, Mike started to walk out of the apartment. "Hey, where you going with my gun?" Duffy cried out. Not answering, Mike just cautiously opened the door and walked out, tucking the gun in his pants. He was not going to leave it behind so Duffy could run down the stairs and shoot him in the back. Mike would later dismantle it and discard the pieces in several different dumpsters along the way so no kid could accidentally find and use it.

It was Christmas day, but Mike was too mentally fried to go home. Instead, he found an open bar and stopped there for a few hours. Sitting on a rickety bar stool in the nearly empty dive, he tried to get a grip on the worries and fears that had now completely consumed him. An already bad situation was quickly spiraling out of control, into nightmarish proportions. Drinking his beer in silence, so many things prayed on his mind. Though only three days had passed since Melissa ran off, it seemed like a month. Only earlier that week he was convinced that everything was going to work out; that the light at the end of the tunnel was drawing ever so near. Now that dark tunnel seemed to stretch for infinity. How could everything have gone so drastically wrong, he wondered. How could it have spiraled into the dire situation it had now become? If there was hope, it was dwindling fast.

Not only was Mike no closer to finding Melissa, but the hole she had fallen into was becoming deeper than he ever imagined. Where was it all going to end? That was the question he feared most. Mike had spent five years behind bars dreaming about that one day when he would walk through those gates back into the outside world. He spent every day in that godforsaken cell telling himself how different – how better – it would be, envisioning a new life. There would be no more drugs, no more hanging with the wrong crowd, no more troubles with the law. That was all in the past. Now there he was, in some dive bar in the city on Christmas day, after sticking a loaded gun in someone drug dealer's mouth. Melissa was somewhere out there doing god knows what with god knows who. His mother was probably sitting at home crying by the Christmas tree. Mike's whole world was unraveling and there seemed little he could do to stop it.

After drowning in an endless pool of "why's" and "how's", Mike finally headed home. Celebrating Christmas could not have been further from his mind, but he knew his mother was at home waiting. He spent the entire trip home thinking of what to tell her. Mike certainly was not going to mention anything about almost getting shot and busting some guy's head. The ride felt ten times longer than it did going to the city. Through the window of the railroad car he watched the drab December sky grow dark as the night slowly devoured the day. With his head against the cold, dirty glass, the slight swaying motion of the train acted like a sedative. Fighting to stay awake, Mike could not peel his weary eyes away from the fading sky. It seemed so peaceful, so calm – so far away from where he was.

Once home, Mike told his mother that he found out that Melissa was definitely with Allison, but had no luck finding out where they were now. He didn't elaborate and she didn't ask. Betty was understandably disappointed, but tried to put a positive spin on the situation. "It's only been three days Michael," she said with an assuring façade. "She'll probably call or come home by the end of the week." Part of Betty actually believed it; she had to as a mother. Yet then again, she didn't know the whole story.

"Yeah, I guess so," Mike tiredly replied, not wanting to worry his mother any more than she was already.

The two then sat at the dining room table and forced down a small meal Betty had made. Mike was famished, not having eaten all day, but nothing seemed appetizing – not even his mother's homemade sauce.

Choking on each forkful, all he could do was look at the empty seat across the table and wonder where his sister was. He wondered who she was with, what she was doing. He kept picturing her with Duffy and Russell. It was a painful, thinking of his sister that way, but Mike could not help it. The inconceivable images ate at him like a cancer. Mike feared that never again would he be able to look at her and see that small, innocent, bright-eyed girl that was supposed to be always sheltered from the evils of the world. Feelings of despair, anger, pain and fear all battled, twisting and tearing every molecule of his body and mind. He tried to put on a brave face for his mother's sake, but could not. There was just no more strength left to muster.

After dinner, Diane came over. They had not seen each other in over a day. After exchanging gifts and talking with Betty for a while, Mike and Diane adjourned to the backyard and sat on the swing. It was a particularly warm night for Christmas and there was no wind blowing. Under the quiet of the night, the two rocked gently back and forth as they talked about what else – Melissa. Mike, as he did with his mother, left out the part about the gun. He had not even told Diane the whole story about the night before with Russell.

After a few minutes Mike pulled out a pack of cigarettes from his jacket pocket. "You don't smoke," Diane immediately remarked.

"I don't," he replied solemnly before putting the cigarette in his mouth.

"Well then what's that?"

Mike pulled the cigarette from his lips. "I don't know. I stopped in a bodega in the city today and just bought them." Mike let out a quick, uncomfortable laugh. "It was the first time I had a cigarette since my second year in the Penn." Then, without saying another word, Mike snapped the cigarette between his fingers and threw it onto the grass.

Diane fought to hold back tears. She wanted to tell him that everything was going to work out and that better days were just on the horizon, but the words had already been exhausted. Instead, she just held him tight.

Chapter 11

ALLISON

Two weeks past and there was still no word from Melissa. New Year's had come and gone and the weather was getting colder. Mike and Betty's fears grew with each passing day as sleepless nights became routine. Every time the phone rang or there was a knock on the door, they shuttered with overpowering dread. Every morning became more distant than the one before, until it felt as though months had slipped away.

In a constant mental and physical state of exhaustion, Mike kept searching, although knowing Melissa might have been hundreds of miles away. Mike questioned everyone she knew. He must have questioned at least fifty people and when there was no one left he started the list all over again. Some people had nothing to tell, some gave suggestions on where she might be. There were even the occasional Melissa sightings, but they always wound up being another dead end. Although finding hope became as elusive as finding his sister, Mike's determination never faltered. Interrogating people and following leads became as natural as breathing air.

Mike returned to work, though he had to force himself to concentrate. As if sleepwalking, he moved around with a blank look, not saying anything. His partners, Carl and Kevin tried to cheer him up, but nothing they said could appease him. All they could do was be supportive, to cover for him if he accidentally dropped or broke something. Normally, Mike would have owned up to his own mistakes, but he was far from normal. He had stopped even caring about his pride. He had stopped caring about everything except Melissa.

During the last week of January, New York, along with the whole eastern seaboard, was hit by a blizzard. In the end, the storm dumped over fourteen inches of snow on Long Island, bringing it and the city to a standstill. For three days schools were closed as were most businesses. The moving company that Mike worked for was no exception. Although snowplows worked around the clock, many of the roads were still impassible. New York was no stranger to the intrusive white visitor, but this was a once in a decade storm.

That Thursday, since work had taken a pause for most people, the neighborhood gang decided to meet up at Baxter's. Diane was coming down with a bad cold, but urged Mike to go without her. She thought that maybe being with all the guys and having a few drinks might pull Mike out of his hole for at least the night. At first Mike was reluctant to go, feeling anything but in the mood to party. Yet despite his reservations, Diane kept pressuring him to go. Finally persuaded, Mike decided that a night out with the guys might be a good escape after all. Around five o'clock, Brain came to the house to pick Mike up. Lately a knock on the door would have brought a piercing fear, but Brian had been expected.

As Mike ran upstairs to put on a jacket, Brian remained in the living room with Mrs. Patterson. However, knowing what she was going through, Brian was not quite sure what to say at first. He wanted to give her encouragement, but wasn't certain how to articulate it. Betty, sensing his loss for words, broke the uneasy silence. "So Brian," she said in a soft but sincere voice, "how have you been?"

"OK Mrs. Patterson," he responded nonchalantly.

"How are your folks?"

Brian shied away from looking Betty straight in the eyes, not wanting to see the pain he knew she was concealing. "They're fine," he answered, trying to keep the conversation simple.

Even without words, Betty could sense his concern. She had known Brian since he was a little boy, playing in their backyard with G.I. Joes and asking to stay over for dinner. Understandably, Betty had negative feelings about many of the people Mike used to hang out with, but not Brian. Sure, she knew that Brian and Mike used to do drugs and get in trouble together, but harbored no resentment towards him. In fact she was glad that he was Mike's friend. Out of all the people that used to consider themselves close to her son, Brian was the only one that ever called to see how she was doing and if she needed anything. Brian was also the only one of Mike's friends that ever visited him in prison.

As Betty asked Brian how his job was going Mike came down the stairs ready to go. "Are you sure you're going to be ok ma," he asked before giving her a peck on the forehead.

"Yes Michael," she answered. "You go and try to have a good time... And be careful."

"All right. If you hear anything, I left the number to Baxter's on the kitchen counter. Just tell whoever answers the phone that you need to talk to me and that it's an emergency."

Hoping that her son would be able to put aside his distress for the night, Betty walked them to the front door. "It was good seeing you Brian," she said, holding the door open for them. "Make sure not to become a stranger."

"I won't," Brian replied as they stepped outside. "And don't worry, I'll keep an eye on Mike for you."

Betty nodded. "I know you will."

After a final wave goodbye, the two old friends went to meet the rest of the neighborhood gang. Wrapped in heavy coats, scarves and gloves they walked along the semi-shoveled path, being careful not to slip on the slick, frozen ground that lay beneath the snow. As they did, thick, white, fluffy flakes the size of silver dollars continued to fall silently from the obscured sky.

"Man, it's been a while since I've seen this much snow," Brian remarked as his boots sank into the soft snow that had already begun to accumulated where the sidewalk had been shoveled.

"Yeah, it's kinda cool," replied Mike.

Brian turned his head and through the flowing white haze saw Mike crack a smile. It was the first time Brian had seen him smile in the last two months. "Man when we were growing up we used to have so much fun in the snow."

"Yeah and it seemed like every winter there was snow on the ground. I remember it being so high that you could barely open the front door. Did it really used to snow that much or did it just seem that way 'cause we were kids?" Stopping momentarily, Mike tilted his head back and let the soft, wet flakes rain gently upon his face.

"What the hell are you doing?"

"Man you should try this," replied Mike with his head still tilted back. "Call me crazy, but this feels great." For the moment, it was as if the unbearable weight that Mike had been wearing like an albatross suddenly became as light as the flakes that fell from the sky. It was the first time since Melissa ran away that she did not gnaw at his every thought.

Brian smiled, happy to see that his friend was able to forget about his troubles for a while. "Do you remember all the great snowball fights we used to get in when we were kids?"

"Yeah," replied Mike, thinking back to those long-gone days.

"Hey, you remember – I think it was the winter of seventy one – we got hit by that major blizzard? The whole state shut down. All the roads were closed."

Starting to walk again, Mike laughed. "Yeah I remember. We were still in sixth grade. I think it was something crazy like four feet of snow. Of course to us it seemed more like ten. Man, I remember the snow was practically up to our fucking shoulders."

"Yeah," Brian replied with a long smile. "I remember me you, Kevin and I think Fat Joey started a snowball war with Dan and those two brothers that used to live on Thompson Street."

Suddenly, the cobwebs of a long, forgotten memory were dusted off as it came back into sharp focus. "Yeah man," Mike said emphatically. "I remember that. We kicked their ass!"

"Yeah, we sure did. I remember we always managed to ambush them, but they could never seem to find us." Brian stopped walking and put his hand on Mike's shoulder while breaking out in laughter. "Hey you remember when the younger brother somehow got separated from the rest of them and walked by where we were hiding? We had just rolled a whole frigin arsenal of snowballs that we had just waiting there."

Laughing himself, Mike started visualizing the entire incident as if he were watching a movie of it. "Oh man, we gave him a pounding."

"Yeah, it was brutal. I remember he started screaming for his brother and Dan: 'where are you guys?' Remember, he went crying all the way home and then his old man came looking for us?"

"He chased us all over the neighborhood."

"Yeah, and then we started throwing snowballs at him. Man, was he pissed."

After about a minute, the two childhood pals stopped laughing just enough to compose themselves. "Man, that was great," Mike proclaimed, still smiling from ear to ear. "It's so strange how you can remember something like that so vividly after all these years. I mean I can still picture that stupid purple ski mask he was wearing. Man, those were great times," Mike said as he reveled in the fond simplicity of the memory.

The two then resumed their walk down the block; a block they had walked down together thousands of times before. "Hey Mike, is that Linda?" Brian asked, pointing down the cross street they were passing.

As if on cue, Mike turned to look. However, before he could ask where, a chunk of cold, wet snow smacked him on the side of the face. He could not believe he had fallen for Brian's set-up; especially right after reminiscing about snowballs fights.

Brian tried to run down the street, but Mike scooped-up a handful of snow and gave chase. "Come back here you fuckin' bastard!" Mike shouted, throwing the ball, but missing.

"Too bad all that working out hasn't helped your throw," Brian yelled back, ducking behind a snow-covered tree. Frustrated at missing, Mike quickly formed another ball and hurled it as hard as he could. Watching it explode in a white powdery haze, Mike swiftly darted for better positioning. As he did, Brian retaliated. Then, just like that, a full-blown snowball fight broke-out, as it had so many times before when they were kids. Suddenly – just like over a decade ago - nothing mattered more than who could cover the other in the most snow. It was one of those rare occasions when the world stopped spinning and everything became simple again.

Despite their fun, Mike and Brian were glad to finally arrive at Baxter's. After pelting each other with snowball after snowball their hands and faces were frozen numb – even with gloves on – and warmth was extremely welcome. Most of the crew were already there and seemed amused at the sight of the two snow-covered friends. Mike and Brian had tried to shake off most of the snow before walking in, but were still blanketed in a layer of white. It was all over them and soon it would be all over the floor of the bar.

Flocking to the neighborhood watering hole during a snowstorm was as much of a tradition as having a barbeque on the Fourth of July so it was no surprise that Baxter's was so packed. There was just nowhere else to go, nothing else to do. Like campers stuck in a cabin, people put their watches away and settled in for the long haul, as everyone became a friend. Old timers mingled with newcomers. Giants' fans shared drinks with Jet's fans. Even guys that never seemed to be able to talk to chicks had girls going up to them. No one was looking for fights. No outsiders were going to come in and start trouble. For one night everyone was a family and all anyone wanted to do was have a good time.

The drinks were pouring and the music blasting. Mike rotated between playing pool and catching up on the latest neighborhood gossip: who was seeing who, who had broken-up and who had gotten themselves into trouble. The gang also reminisced about the "good ol' days", even though none of them were a day over twenty-six. As the night rolled on, more people came in and the crowd grew louder. The place was rockin'. Everyone was ordering rounds of shots and downing beer as if it was the last time they would be able to drink. Mike was restrained compared to everyone else, but still had a good buzz going. Somehow he was able to push everything that was going on to the back of his mind for the night. Maybe he was just caught up in the festivities. Maybe his mind automatically took a seven-hour vacation from all the pressure. Whatever the reason, Mike was enjoying himself for the first time in a while. Later that night he even joined Brian, Dan and a few others outside for another snowball fight in the parking lot.

When Mike opened his eyes the next morning, he was surprised to see Diane sitting next to him on the bed. "Rise and shine," she said softly with a welcoming smile.

"Diane," Mike replied in a hoarse voice, his throat as dry as desert sand. "What are you doing here?"

"Your mom let me in. It's eleven o'clock."

Mike may have been groggy and hung over, but was happy to receive such a pleasant and unexpected wake-up call. "How are you feeling?" he asked while stretching out his arms.

"A lot better."

As his vision began to come back into full focus Diane's silhouette transformed into a detailed face. With the heavy down comforter still draped around his legs, Mike sat up in the bed. "Well you look good."

"Why thank you," Diane responded in a sly, seductive voice.

Mike smiled. "Well you always look good, but I mean you don't look like you're sick anymore. But just 'cause you look and feel better doesn't mean you should be walking around in the snow. That's how you catch pneumonia. And I hope you wore a hat and gloves."

"Yes father, I bundled myself up real good," Diane replied as she lied down on the bed next to him. "I just couldn't resist coming to see you. You can't blame me for that. Besides, we're supposed to spend the whole day together – remember."

Still lying down Diane began to gently brush her nails back and forth along Mike's bare arm. It was something that she knew drove him crazy. It was enough for Mike to rip off her clothes and lock the bedroom door for the rest of the day, but he knew that his mother was awake and could be walking around right outside the door. The throes of passion would have to wait for another time, but that did not mean he wanted her to stop. In fact he could have lain there in bed all day with her hands combing across his arm. "Oh babe, you don't know how good that feels," he proclaimed as his body melted into the mattress. "You don't know how much money people would pay for this."

"Well I charge twenty bucks an hour. Do you think I should raise it to thirty?"

"Sure, just put it on my tab," he replied with a smile. Still in a trance, Mike asked if it was still snowing out.

"No, it finally stopped this morning," she answered. "I think everything's going to be covered in snow for quite a while though."

Still feeling the effects of the night before, Mike finally ventured downstairs with Diane, where his mother was cooking a late breakfast. All three were ready for a leisurely, "do nothing" day. For the second day in a row they all had off from their respective jobs because of the storm.

Although snowplows worked around the clock, many of the roads were still too dangerous to drive on. Schools were closed, as were many offices and retailers. Although the bank where Diane worked as a teller was open, it was only operating with a skeleton crew, which did not include her.

Dressed in sweat pants and a t-shirt, Mike sat at the kitchen table as his mother served-up him an over-stuffed ham and cheese omelet, complete with bacon and toast. She had offered to make an omelet for Diane, but she had already eaten. Mike was hungry, but it was going to take plenty of empty room in his stomach to wolf down the behemoth size plate that his mother had prepared. "Wow ma, is it some special occasion or something," he asked with fork and knife in hand.

"No special occasion," she replied matter-of-factly. "I just figured that you could use a nice, big breakfast after a night out with the boys."

Betty then went into the living room, leaving Mike and Diane to talk amongst themselves. In between bites, Mike updated Diane on who was at Baxter's and what everyone was up to, making sure to say that they were all asking about her. Occasionally Diane would steal a piece of bacon. Mike was feeling better by the forkful and as the two tossed around friendly gossip and what they were going to watch on television, the phone rang in the background. Although there was a phone in the kitchen, Betty yelled out from the other room that she would get it. "It's probably Brian," Mike yelled back. "He probably wants to trade hangover reports," he then said to Diane. "I know he's a lot worse-off than me. Actually, I'm surprised he's even up and about."

"Why, he was that wasted?" Diane asked as she stole Mike's last piece of bacon.

Mike shook his head. "You should've seen him. I mean he didn't get out of hand or anything, but he kept on doing shots of tequila."

Diane smiled, picturing Brian stumbling around the bar, trying to pick up on every girl in sight. "You didn't do any shots?"

"I did two," Mike replied with a squeamish look on his face as if remembering exactly how it tasted. "I just can't do 'em like I used anymore. I don't know, I guess my stomach isn't as cast-iron as it used to be."

At that moment, Betty walked into the room with a silent, ghostly stare on her face. Before even opening her mouth, Mike and Diane knew that something was terribly wrong and just like that the light casual atmosphere that had just embraced the room became thick enough to choke on. "That... That was the hospital," she sputtered forcing each word to come out.

As his mother's words hung in the air, Mike's heart came to an abrupt stop. Everything came to a standstill. He had prepared himself for this in his worst fears and nightmares. He had envisioned the moment time and time again: the phone ringing, the blank stare on his mother's face. Still, imagining it and living it were two completely separate things and despite all the times it played out in his head, the reality of the moment dropped like a bomb from the clear blue sky. He wanted to ask what happened, but was too afraid to face the answer.

Seeing how petrified Mike was, Diane, who was also obviously shaken by the news, intervened. "Is Melissa all right?" She asked, with great hesitation.

"It's not Melissa," Betty crackled, as streaks of tears rolled down her face. "It's Allison. She was raped."

Diane and Mike looked at each other in sheer horror. The fact that it was Allison and not Melissa did little to put them at ease. There was no sighs of relief or "Oh, thank god it's not Melissa." Maybe that would come at a later time, but what they had just heard was too shocking and horrendous for even the slightest sliver of optimism.

"Raped?" Diane repeated in a hollow voice, perhaps hoping she had heard it wrong.

"Yes," Betty answered back, still trembling with tears pouring down her face. "Supposedly, Melissa went out for a while by herself and when she returned to where the two of them were staying she found Allison..." Betty paused to let out a bellowing cry that rang through the entire house. "She immediately ran and called 911."

By this point, Diane had also broken into tears. "Where's Melissa now?" She asked, knowing that Mike was still too overcome to speak.

"She's at the hospital – Beth Israel in the city. The woman on the phone – a police officer – said that they were asking her questions about what happened and would keep her there until we arrived." Betty stopped to wipe away more tears. "I don't want you driving though," she said to Mike. "The roads are too dangerous. Diane, could you please call a cab dear. I think I'm too nervous to talk to anyone right now."

"Sure," Diane replied, busy wiping away her own tears.

Mike, who had not said anything yet, was still frozen in shock. He was not crying, he was not banging things around or grimacing in dismay. He was just sitting there, with a blank stare, still trying to digest what he had heard. "No, it's all right ma," he said with bated breath, "I'll drive. Who knows how long it'll take a cab to get here."

"Michael I don't want you to drive. The roads are too dangerous and..."

Before Betty could finish her sentence, Mike grabbed the car keys from the key rack on the kitchen wall. "Too dangerous? What, it's not going to be dangerous for the cab?"

"Michael, look at you," she replied in a frantic voice. "You're too emotional to drive. You'll wind up speeding and we'll get into an accident. If you don't want to wait for a cab, we can take the railroad. Actually that'll probably get us there the fastest."

With the keys in hand, Mike realized that his mother was right. On a good day it took almost two hours to drive into the city. With conditions the way they were it would probably take double that time. However Manhattan was only an hour and a half by train and one came just about every half hour.

Frantically Mike ran upstairs to get dressed as Diane called for the railroad schedule. Betty remained in the entranceway to the kitchen and continued to cry. In less than ten minutes they were in the car headed for the train station. No one told Diane to go or not to go. It was just instinct that made her jump in that car and head to the hospital. The thought of not going never even crossed her mind.

Once in Manhattan, they hailed a taxi to get to the hospital. Both the train and cab ride were filled with an ominous silence, as no one knew what to say. Perhaps there were no words to say. It seemed much too late for "everything will work out" and too selfish for "at least it's not Melissa." Instead, the three of them sat there staring at their watches and trying to figure out the many unanswered questions. How critical was Allison's condition? Why did Melissa leave her alone? Was Melissa just lying about being ok? But questions were not the only things going through their minds. Each of them fought back pictures of Allison and the sheer terror of what she must have gone through. Although Mike may have thought Allison was a bad influence on Melissa, he would not have wished that atrocity on anyone. Like Betty and Diane, he was sickened by it.

Mike had thought that there was no way his heart could beat any faster, but after taking the first step into the hospital, it did. Trying to catch his breath, he felt the entire room starting to spin. At one point he had to lean on the reception desk to keep from passing out. His knees started to buckle and even after coming in from the fifteen-degree weather, sweat ran profusely down his face. Fighting vigorously to pull himself together he listened as the receptionist told them where to find Melissa.

From the elevator, through a maze of narrow and crowded corridors, they followed the receptionist's directions. With each step their apprehension grew. With each bated breath, the noose of anxiety pulled tighter around their necks. Then, as they turned one last corner, Mike spotted Melissa sitting by herself at the other end of the hallway. He wanted to run to her, but his legs turned to gel. Suddenly everything was again in slow motion. Blocking out all sounds except the pounding of his heart, Mike kept walking, but it was as if he was walking in place. Doctors and nurses going the other way bumped into him as if he wasn't even there. The usual commotion of a big city hospital was going on all around him, but somehow seemed to make no noise. Then, as it appeared he was finally drawing near, Melissa lifted her head from her hands. Still in slow motion, Mike realized that the closer Melissa became the less familiar she looked. Her hair was dirty and tangled and the clothes she was wearing looked like they had not been washed in weeks. Her face was gray and worn. As Mike approached, he noticed that he was steps ahead of his mother and Diane. In reality, he had run down the corridor and what seemed like minutes was in fact less than a second.

Getting there before anyone else, Mike kneeled in front of Melissa and placed his hands upon her shoulders. Gazing into the void where her bright, blue eyes used to be, Mike no longer felt his heart pounding. Instead, he could feel it breaking into tiny pieces. There were so many unanswered questions, but it was neither the time nor the place. Without saying a word, Mike wrapped his arms around his sister as she broke helplessly into tears. "Oh Mike," she cried, trembling into his shoulder.

Before Mike could respond, Betty kneeled down and grabbed Melissa from him. "Oh my baby," she cried, "are you all right?"

As Melissa and her mother shared tears in a heartfelt embrace, two detectives walked up. "Excuse me," one of them said in a tentative voice, "are you Mrs. Patterson?"

Still shaking, Betty lifted her head. "Yes, I'm Mrs. Patterson."

In a business like fashion, the detectives introduced themselves. "I think we have all the information we need right now," said the older looking detective. "So you can take your daughter home when you're ready. However, as we told Melissa, someone from the DA's office will probably be giving her a call."

"Did you catch the guy?" Mike asked apprehensively.

"Well according to your daughter's friend it was actually two men that attacked her. Fortunately though, she was able to give us full descriptions of what they looked like and we've put out an all points bulletin. So although they're not in custody yet, every cop in the city is looking for them."

"How is Allison?" Betty asked, fearful of what the answer might be.

Before responding, the detective motioned them to walk down the hall, away from Melissa. Then it was time for the graphic truth. "Your daughter's friend is in pretty bad shape I'm afraid. The guys that did this to her really did a number on her. The doctors say that there's extensive damage to her uterus and a couple of cracked ribs that they say just missed puncturing her lung. She also has substantial head injuries; a fracture in her skull, a broken nose and jaw and two black eyes."

Feeling lightheaded, Diane clutched onto Mike's arm. "Oh my god," she cried out in a quivering voice.

"Yeah, there's some sick people out there," replied the younger detective.

Shaking his head in agreement, the other detective continued. "According to Melissa, the two of them were staying by themselves in an abandoned apartment building down by the Bowery. Well actually it's supposed to be abandoned, but we get a lot of squatters over there."

"Squatters?" Betty asked, not knowing what it meant.

"People who are there unlawfully," he replied. "Mostly homeless people. Melissa said they had been staying there for the last several days." The detective then paused as they all moved over to let a nurse wheeling a patient pass by. "Anyway, according to your daughter, they were supposed to meet a friend early this morning who was going to lend them some cash. However Allison wasn't feeling good so Melissa went by herself. When she came back two hours later she found her there on the floor, unconscious. She immediately ran across the street to the payphone and called 911. The doctors say that if your daughter didn't get there when she did Allison could have slipped into a coma or even died."

A doctor walked by with a man and woman and gave the detectives a nod. "Those are Allison's parents," replied the younger detective.

Surprisingly, neither Betty nor Mike had ever before seen them. As her parents reached the end of the corridor, just past where Melissa was sitting the doctor escorted them into a room. No more than a second later a god-awful scream reverberated through the entire hospital. "That's where they're keeping Allison until she's ready for surgery," the detective pointed out. "Unfortunately they're bringing in a lot of people today so she's still waiting to be operated on."

"Yeah, well we better get over there and talk to them," remarked the other detective. With that, Mike Betty and Diane were left to ponder the devastating details that they had learned.

The trip back to Long Island was filled with even more silence than the ride into the city. Melissa sat lifelessly, staring out the train's dirty window. There were many questions that Mike and Betty wanted to ask her not only about Allison, but also about the entire time she was gone. Where had she been staying? What had she been doing? Had anything else traumatic happened that they didn't know about? Mike wanted to know if she ever saw Russell or Duffy again; if she ever found out about his altercations with them. However both Betty and Mike knew that it was not the time to bombard Melissa's broken psyche with questions. She had been through enough for the day. Besides, perhaps they would really rather not know the answers to some of the questions.

Betty sat next to Melissa, saying nothing as she gently rubbed her daughter's arm. Silently she thanked the lord that Melissa was not raped, but at the same time was devastated by what had happened to Allison. She thought about the pure horror the seventeen year-old must have gone through. She thought about the physical and emotional scars she would have to carry for the rest of her life. Betty could also not stop thinking about Allison's parents – especially her mother. With a daughter of her own, Betty could only imagine the torment she must have been going through. It was a pain only a mother could feel. It was the pain of knowing that her child was violated in the most horrendous of ways. Before leaving the hospital, Betty had introduced herself to Allison's mother, Millie. Betty knew she was in no state of mind to talk, but felt the need to offer support. Now on the train, she could still picture the sheer wreckage in Millie's watery eyes. It was an image that had burned itself into her mind.

Mike too, was shrouded in silence. There were just no words that seemed good enough, meaningful enough, to say. So he just sat there in his own world of battered thoughts. His mind felt as though it was going as fast as the train. One minute he would picture Allison the way he saw her so many times before – carefree and glowing with life. Then he could not help but picture how she must have looked lying unconscious on the floor bleeding and with her clothes torn off. It disgusted him. It angered him. It frightened him. However, at the same time, like his mother, Mike was also relieved that Melissa was not physically harmed.

The first thing Melissa did when they arrived back home was go upstairs to take a long hot shower. As she did Betty, Mike and Diane stood in the kitchen and for the first time talked about what happened. Everyone was still in a state of shock. It was hard for them to conceive what had happen, let alone discuss it, but somehow they acted as each other's crutch. After about a half hour, Diane went home, feeling that Mike and Betty needed to have time alone with Melissa.

After hearing the shower stop, Mike slowly made his way upstairs and knocked on his sister's door. Looking much better, but still obviously distressed, Melissa opened the door dressed in pajamas and a robe. "If you want to be alone I can come back later," Mike half-whispered.

"No, it's ok," she replied in an exhausted voice. "C'mon in. Just close the door behind you."

Before Mike could utter another word, Melissa threw her arms around him and burst into tears, holding back nothing. As her small body trembled against his chest, Mike began to shed his own tears. It was as if her pain, her sorrow, her fear were pouring out of her body and into his.

Mike only wished that he could take it all from her. "I'm so sorry Mike," she cried.

"Sorry? You don't have anything to be sorry about," Mike whispered, while gently caressing his sister's hair.

"I said all those horrible things to you the last time you were in my room. I didn't mean any of them. I know you were just tryin' to watch out for me."

Mike grabbed his sister by the shoulders and looked straight into her teary eyes. "Melissa, I love you. I don't care what you said to me in the heat of the moment. I know you didn't mean it. Besides, even if you did – even if you burned all my stuff and had someone beat me up – I would still love you. I will always love you and I will always be here for you... and that will never change. "

After letting a smile escape from her face Melissa fell back into her brother's arms. "Oh Mike, I love you too. I only wish I would have listened to you. It was so awful out there. I don't know what I was thinking."

"Shhh. Everything's going to be ok. The important thing is that you're back home," Mike replied, wishing he could keep her in his arms forever. "But Melissa, you've got to want to get help. You..."

"I know." She interjected. "I really do. There's no way I can go on like this – especially after seeing what happened to Allison. Oh Mike, I'm just so scared."

As she continued sobbing and trembling in Mike's arms, his hand ran gently along her blonde hair. It was hard for him to see her in such despair, but knew she had to let it all out. For a while he just held her there saying nothing; hoping that this would be the start of a long healing process. Then, after about five minutes, Melissa emerged from her brother's embrace. As she sat there on the bed, Mike handed her a box of tissues that were on the dresser. "You know Missy, you're gonna have to go back to rehab," he said in a soft, but direct tone. "It's the only way you're gonna get help."

"I know," Melissa said in a nasally voice before blowing her nose into a tissue. "And I will. And I promise I won't leave this time. I know it's not gonna be easy, but I can't go on like this. I just can't."

Mike put his arm around his sister's shoulder. "It won't be easy, but I'll be here for you every step of the way – and so will mom. I want you to know that. And I'll come visit you every chance I get. We'll get through this together Missy. I promise."

Melissa stayed inside the house for the entire weekend, watching TV, getting her nourishment back and catching-up on some much-needed sleep. She felt good being back home. It felt good to be able to take a long hot shower, lie on the couch without worrying who else was in the room, eat home cooked meals and sleep in her own bed. However, on Monday, it was back to rehab. Yet it was not the same center she had been in before. Understandably displeased with the way The North Shore Center handled her last stint; Mike and Betty contacted another facility over the weekend – The RiverDale Center – that was further out on Long Island.

When Monday morning came, Melissa put her own bag in the car and willingly climbed in for the ride. It could not have been more different than her last trip. This time there was no surprises, no kicking and screaming. This time when the staff met them at the door, Melissa gave her mother and brother a gentle kiss goodbye and said she would see them soon. Finally, a sense of hope had been restored. For the first time Mike and his mother felt that Melissa *wanted* to get help. She *wanted* to change her life. Mike and Betty left the treatment center once again feeling that perhaps everything was going to work out.

Chapter 12

A TIME TO HEAL

"C'mon ma, I don't want to be late," Mike yelled up the stairs.

"It's not like we have an appointment Michael," she yelled back.

Mike, who already had his coat on, was standing by the front door. "I Know," he replied. "It's just that I'm anxious to see her."

Checking to make sure if her earrings were on, Betty came walking down the stairs. "I know. I'm anxious to see her too. But can you just let me get my jacket on."

It had been two weeks and they were making their first trip to see Melissa. Up to that point they had not even talked to her on the phone. Like the North Shore Center, the RiverDale Center prohibited any outside contact for an initial period.

After meeting briefly with one of the counselors, Mike and Betty were escorted to the visiting area, where Melissa was waiting. After hugs and kisses, the three of them sat down around one of the visitor tables. Immediately they noticed how rested Melissa looked. She looked like a completely different person from when they saw her last.

The first thing Melissa asked after they sat down was if they had heard anything about Allison. Betty explained that she had spoken to Allison's mother and that Allison was supposed to be coming home in a few days. However she would have to go back for several more plastic surgeries to fully repair her face. Betty also let Melissa know that the police had caught both of the suspects. The conversation then turned to a lighter side as Melissa explained her daily routine. After about a half hour, Mike asked if his mother would mind giving him some time alone with Melissa. So with a tight hug and kiss on the forehead, Betty said goodbye to Melissa and told Mike to meet her by the reception area.

"So, Doctor Crowley says you're coming along well," Mike said with encouragement. "You're also looking a lot better."

"Compared to what?" she asked with a smile. "No, I'm just kidding. The truth is I feel a lot better. I mean the first week was pretty rough, but I think now I'm starting to settle in. You know, do some thinking." Melissa paused to let out a sigh. "I'll tell you, now that I've had time to clear my head and look back – even though it's only been two weeks – I can't believe that that was me doing some of those things."

"I know the feeling."

Melissa pushed back the hair from her face. "I just can't believe that things got so out of hand. But I want you to know Mike," she said, putting her hand on his knee, "that it had nothing to do with you. I mean it's important that you know that it had nothing to do with you being away. Whatever I did, it's not your fault. It's not mom's fault either. I mean I couldn't have asked for a better mother than mom. No, I have no one to blame but myself." As his sister searched her soul, Mike listened without interrupting. He knew that searching for answers was the first step in the healing process and that having someone there to listen without passing judgment made it easier. "It's funny," she continued. "I always used to look down on the kids that came to school high, make fun of them. I used to hear the kids in school talking about getting high and doing coke and think 'what a bunch of losers'. Now I'm the loser. Now I'm the one who people look to and point their fingers at."

"Don't worry about what other people think Missy," Mike replied. "You don't know what kind of skeletons they have in their closets."

"It's just hard to believe how I got to this point," she continued, not really paying attention to her brother's remark. "I mean I can't believe how fast everything spiraled out of control. It's crazy to think how I got from point A to point B in such a short time. Everything started out so innocently - getting drunk at a party, maybe taking a couple of hits off a joint. I wasn't trying to suppress any feelings or hide from anything. It was nothing deeper than just having some fun – having a good time. But then somehow, somewhere along the line I started getting into heavier things and it became more than just having a good time. It became a way to get away, to escape. The only thing is that I have no idea of what I was trying to escape from. I felt so discontent inside, but I didn't know why. I mean what did I have to feel so unhappy about? But I did. For some reason everything just started to seem so bleak." Melissa's tone of voice was subdued, but continued to grow with frustration. "I don't know Mike, for some reason I just didn't see anything promising out there. Almost all the people I know, all they do is sit around and get high everyday. I know that most of them are still in high school, but it's like none of them are going anywhere. I mean even the people you know – I'm not putting them down or anything – but most of them still live at home with their parents. It's like everyone is just stuck in place. Is that what I have to look forward to? Am I gonna live on Franklin Lane for the rest of my life?" Melissa paused to exhale a deep breath and then continued in a more relaxed tone. "Don't get me wrong, Massapequa is a lot better than the city. I never want to go back to Manhattan ever again. But it's just that it feels like there's this invisible barrier that I can't break through. I just wish we could go far away – somewhere far away from here."

Mike put his arm around Melissa as her head gently fell on his shoulder. "Maybe you're right. Maybe what we need is to just pack-up and a get a fresh start somewhere new."

Melissa lifted her head. "What, you mean like move?"

"Yeah," he replied with confidence. "Maybe somewhere out west, like Arizona or Texas."

Melissa gave her brother a look like he was crazy. "Mike, I was just blowing off steam. We can't actually move."

"Why not?"

Melissa smiled, looking her brother in the face. "Why not? I'll tell you why not. How about your job? What about mom's job? What about Diane? You know Mike; she really cares about you. You're very lucky to have found some one like her. Have you told her that you love her yet?"

"Listen. Diane is very special to me, but you and mom have to come before anything else."

The two talked for another ten minutes before bidding farewell with a hug and an "I love you". Mike assured his sister that he would visit again the following weekend.

Mike came away from the visit feeling positive, as did his mother. Although he knew that there was still a long and onerous road ahead, he could sense that Melissa was on the right track. In fact both he and his mother were surprised by how far she seemed to have come in only two weeks. Mike was glad to see her talking about her problems and trying to understand the choices she had made. Admitting there was a problem may be the first step in the healing process, but it was meaningless without secondly understanding why the problem developed in the first place and that was done only through extensive soul-searching and self-evaluation. The counselors and the shrinks could point a person in the right direction, but inevitably the person has to go there themselves. It was often a dark and lonely journey into the deepest corners of the mind and center of one's soul and sometimes there was no telling what a person might find. Yet getting to the root of the problem was still only half the work. A person that's addicted may know they're an addict and understand why they wound up that way, but ultimately they still had to fix the problem and that meant dealing with one of the most feared words in the human vocabulary: willpower. Willpower is to the alcoholic and drug addict what white blood cells are to a person fighting an infection. All the medicine and outside help in the world was not going to heal a person if their body rejected the treatment.

Over the next couple of weeks, Mike thought a lot about the conversation he had with Melissa during that first visit. Her words about wanting to be far away weighed on his mind and the idea of moving from New York was something that was starting to keep him up at nights. It was not that Mike had any illusions that they were going to move somewhere that was immune from the inflictions and perils drugs. He knew that unfortunately there was no such place. He worried that once Melissa was released, she would once again be surrounded by all her old cohorts, especially in school. Melissa was supposed to have graduated in June, but now, because of her troubles and running away, she would have to make up the whole school year. Everyday she would come face to face with some of the same people with which she used to party and do drugs. Temptation was hard enough without it being crammed in your face. Sometimes all it takes is a phone call or friendly invitation to lure even the strongest of wills. Mike feared that letting Melissa go back to the same school with some of her old friends (most would have already graduated and moved on, but she surely knew people in lower grades and still others that had to go for a fifth year) would be like giving a bank robber a job at a bank. Sure, Mike had gone back to the old neighborhood and even hung out with his old friends, but it was not the same. He had been removed for five years and had time to develop into a different person. He was also older and didn't have to deal with the constant peer pressures of high school.

Mike was convinced that Melissa needed a fresh start somewhere where she could meet new friends and not be constantly reminded of a past that she was trying to leave behind. Was moving realistic though? Mike was ready to do anything to help his sister, but there *were* certain realities that could not be ignored. What about his and his mother's jobs? How easy would it be to sell the house and find a new one? Lying awake at night, Mike would keep going back and forth. One minute he would realize that picking-up and moving cross-country was easier said than done. However, the next minute he would tell himself that it was something that people did all the time. It was not like he or his mother had perfect jobs with fat salaries that they couldn't afford to loose. Then again, Mike didn't have any specialized skills and was lucky to have the job he had. His mother was a manager at Macy's, which was not particularly a hot commodity in the job market. There was also a recession going on, which made getting a good job that much harder. It would also make selling their house a lot harder. Yet Mike kept on going back to the fact that if other people did it, why couldn't they. Then he would think about Diane. If turning Melissa's life around meant moving, than Mike was willing to sacrifice his relationship with Diane, but it would not be without grate pain. In Diane, Mike had found something that for a long time he thought he would never find again: a partner, a soul mate. Although they had only been together for about six months, Mike could not imagine himself without Diane.

After sleepless nights of playing ping-pong with his thoughts, Mike finally went to his mother. After all, the decision was ultimately hers to make. Betty agreed that having Melissa go back to her old school and be around the same friends might be too much pressure. However, she also agreed that moving may not have been realistic. Besides the difficulties of selling house and looking for a new one, Betty pointed out that her job – the same place she had worked for the last nine years – made it possible for them to live comfortably. It also provided health and life insurance. Over the years she had worked her way up through promotions and raises. If they had to move in order to save Melissa they would, but it would not be easy. Then finally, they came up with a plan. Melissa would go to private school for a year to make up for her senior classes. Hopefully, Mike and Betty rationalized Melissa would make new friends in private school, making old bonds easier to break. Then after she graduated, the hope was that Melissa would go away to college. That did not necessarily mean out of state. There were some very good schools in New York – NYU, Fordham, Cornell – where she could live on or near campus and still be close enough to come home for the weekends. It seemed a practical solution to an impractical problem. However, for the time being, they kept their plan from Melissa. She had enough to deal with at the moment.

Mike was relieved that they had decided not to move and it was for one reason only: Diane. Though he had been willing to leave her for the sake of Melissa's well being, it would have been difficult. While incarcerated, he could only think about getting out so he could watch over his sister and mother. Mike lived for them and although they were still the center of his universe, Diane proved that he also had a reason to live for himself.

Mike had not discussed moving with Diane. A part of him felt guilty for keeping it from her, but had seen no need to worry her about something without knowing if it was going to happen. Now though, having decided to stay in Massapequa and with Melissa finally getting help, it was time for their relationship to take the next step. For some time Mike knew that he was in love with Diane, but had never told her. However, the time had now come and what better day to do it on than Valentine's Day.

Valentine's Day fell on a Friday that year. Mike had made plans to take Diane out to an upscale seafood restaurant and then surprise her with a hotel room for the night at the Hilton. He was both excited and nervous. He had loved Diane for a while, but saying it for the first time was still a big step. Yet there was no doubt that he was ready. Before leaving for work that morning Mike made sure to wish his mother a happy Valentine's Day and asked again if she would be all right being alone for the night. Like she did when he first told her of the plans to stay at a hotel for the night, Betty said she would be fine. She was just happy that Mike had found someone like Diane and knew it was important for them to be together on Valentine's Day.

That afternoon, Mike had a dozen red roses delivered to his mother's work. Taken by complete surprise, Betty paraded the vibrant, red flowers around to all her co-workers, making sure to say from whom they came. When Mike came home from work, she met him with a hug that even a bear would envy. After thanking him for the flowers, she then began to cry. Only this time her tears were tears of joy. Betty was so proud of her son and could have stood there holding him all night. However, she did not want him to be late for Diane.

After taking a shower and putting on his only suit, Mike packed an overnight bag. The time to tell Diane his true feelings had arrived. Before giving his mother one last kiss goodbye, Mike straightened his tie and made sure that not a single hair was out of place. He then drove the few blocks to Diane's feeling so alive and full of life. Slapping his hand on the steering wheel to the beat of Led Zeppelin, he made a mental note of how clean and light each breath felt. Nothing felt like it was weighing over his head or clouding his mind. It was time for once to just sit back and enjoy the moment.

As soon as he pulled up to the house, Diane came out the front door holding her purse and a small black bag. Yet Mike was not concentrating on what she was carrying. He was too busy looking at what she was wearing – a short, but formal black dress that fit her every curve, covered by an elegant, black cardigan. Being a gentleman, Mike stepped out of the car to open the passenger door. Of course, he first greeted her with a kiss. "You look beautiful," he proclaimed as he looked her over. "I mean you're always beautiful, but you look absolutely stunning. You look like a movie star or something."

Diane blushed. "Well, you don't look so bad yourself," she replied with a sheepish smile. "I've never seen you in a suit before. You look so debonair."

"Well it is a special occasion."

After exchanging a few more words of admiration, they climbed into the car and were on their way. "I'm so excited," Diane declared. I hear that The Oceanic is the best seafood restaurant on Long Island."

Mike shook his head in agreement. "Yeah, everything's supposed to be real fresh there. They say the lobster is incredible. But I can't wait to start

off with the cold seafood platter; shrimp, crab legs, clams and oysters. You
know, they say oysters are an aphrodisiac."

"Aphrodisiac, huh? That should be interesting," Diane replied as she
put her hand on Mike's knee. "They say the atmosphere is very romantic
there too. I made all the girls jealous at work when I told them where you
were taking me."

Mike let out a laugh. "Good. That's important."

"I just feel bad for your mother. I mean it's Valentine's Day and she's
all alone. She doesn't even have Melissa there."

Mike nodded. "Yeah I felt bad too, but she was happy that we were
going out. Oh, by the way, she said to wish you a happy Valentine's Day."

"Your mother is so sweet."

Stopping for a red light, Mike turned to look at Diane. "And Melissa
was asking how you were doing too."

"You talked to Melissa?"

As the light turned green, Mike turned both eyes back to the road. "I
got a letter from her yesterday" .

When Mike and Diane made their entrance into the restaurant, it
was everything they had expected and more. Elegance gleamed from wall
to wall; from the crystal chandelier to the extravagant aquarium that greeted
patrons when they walked in. The hand painted mural of a quaint ocean-
side villa, the spacious yet cozy dining room, the burning candles on every
table, were all meant to seduce the senses. They were all meant to take one
on a romantic dining journey.

As Mike sat down across from Diane, he was suddenly overcome by
a sense of pride and accomplishment. The past five years had been a long
and laborious journey. Six months earlier Mike was wasting away in a tiny,
rancid cell, deprived of even the most fundamental of liberties. Now there he
was in a suit and tie at one of the most elegant restaurants on Long Island,
sitting across from a beautiful young lady. There he was sitting shoulder to
shoulder with the cream of society and did so with dignity and confidence.
No one there besides Diane knew about his past. There were no

preconceptions or judgment. For all the waiter or people at the next table knew, Mike was a doctor or owned his own business. If they pointed, it was to remark what a nice suit he was wearing or how beautiful Diane looked. Mike felt just as important as anyone else in that restaurant – and for what anyone else knew, he was.

In between appetizers and the main course, Diane pulled out a small gift wrapped box and card, from the bag she had been carrying. "Happy Valentine's Day honey," she said in a soft, but proud voice as she handed them to Mike.

"I was wondering what you had in that bag," Mike replied with a smile. He then reached into his inside coat pocket and pulled out a box of his own. "I have a confession though. I don't have a card."

Diane smiled. "That's ok."

"But there's a reason why. You see I actually did buy you a card, but then I realized that what I was going to write in it was something I had say to your face." With a stomach full of butterflies, Diane leaned across the table waiting for what he had to say. Nervous, Mike stopped beating around the bush and went for it. "Well Diane, I just want you to know how much I love you. I've loved you for a long time and I hope you know that. I'm just sorry that it took me so long to tell you."

Diane grabbed hold of Mike's hands as tears began to swell in her eyes. "Don't be sorry Mike. I love you too. I love you so much, you'll never know."

Suddenly Mike felt like a kid again – when everything was milk and honey. He knew what Diane's response was going to be, but hearing those words filled him with exhilaration beyond what he could have ever expected. They were simple words that too often became as mechanical as "hello" or "good morning", but when someone meant them and said them for the first time, they still held that magical meaning that some people spend their entire lives trying to find.

"Well I'm glad you feel the same way, but I didn't want you to cry," Mike replied as he wiped away a tear from her cheek. "I mean you know I think you look beautiful without any make-up at all, but you probably spent so much time putting it on."

Diane let out a quiet laugh as she wiped away another tear. "You're right, I did. I guess I should go freshen up." With that, Diane excused herself from the table, but not before walking over and giving Mike a kiss.

When she returned, they finally opened each other's gifts. Diane had given Mike a new watch and although he didn't know much about watches, it looked expensive. Immediately he replaced his old watch and showed Diane how it looked on his wrist. Happy that he liked it Diane anxiously opened her gift. It was a gold bracelet with hearts hanging from it. Like Mike did with the watch, she immediately put it on.

In the midst of praising their gifts, the main course arrived: lobster Fra Diavlo for Mike and for Diane, a broiled Maine lobster tail and thick filet mingon with béarnaise sauce and sautéed asparagus. It looked and smelled as good as it sounded and they would soon learn that it tasted even better. The night continued as perfectly as it started. Everything was exquisite: the food, the wine, the service, the ambiance. Neither could have asked for anything more. It was a night they knew they would remember.

When the bill finally came, Diane pleaded that they at least split it. "C'mon Mike, it's expensive," she said, trying to snatch the $97 bill out of his hand. "I had a great time. At least let me pay for half of it."

"What are you kidding," Mike replied. "It's Valentine's Day."

"So that's even more of a reason. Why can't I take you out for dinner?" She asked, still trying to take the bill from his grip.

Finally Mike won the tug of war. "Listen, it's not every day we get to live it up like this. I wanted it to be a special night and it has been. Believe me when I tell you that this is the best money I've ever spent. I mean everything's been perfect. However, I do have another surprise."

Diane leaned over the table. "Another surprise," she said wondering what it could be.

"We have a room waiting for us at the Hilton on Hempstead Turnpike."

"Are you serious?"

Mike slyly leaned back in his chair. "Yep. I already have an overnight bag in the trunk. We can swing by your house so you can pick up yours. I was gonna tell you yesterday so you could put some stuff together, but I wanted to make sure everything worked out with this whole 'I love you' thing first.

Diane laughed. "What'd ya think I wasn't going to say that I love you back?"

"I was hoping you would, but I didn't want to take anything for granted." Mike shrugged his shoulders. "You know, I just didn't want there to be any extra pressure or anything. However, I know it's already ten o'clock – I can tell by my beautiful new watch... and if it's too late... I mean I don't want you getting in trouble with your parents or anything like that."

Diane leaned even further across the table and grabbed his hand. "It's not too late," she whispered. "It'll take me ten minutes to throw some stuff together and don't worry about my parents. I'm twenty-three years old. But I'll tell you what – if you thought the night's been perfect so far, just wait 'til later. "

It was what Valentine's Day was all about: a romantic dinner, a confession of love and a passionate night together. The next morning they would wake-up in each other's arms happier than ever that their paths had crossed.

Inevitably, winter began to fade as the days slowly became warmer with each passing week. The last remnants of snow had long since melted and the air told that Spring had once again arrived. As the calendar peeled away, things continued to look up for the Patterson family. The dark clouds that had loomed over them in recent months seemed like they were finally starting to dissipate. Melissa was able now to have routine visits from her family. Every time Mike and his mother talked to her, her voice seemed stronger and more confident. With each visit, she appeared healthier and more ready to move on. The counselors and psychologists were all pleased with her progress. Though there were always disclaimers, all signs were pointing to a long-lasting recovery. Inside the Patterson house, the air started to become easier and easier to breathe. It appeared as if Melissa would soon be coming home and they could finally be the family again.

April 15th would have been Katie's twenty-third birthday. It was a day that Mike had on his mind weeks before its arrival. It started with just noticing the date on the calendar, but as it drew closer, it grew to the forefront of his thoughts. Every April Mike paid homage in his own way, but this year was different. This would be the first year – the first time ever – that he would visit her grave. It was something that he had awaited with both anticipation and trepidation. Yet Mike kept it all to himself. He saw no purpose in talking to Diane about it. Their relationship had been going so well and Mike did not want her to feel that she would never live up to Katie's ghost.

Not wanting to run into Katie's parents, Mike decided to go to the cemetery the day before her birthday. It was not that he was afraid to run into them, but rather he did it out of consideration. The last thing they needed to see while visiting their daughter's grave was the man they thought was responsible for putting her there. Mike could still see her mother's tormented face and still hear her screaming "murderer". So without telling Diane or his Mother, Mike made arrangements to work only a half a day. From work he would take a cab to the cemetery. Mike could have asked his mother to borrow the car for the day, but did not want to arouse any suspicion.

Mike had the taxi stop by the florist before going to the cemetery, which was only a twenty-minute drive. Yet it was the loneliest twenty minutes that he had experienced since being in prison. So many thoughts streaked across Mike's mind that he could not concentrate on a single one. However, there was only one image: the image of Katie's glowing blue eyes

and soft-witted smile. It was a picture that brought with it so many emotions
and memories. Some of them were difficult bear, but most were of joyous
times. As they drove past the tall, cast-iron cemetery gates, Mike was
overwhelmed by a cold, eerie sensation. Confronted immediately by a
dozen arrow-shaped signs that pointed out in every direction, Mike told the
driver which lot to go to; knowing it himself only because he had called the
cemetery earlier that day. As the taxi snaked through the labyrinth of
narrow, gravel roads, Mike gazed out the window at the endless sea of
headstones. Some were elaborate, some simple. Some looked like they had
been there since the beginning of time and some appeared unmistakably
new. Each one though had their own unique story to tell. At one point, they
drove past a funeral recession. Mike looked at the small, somber crowd all
dressed in black and wondered whom it was they were laying to rest. Was it
someone young? Was it an elderly person who had lived a full and
prosperous life? How did they die? Who were they leaving behind? The
cemetery held so many untold stories.

"I think this is it sir," said the driver as the car rolled to a stop.

Mike looked over at the meter. "Thanks," he replied in a solemn
voice as he handed the money to the driver.

"Listen, I'll tell you what I'll do. I'll wait for you, but I won't run the
meter." The driver must have known someone that had just passed away,
because a New York cabbie – even in Long Island – would never make
such a generous offer.

Mike thanked him and then stepped out of the car to find Katie's
grave. With the bright bouquet of flowers in hand, he walked slowly along
the grass, looking at each and every headstone. As he did, there was no
escaping the overwhelming feeling of finality. The dead seemed so lonely. In
fact Mike could not help but feel guilty for even being alive. Oh, how envious
the dead must be of him, he thought, if only they could feel at all. Walking
across the grass, searching for his lost love, one gravestone in particular
caught his eye. It was that of a little girl, which read: "Kelly Jean Andersen,
We will always love you, 1980 – 1984." He looked at it twice, hoping he had

read the dates in err, but reality would grant no such wishes. Standing frozen in a state of disbelief, it was as if someone had stolen the breath right from him. Mike wanted to yell, to protest that it was not fair that he was alive when this little four-year-old girl was not. It wasn't right at all. He knew how cruel and unjust life could be and now the evidence was right there before him. Wearily, Mike continued his search, but could not get those dates out of his mind.

Finally, Mike stumbled upon the headstone that he had seen in his dreams over and over again, for the last five-odd years. Falling to his knees as if on command, Mike noticed that it looked just like he had imagined. Etched in it were the words: "In the loving memory of our daughter, Kathleen Ann Fuller, 1964 – 1980". It was a simple stone; one that hundreds of people probably past every week, without even noticing. To them, it was just another untold story, nestled in the endless rows of graves. Mike, however, knew differently. He knew not only of her story, but was part of it – and as long as he lived, so would the story.

Carefully Mike reached out and glided his hand along the cold, smooth surface of the granite stone, not believing that he was actually touching it. It felt so tangible, yet so surreal. Then the realization hit him that Katie was actually buried beneath. There, six feet under the hard soil was her final resting place. As if to make contact, Mike gently combed his fingers across the ground. "Hey Kate," he said in a whispering voice. "I brought you some flowers." With a smile, Mike placed the colorful arrangement by the foot of the stone. "I'm sorry it's taken me so long to come visit you. I know your birthday is tomorrow, but I came today because I didn't want to... well anyway... things are going real good. We visited Melissa yesterday. It seems like she's really coming along. In fact the counselors say that she'll probably be released next month. Hmm, I can't believe it's already been three months. Anyway, I think she's ready to put everything behind her now and move on. I know. I'm not dumb. It's still going to be a long, bumpy road. If all it took were three months in a rehab, there'd be a hell of a lot less people with drug problems out there. But you should see how much better she looks. She even sounds so much stronger. My mother and I decided that it would be best if she goes to a private school when she gets out. You know, so she doesn't fall back in with all her old friends. Yesterday was the first time we discussed it with her and she went right along with it. I think she wants to make new friends. She wants to change her life around. I really think everything's going to work out."

With a smile, Mike continued talking to her grave; his hands clasped between his folded knees. "My mother's been doing good. Of course she's happy that Melissa might be coming home next month. I think it was a tease for her, having both Missy and me home when I first got out. She had waited so long for it and it only lasted for a little while. She's been through a lot, but you know her, she's always been strong."

"Things are also going good with Diane." Mike let out a deep breath and paused. "I told her I love her... And I do, Kate. Believe me, no one will ever replace you and that's not what I'm looking for. But she's really been good to me Kate. She's been right there for me through this whole Melissa thing.

Anyway, things are really looking up. Everything's going good with my job. My boss loves me. Imagine me, not only working, but actually enjoying it. I feel like I've come such a long way. You'd really be proud of me Kate." Mike paused as the smile ran away from his face. "I only wish that you were here to see it all." As his words faded into the air, Mike broke into tears. "I miss you so much Katie," he cried aloud. "It's just not right! It's just not right that you're not here! Oh Kate, there's so much to life that you didn't get to see." For the next five minutes, Mike sat there crying into his hands. As he did, pain, guilt and anger all poured from his body into the still cemetery air.

When there were finally no more tears left, Mike lifted his head and wiped his eyes dry. "Well, I guess I should be going. But I promise I'll come visit you more often," he pledged, staring at the small, granite memorial. Then, while observing one last moment of silence, a smile slowly reappeared on his face, emerging from the depths of sorrow. Before getting up, Mike kissed his hand and then pressed it gently on the headstone.

"Happy Birthday Katie."

Chapter 13

MELISSA,
WELCOME HOME

Eight months earlier Betty and Melissa picked-up Mike from prison and welcomed him home. Now it was Betty and Mike's turn to welcome back Melissa. Yet before seeing her, they first met with one of the counselors. Dr. Ilene Dawson, who had been assigned to Melissa, had already met both Betty and Mike on several occasions. Anxious to finally take Melissa home, they walked into the brightly lit office and sat across from the young, attractive psychologist. If there was a stereotype of psychologists – especially ones that worked in drug rehabs – Dr. Dawson certainly did not fit it. She was slender, had a striking face with big brown eyes and didn't look a day over thirty. She looked more like a model than a shrink that worked with troubled kids. However, the degrees and certificates on her wall said otherwise.

From across her neatly cluttered desk Dr. Dawson handed Betty a few papers to sign. "So," she said in a soft-spoken voice, "I guess you're both excited to have Melissa coming home."

"Yes," Betty replied while looking over the papers.

"We're very excited," added Mike.

Dr. Dawson smiled as she shook her head. "Well, like I told you during our last visit, we're very pleased with Melissa's progress and think she's ready for that step. However, like I also explained, that doesn't necessarily mean she still doesn't have a long and difficult road ahead of her. Chemical dependency is a lifelong battle. Even with the best treatment, there is always a chance of relapse. I don't want to scare you. I think Melissa is sincere about turning her life around and has an excellent chance of doing so. I think she has a bright and productive future waiting for her. Nevertheless, it's important to understand that Melissa going home is just one step in her recovery – albeit a very significant step."

"No, we understand," Betty, replied. "We know that she's not quite out of the woods yet."

"Well, the most important thing is that she has support. Now Melissa is very fortunate to have you both and I have no doubt whatsoever that you'll both be there for her – as you've already been. However, it's also essential that she attend the support group meetings we talked about during our last visit."

Mike leaned forward. "They're twice a week right?"

"Yes and I'll give you a packet with various information, which will include the different locations and available times. Most of the ones during the week are in the evening in order to accommodate working parents, but there's also a couple on the weekends. You'll see that they're very flexible and they're only about an hour long." Dr. Dawson then opened one of her drawers and pulled out a light-blue folder. "Here's all the information." Since Betty was still busy with papers, Dr. Dawson handed the dossier to Mike. "Now Betty, there's also information in there about the Al-Anon meetings I talked to you about. That's the support group for parents who have children with substance abuse problems."

Betty handed the signed papers across the desk to Dr. Dawson. "Thank you doctor, I will look into that," she replied. "Oh, I wanted to tell you, we finally found a private school – the Deer Park Private Academy."

Dr. Dawson nodded. "Oh yes, I've heard of it. It's supposed to be a very fine school."

"Oh, I'm glad you've heard of it," Betty replied. "We've also signed her up for a few summer classes, but the first ones don't start until June fifteenth." Betty let out a nervous sigh. "I'm just worried that that leaves almost a month that Melissa's going to be home by herself all day. However, I took the rest of this week and Monday and Tuesday of next week off so I can at least spend some time with her."

The young doctor digested what Betty said before answering. "Well that's a good idea. In fact you should use this as an opportunity to spend time and go places together. Go out to lunch together. Go to a museum or maybe even see a play. I think it will be a healthy experience for both of you. Also, this way she won't feel as if you're staying home just to watch over her."

"That's a good idea," Betty answered, as Mike too, shook his head.

"As far as the other three weeks or so that she'll be home by herself. Well, all I can say is that in the end it's all about trust – not only you trusting her, but more importantly Melissa trusting herself. Eventually, there's going to be temptations and its how she deals with those temptations that will ultimately determine how well she does in her recovery."

The three talked for about another ten minutes before Dr. Dawson finally walked them to the room where Melissa was waiting. Although there may have been concerns and questions, it was a joyous occasion. She had been away for nearly four months and though Mike had gone years without being home, it was by far the longest Betty had gone without being with her daughter. Yet it was more than the three of them just missing each other.

Melissa coming home signified a new start for the family – a start that was supposed to begin eight months earlier with Mike's release from prison.

The house felt full again. Their lives began to feel complete again. Betty followed Dr. Dawson's advice and used the days off to do things with Melissa. They went out to lunch everyday and went shopping together. They went to the movies together. They even went into the city to see the matinee showing of Cats and then hopped on a train to the World Trade Center. Although Melissa had lived in New York her whole life, she had never been to the Twin Towers. Now she was able to get her chance. The two had nothing but fun together. Betty's worries and fears had turned to smiles and laughter. It felt more like they were sisters then mother and daughter. They told jokes to one another. They talked about shoes and clothes and which actors were the most handsome. What they didn't talk about was anything serious. There was no talk about rehab or drugs or Allison and because of it, there was also no friction. It was not that Betty did not know how to talk to her daughter about such things, but they had already been talked about to death. Melissa had spent the past several months discussing her feelings to counselors and to her mother during visits and in letters. It was time to enjoy life and have fun for a change. It was about Betty and Melissa getting reacquainted and putting the past behind them. Though Melissa had always been close to her mother, it had been years since they had spent quality time together. It felt good to be able to smile and joke around with each other again. It felt healthy and much more constructive than discussing who did what and what new rules were going to be in place.

Mike was glad to see his sister and mother spending so much time together. During dinner they would fill him in on their daily adventures, always talking with a sense of elation and enthusiasm. Mike would just sit back and listen to their stories as they finished each other's sentences. It was like they were girlfriends and Mike could not have been happier. He was pleased that things were going so well with Melissa's return home. She seemed in such high spirits and full of life. It was as if she had been born again. Seeing her laugh and smile, seeing that long lost twinkle in her eyes return, filled Mike with a sense of renewed hope.

On Memorial Day weekend, Diane treated Mike, Betty and Melissa to dinner. She had wanted to show her appreciation for making her feel like one of the family. They were reluctant for Diane to pick up the tab, but she would not take "no" for an answer. So that Saturday night they went to a well-known Italian restaurant in Hicksville that Diane had picked out. She even picked them up.

As Diane checked on the reservations, Betty and Melissa looked around at the rustic décor and inhaled the fresh and lustrous aroma of sautéing garlic. Betty made a comment about how wonderful it smelled and Mike, in an almost aromatic trance, eagerly agreed. Melissa was busy checking out a couple of cute guys that were also waiting for a table, though it looked like they were with their girlfriends. As the maitre d walked them to the table, Betty nonchalantly peeked at what other people were eating and remarked to Diane how delicious everything looked.

Once seated, the four of them talked about the menu and what each one was thinking of ordering. Mike, who had been to the restaurant once before, told his mother to try the Eggplant Parmigiana. He then pointed out to everyone an autographed picture of Thurman Munson that proudly hung on the wall. The atmosphere was light, but festive. They were there to relax and have a good time and that's exactly what they were doing. While Mike talked about other pictures on the wall, Melissa commented to Diane how much she liked her earrings. They then broke into a conversation about jewelry and pocketbooks. When the waitress came to ask everyone what they wanted to drink, Mike was going to get a beer, but then looked at his sister and ordered a soda instead. Knowing that everyone was probably reluctant to get appetizers because she was paying for the dinner, Diane took it upon herself, ordering baked clams and cold antipasto. She remembered Betty saying how good the baked clams looked when a waiter passed the table carrying a plate.

The restaurant was crowded and the service slow, but no one seemed to mind. They were not there to be rushed. They were just enjoying being out and talking to one another. After all, it was the first time they were all out together. It felt like a special occasion; like somebody's birthday. No one was paying attention to their watches or had anywhere else to be. Of course they were getting hungry from the constant fragrance of garlic and basil, but one of the bus boys kept bringing a fresh basket of bread to the table.

When the food finally arrived it was delicious, from the appetizers to the main course. "Mmm Mike, you were right," Betty declared with a look of ecstasy on her face. "This eggplant is delicious!"

Mike finished chewing and wiped a thin string of cheese from his mouth. "I told you. And you know how picky I am about my eggplant."

"Well I'll tell ya', this Chicken Marsala is delicious," Melissa eagerly added. "The chicken is so tender and the sauce is perfect. Diane, how's your Linguini and clam sauce?"

"It's very good," she replied. "In fact, it might be the best I've ever had."

Melissa looked up at Diane as she cut another piece of chicken. "So, I heard Mike took you to The Oceanic for Valentine's Day."

Diane paused as if transporting herself back to that night. "Yes," she replied with a glowing smile. "It was so romantic." As the words rolled from her mouth, Diane turned and stared at Mike with puppy-dog eyes.

"Aww mom, look at that. It's so cute." As Melissa stared at them like two oversized, fluffy teddy bears, Mike gave her a friendly kick under the table. "What? I think that's so romantic." Seeing that Diane was getting slightly embarrassed though, Melissa changed the subject. "So, how was the food?"

"It was superb," Diane answered. "Everything was so fresh."

Melissa stopped to take another bite of her Chicken Marsala. "I've always wanted to go there. It's always ranked one of the best restaurants on Long Island, especially for seafood and I love seafood."

Diane turned to look at Mike. "Did you tell Melissa about Montauk yet?"

Melissa's eyes opened wide. "What about Montauk?"

Mike finished chewing the piece of eggplant he had just put in his mouth. "Well, I was going to tell you tonight. How would you like to go up to Montauk for the weekend next Friday?"

Melissa sat straight up in her seat. "Are you kidding?"

Betty was mutually surprised. "Montauk? You're going to Montauk?"

"Yeah. Well at least that's the plan," Mike replied. "I made arrangements to take this next Friday off of work," he said, turning his attention back to Melissa. "If you want, we'd go up there Friday morning and then Saturday Diane would come out and meet us there. We'll come back Sunday afternoon. It's only about a three hour train ride."

"Of course I want to go!" It wasn't California or the Bahamas, but the idea of just getting away sounded appealing. Besides, even though it was still Long Island, Melissa had never been there before.

Mike was happy that his sister was so excited. "You'll love it up there. The beaches are beautiful. You don't even feel like you're in New York."

"And if you love seafood, that's the place to go," added Diane. "They actually have restaurants that overlook the dock where all the lobster boats come in. It's great. I went there a couple of years ago with some of my friends and we loved it. You can lie on the beach all day or if you like they even have a small town there to go shopping. And let me tell you, the food is fantastic. I don't know if it's still there, but there was this place that made these lobster rolls that were to die for. We were there for four days and ate them for lunch every single day."

While finishing dinner, they continued to talk about Montauk, which was on the eastern most end of Long Island. In fact it was commonly referred to as "The End", because if you drove any further you would be in the Atlantic Ocean. Mike explained that he had originally thought about going during Memorial Day weekend, but then realized it would probably be too crowded. Mike asked his mother if she wanted to go out of courtesy, but Betty politely declined. She liked the idea of Mike spending some time alone with Melissa – just as *she* had the week before.

As the bus boy removed the empty plates from the table, the conversation quickly turned back to how scrumptious the food was. Diane commented on how delicious their desserts were supposed to be, but everyone was too full to eat another bite. Not only was it good, but also the portions were big. Not wanting to break-up the party, Betty suggested that they all go back to the house where, after digesting, they could have some ice cream and Entenmann's cake. Diane graciously accepted the offer.

When the check finally came, Betty tried to grab it from Diane. "C'mon Diane, it's not right that you pay for everything. Please let me get it."

"Please Mrs. Patterson, it's my treat. I told you that before," Diane said, as she was able to wrestle the bill out of Betty's hand. "I want to thank you guys for being so nice to me. Besides, all the times I've eaten dinner at your house…"

"Oh Diane," Betty replied. "What does that mean? We enjoy your company and love having you over for dinner."

Mike put his hand on his mother's arm. "Forget it ma'. I already argued with her about the same thing. She wants to pay for dinner."

Realizing that it was a done deal, they all thanked Diane for the wonderful meal. To hear their appreciation and see the smiles on their faces made it all worthwhile for her.

It was a quiet Memorial Day. Mike cooked hot dogs and hamburgers on a small charcoal grill he had bought the week before. For the most part, it was just Mike, Melissa and their mother. Diane would stop by later on. Mike had been invited to a big barbeque at Dave's, but did not go. A part of him wanted to, but he did not want to leave Melissa alone. Memorial Day is traditionally a day to party – to drink coolers full of beer and get wild. Even though Mike felt that Melissa was turning over a new leaf, he knew that at least a small part of her must have had a yearning to celebrate with all of her old friends. It was only natural. Yet the yearning would have been greater if he was out drinking beers and partying with his friends. It also would have been hypocritical. However, just because it was a subdued Memorial Day, did not mean that they did not have a good time. The weather was perfect and so was the food. As the Scorpions played on a portable tape deck, Mike commanded the grill as Melissa lied on a lounge chair, trying to get a tan. Later, they would trade stories about past family barbeques.

When that Friday morning arrived, Mike and Melissa were ready for Montauk. Earlier in the week, Betty had made arrangements for somebody to drive and pick her up from work so Mike and Melissa could drive to Montauk instead of taking the train. Although Mike had no problems with the train he was glad that his mother offered them the car. It just made everything easier. Now they could stop wherever they wanted and would not have to take cabs to get around town. Besides, Mike liked to drive, especially on the open road. There was a certain sense of freedom about it. So with the car loaded up with their overnight bags, tapes to listen to and plenty of snacks to munch on, Mike and Melissa embarked on their first ever road trip together. They had been on family trips together when they were younger, but never just the two of them.

The drive out to Montauk was long and straight. In fact once on the highway, there was only about three turns the whole rest of the way. Scenically though, the trip was split into several different parts. During the first part, which lasted for about an hour, there was not really much to look at through the windows. The landscape was flat with sporadic patches of houses and shopping centers that could have been "Any Town USA". However all that changes once you start hitting the wineries. Some people may not know, but Long Island is second only to California in American wine making. In fact many people refer to this part of eastern Long Island as "Wine Country". As the road narrows into one lane, the drab backdrop of the highway quickly transforms into picturesque vineyards. Rows of endless grapes stretch along the landscape as wood-carved signs welcome you to the wineries. Suddenly, the feeling that you were in New York begins to escape you. Then you hit the Hamptons – the Palm Beach of New York. Quaint little shops line a narrow, one-lane-street that formed a scenic façade in which million dollar mansions laid behind. Mercedes and Rolexes were everywhere as the rich and curious walked casually from store to store. However, the swank cafes and antique stores slowly morphed back into a more tranquil landscape before entering the final stretch into Montauk.

It was a perfect day to be driving out to Montauk. There was hardly any traffic and the sky was a pristine blue. It was warm, but not hot enough that the air condition was a necessity. So Mike rolled down the windows and let the fresh June air rush in. The two spent most of the drive remising about past family trips. They laughed about the time they all drove down to Disney World when their father was pulled over for speeding. They remembered how he tried to get out of it by telling the cop that his brother was a New York police officer. Of course the officer wound up catching their father in the lie and gave him the ticket along with a long drawn-out lecture. They also talked about the time the whole family flew to Washington D.C. for vacation. It was the only time they had ever flown anywhere together. It was the only time Melissa had ever been on a plane. In between stories, they munched on chips and candy bars and joked with each other. Mike teased his sister about putting on music that *she* used to make fun of him for listening to.

"When the hell did you start listening to Neil Young?"

"What? You know I listen to a lot of the stuff you used to listen to."

Mike looked over to his sister, who began softly singing the words to the music. "Yeah, but Neil Young? I remember you used to say he sounded like whiney old man."

Melissa laughed, remembering that those were her exact words. "Well what can I say, my taste has changed," she replied as she turned the volume up another notch. "I love After The Gold Rush."

Mike nodded in agreement. "Yeah and it's perfect driving music."

As they entered the final stretch into Montauk, Melissa glanced out the window at the Atlantic Ocean that suddenly appeared from nowhere. Mike turned off the radio and announced that they were almost there. Not taking her eyes off the calm, vast water, Melissa commented that she could not wait to lie out on the beach. Not more than ten minutes later came the small, green sign: "Welcome to Montauk". As Mike slowed down to read each sign, Melissa remained glued to the window, though the mighty Atlantic had disappeared just out of sight. As they rolled down the only main street into town, she pointed at each motel asking if that was the one they were staying. To each one, Mike replied no. Having never been to Montauk before Melissa was seeing everything for the first time and it showed in the excitement in her voice. It might have still been Long Island, but it was a different world than Massapequa or anything to which she was accustomed. It looked so serene. No one was beeping their horn or shouting from the sidewalk. There was no traffic. It did not have that overpopulated suburban feel. Everything was so quaint and clean. Every shop in town – though there weren't many – was a mom-and-pop store. People rode down the street with bicycles and mopeds. Everyone was wearing shorts and sandals and looked so at peace. The whole place permeated with happiness and relaxation.

When Mike turned down a side street the ocean reappeared. As Melissa remarked how beautiful it was, Mike pulled into a small, gravel parking lot. "This is where we're staying?" she asked in excitement.

Mike casually shook his head. "Yeah. It's not the Hilton, but…"

"Are you kidding me? It's right on the beach. You said we were going to be by the beach, but you never told me we were going to be right on it!"

As Mike parked the car, he gave his sister a smile. "I wanted to surprise you. And not only are we on the beach, but our room overlooks the water. You can sit on the balcony and look right into the ocean."

Melissa gave her brother a big hug and kiss on the cheek. "Oh Mike, you're the greatest. What brother would do this for his sister?"

Mike was happy that Melissa was excited. It was already turning into a great time and they had not even stepped out of the car. "Are you sure you don't mind sharing a room for tonight?" he asked, opening the car door.

"Mike, you're my brother. I think its o.k." Melissa stepped out of the car and stretched her legs and arms. "I can't believe how fresh the air is."

"Yeah," Mike replied before taking a deep breath. "It's so crisp and clean."

The two then walked a few yards into the small front office, where a short, white-haired elderly lady greeted them. "How are you folks this morning?" she asked with a wrinkly smile.

"We're doing very well, thank you," Mike politely replied. "My name is Michael Patterson. I have reservations staring today."

The pint-sized woman paused as she tried to recall the name. "Oh yes, you're that young man from Massapequa I talked to over the phone."

"Yes. I didn't realize that was you on the phone."

"Yep, that was me. You know I have a son that lives in Massapequa," she said as she opened a black ledger containing the names of the guests.

"Yeah, you were telling me that over the phone," Mike replied.

Wearing a thick pair of glasses, the woman ran her finger down the ledger. "OK, here you are. Lets see, you have one room for tonight and then for tomorrow you have two rooms reserved." Suddenly the phone rang. "Excuse me for a second," she said as she went to answer it.

As the woman talked on the phone, Mike turned his attention back to Melissa. "So I figure we'd put our bags in the room and then go get lunch. Then when we come back we can go out to the beach." Melissa said that it sounded good to her.

After a full day of going out to eat and lying on the beach, Mike and Melissa sat outside on the balcony to kiss the day goodbye. Under the star-drenched sky the two talked while gazing at the beach. Only hours before it was sprawling with people, beach towels and umbrellas. Now it was empty, except for the occasional couples that passed by, holding hands. The raucous chatter of a thousand people's conversations had been replaced with the soft, tranquil roar of waves slapping gracefully against the shore. On a lounge chair Melissa watched the waves in awe as Mike sat by a small plastic table, sipping a 7-Up. All the while, a cool breeze rolled in from the ocean.

"It's so beautiful here at night," Melissa said softly while staring at the vast, black ocean.

"Yeah, it's just so calm and peaceful. I was thinking that tomorrow night when Diane's here, we can all go down to the beach and have a little bon fire."

Melissa peeled her eyes away from the ocean and looked at Mike. "You can do that?"

"Yeah – at least you used to be able to. It's great. You just sit out there right on the beach watching the waves roll in. You can even roast marshmallows."

"That sounds so romantic," Melissa replied in a sighing voice. "Maybe you should just go down there with Diane. They say there's nothing like making love on the beach."

"That's more information than I need to know from my sister."

Melissa let out a fleeting laugh. "You're so uptight about those kinds of things. There's nothing wrong with sex between two people who love each other."

"All right, all right. Can we change the subject already."

"OK, I won't harass you anymore." With that, Melissa leaned back in the lounge chair, tilting her head towards the sky. "Mike, look at the stars," she exclaimed as if seeing them for the first time. "I can't believe how clear they are. And there's so many of them. I feel like I'm in a planetarium. I love the beach. I love summer."

"Just think, in a few more weeks it'll be your birthday. I can't believe you're gonna' be eighteen."

Melissa laughed. "Yeah, neither can I."

"Melissa," Mike said tentatively, without taking his eyes off the night sky. "You don't still have that empty feeling inside, do you?"

"No," she softly replied without any hesitation. "I think I'm learning to take one day at a time. They drill that into your head in counseling – take one day at a time – but I can see why. It works. Like right now, I'm just enjoying being here, by the beach, listening to the waves. But I've been feeling good about things since I came home. I guess most importantly, I've been feeling good about myself. I just feel like I'm able to enjoy things now without having to be high. Like today – I had a blast – and I'm looking forward to tomorrow." Melissa let out a deep breath. "It's funny. Looking back, I don't know if I started getting heavier into drugs because everything seemed so depressing or if doing drugs was what made everything seem so depressing. Either way, I'm just glad I've put it all behind me."

Mike turned his head towards Melissa and smiled. "So am I."

Chapter 14

FAR AWAY

M ost teenagers loathed the idea of going to summer school. That was because most of them wanted to spend their summer days hanging out with friends and partying. However, other than going to Montauk, spending the one-week with her mother and the twice a week outpatient sessions, Melissa had spent most her days just hanging around the house and welcomed the opportunity to make new friends and interact with people. Besides, it was only two classes and summer school was never as hard or had as much homework as regular school. The teachers didn't want to spend any more time grading papers than the students wanted to spend doing them. Although there was of course a certain sense of expected nervousness about being in completely new surroundings, Melissa was excited. Since there were no school buses during the summer, Betty was able to change her schedule at work in order to take Melissa to school in the morning. However, for the way home, Melissa would have to rely on public transportation, which meant taking a bus, as well as a good deal of walking. The entire trip was about an hour, which may seem long in other parts of the country, but not in New York, where every destination seemed to involve a lengthy commute. Besides, Melissa was still usually home by 2:30pm.

June 29th, the last Saturday of the month, was Melissa's eighteenth birthday. For most teenagers that meant a night of wild partying with obscene amounts of booze and sex. It was supposed to be a night they would remember the rest of their lives and to teens that meant it had to be surrounded by pure decadence. It was a day when even the kids that normally didn't get wild came out to party. That's why when Melissa said that two new friends she had made in summer school wanted to take her out for a birthday dinner, Betty was at first reluctant. However, feeling bad that Melissa would be spending her eighteenth birthday sitting at home all night she finally gave in. Besides, both she and Mike knew that Melissa would be going out with her new friends sooner or later. After all, they're the ones that wanted her to meet new people.

To accommodate Melissa, Mike and his mother changed their original plans of a birthday dinner to an afternoon barbeque. They ordered a cake and put up some balloons and a banner. Mike went to the store and bought hamburgers, hot dogs and chicken to grill. Diane came by with potato salad and coleslaw. Dave even stopped by with his new girlfriend. However there was also an unexpected visitor. With everyone else outside, Mike was in the kitchen getting a new bottle of ketchup when the doorbell rang. Since Diane and Dave were already there, he wondered who it was, but did not think much of it. However, after opening the door, his jaw immediately dropped. It was Allison.

"Hi Mike," she said in a tender voice. "I just came by to wish Melissa a happy birthday and drop off a gift I got her."

"C'mon in," he said, as he inconspicuously looked her over. Marks from the attack were still visible on her face and her hair had still not fully grown back from the surgery. A blue bandana concealed the long scar that had been left behind. Walking with a strong right limp, reminders of her brutal encounter were everywhere. "It's good to see you," Mike remarked as he led her through the house and into the back yard. As the sliding glass door opened, Mike could tell by the look on his sister's face that she had no idea Allison was going to show-up. It was evident that the two had not had contact with each other in quite some time.

Allison could see that her old, best friend was at a loss for words. "I didn't mean to interrupt anything," she said in a soft voice. "I just came by to wish you a happy birthday."

As Melissa looked at Allison for the first time since that horrible day, she was not sure how to react at first. She was happy to see her, but it was just so unexpected. "No... No, you're not interrupting anything. I'm glad you came," she said, feeling guilty for not calling Allison since getting out of rehab. "I can't believe you remembered today's my birthday."

Allison looked over to Betty, who was just as surprised as her daughter. "Hi Mrs. Patterson."

"Hi Allison," she replied in an uneasy voice. The last thing Betty had wanted was for Melissa to start hanging out with Allison again, but suddenly that concern was the furthest thing from her mind. Suddenly all she could think about was how sorry she felt for the seventeen year-old. In fact, just looking at Allison nearly brought Betty to tears.

"I can't stay long. My parents don't know I'm here."

As Melissa led Allison back inside to talk, everyone looked at each other. With the exception of Dave's girlfriend, they all knew about what happened. They knew the gruesome details of that fateful winter day. As Dave whispered in his girlfriend's ear, Mike, Diane and Betty stared speechless at each other. Yet each one knew what was going through the other's mind. It was the memories of that trip to the hospital and the realization that the suffering was far from over.

As the atmosphere in the back yard slowly started to lighten again, Melissa came out and told Mike and her mother that Allison wanted to talk to them. Curious, Mike and Betty looked at each other before following Melissa inside to the kitchen. Waiting there for them was a frail and sheepish looking

Allison. "Mike, Mrs. Patterson," she began with a subdued voice as she looked away from their eyes. "I don't want to keep you from anything so I'll keep this short. I just wanted to tell both of you in person that I'm sorry for any troubles I may have caused you in the past."

Moved almost to tears, Betty put her hands on Allison's shoulders. "Allison honey, you have nothing to apologize for. We just want the best for you."

"Thank you," Allison replied softly, before pausing. "I also wanted to let you know – I just got finished telling Melissa – that we're moving to Texas. My uncle owns a small chain of electronic stores out there and my father's going to run one of them. The main reason we're moving though is because of me. I guess my parents thought it would be a good idea if I got a new start somewhere else. They say that there's too many bad memories here. Anyway, we won't be moving until the end of the summer. My parents wanted to move sooner – my father already went out there and found a house – but I still have to go back to the hospital a couple more times for some reconstructive surgery." Looking towards the floor, Allison placed her hand over her scarred and crooked jaw. "I could have it done in Texas, but it's just easier to do it here because I'll have the same medical team that's already been working on me."

Betty was able to fight back her tears, but it was not easy. No child should have to go through what Allison did. It killed Betty to look at her and know the truth and wondered how Allison was able to cope with it all: the pain, the anger, the fear. The nightmares must have been insurmountable. Betty could sense though, just how much the teenager wanted to start anew. "Well Allison, we wish you and your family the best. I really mean that."

"I know you do Mrs. Patterson," she whispered back. "Thank you."

Betty then gave her a tight hug. "Please come visit us before you go."

"I will."

Mike looked at Allison and like his mother, had to fight back tears. Yet he felt a reassuring sense that she was not only going to make it through it, but would wind up making something great of her life. With that sense of hope, Mike grabbed hold of her small hand. "I know everything will work out for you."

"Thank you," she replied with a frail smile.

With that, Melissa led Allison to the door. Mike and Betty then adjourned to the living room to give the two girls a moment by themselves. After hearing the door close, Melissa walked into the room and filled them in on something that Allison had left out in the kitchen. Before they came into the house, she had told Melissa that the reason she did not have to stay in New York for the trial was that both of the guys that raped her had accepted plea agreements. One of them, who was actually out on parole for a rape conviction at the time of the attack, was sentenced to fifteen years – with the possibility of parole after ten. Allison said that the other one, because of rolling on his partner, would probably wind up spending no more than three years in jail.

Around six o'clock, Melissa's two friends came to pick her up. Before leaving, Melissa kissed her mom on the cheek and thanked her and Mike for the barbeque. She also assured them once again that she would be home by 10:30. After she left, Mike, Diane and Betty finished cleaning up the backyard. It wasn't a big mess, but little things can pile up. Once everything was put away, the three sat outside for a while talking about Allison, before finally finding their way on the couch in front of the television. There, they flipped through the channels until Betty announced that she was going to bed.

Now that it was just the two of them, Diane laid down on the couch with her head on Mike's lap. As they talked and watched TV, Mike gently brushed his fingers along her arm. It was a peaceful ending to a long day.

At 10:15pm, Melissa walked through the door, just as she had promised. Hearing that the TV was on, she walked into the living room. After a brief conversation about where she went for dinner, Diane wished Melissa one last happy birthday and went home. Melissa then joined her brother on the couch. As she did, Mike caught the unmistakable scent of alcohol on her breath.

"Missy, have you been drinking?" he asked in a calm but blunt tone of voice.

Melissa looked like a deer caught in headlights. "No," she replied, but then quickly changed her story. "Well I had one drink."

Mike immediately sat straight up. "Melissa..."

"Mike wait," she interjected before he could say another word. "I know what you're thinking, but it's not like that. I just wanted one drink to celebrate turning eighteen. That's all. I could've had more, but I didn't. It was just an innocent drink."

"Melissa, you know that's exactly how it starts." For whatever reason, Mike did not question why her breath still smelled of alcohol after only one drink.

"I know, I know. But it was just because it was my eighteenth birthday," she tried to convince him. "Mike, that's all it was. I'm never going back to the way I was before. I mean especially after seeing Allison today. How can I ever go back to that life?"

Mike let out a deep breath. "I wanna believe you Melissa."

"Than do," she replied, staring her brother in the eyes. "I mean c'mon Mike, I've seen where all that can lead. When I think of the drugs I used to do and what I became, it turns my stomach. And I know that alcohol can be just as dangerous as cocaine or pills, but all it was tonight was just like having a glass of Champaign on New Years – that's all. C'mon, you know I've changed." Melissa could see by the expression on his face that Mike was beginning to soften-up. Grabbing a hold of his arm she flashed her best puppy dog eyes. "Just please don't tell Mom."

Reluctantly, Mike gave in. "OK, I won't tell mom, but only because you had enough control not to get drunk. But let me tell you something, a drink of Champaign on New Years Eve better be the next time you so much as smell alcohol."

"I promise," she replied.

In the following weeks, Melissa started spending more time with her newfound friends, but never came home smelling of alcohol or acting like she was high, so Mike did not bring up the incident again. Perhaps it was – as she had said – just a harmless drink to celebrate her birthday.

As summer progressed, it looked more and more like everything was going to have a happy ending. Melissa brought home papers showing how well she was doing in summer school. She was making new friends. She also continued to go twice a week to support group sessions that Dr. Dawson had suggested. Because she seemed to be doing so well, Betty began trusting her more and felt less and less nervous every time her daughter walked out the front door. On several occasions, including the Fourth of July, Melissa was even allowed to sleep over one of her friend's house. However, Betty now required meeting all of Melissa's friend's parents, especially before letting her sleep over. Betty's trust in Melissa may have been growing back, but she still wanted to be careful and take every precaution.

For Mike, in August, things started slowing down at the moving company. However, Dave promised everyone that things would start picking up again in September, so no one was too concerned. In fact they all saw the light workload as a welcomed opportunity to enjoy what was left of the summer. One Friday in mid August, everyone was finished with their jobs around 11:00am so some of the guys decided to have a few drinks at one of the local bars. Mike usually didn't get a chance to hang out with them, so he happily went along. Over fried bar food and pitchers of beer, they sat around a table and talked about women, baseball and the summer coming to an end.

"Hey John, you see the tits on that girl sitting over at that table? They probably have their own zip codes."

Instinctively John turned to look. "Holy shit," he replied in amazement. "Are those fuckin' real?"

Carl gave John a smack on the arm. "Do you gotta be so fucking obvious? Why don't I give you a camera and you can walk over there and start taking pictures."

"You tell me there's a girl over there with big tits – I'm not gonna turn and look. You fuckin' told me, 'John, you see the tits on that girl sitting over at that table?' How the hell am I supposed to see her if I can't look? Whatdya' got some special fuckin spy glasses you want me to wear?"

Everyone at the table started laughing. "You guys should be in a fuckin movie together," Kevin said in his usual deep, husky voice.

"I don't know," Mike replied before pausing to take a drink of beer. "I think our waitress is hotter than that."

John leaned across the table towards Mike. "You greedy motherfucker. You already have a woman at home – and a hot one at that."

Mike shrugged his shoulders. "Hey, I can still look can't I? I mean I ain't fuckin dead."

Mike had barely finished his sentence when the waitress walked up to the table with another round. She must have known something was up, because everyone was suddenly silent and looking straight at her. In fact it was the first time any of them had shut-up since they walked into the place. Working for her tip and just to tease them a little, she smiled and bent over the table to fill their mugs. As if caught in some kind of tractor beam they all focused in on her cleavage as she knowingly toyed with them. She even gave Mike the old "have I seen you before" routine. When she left their tongues were still hanging out of their mouth. Then, all eyes turned to Mike.

"Have I seen you before?" Carl repeated sarcastically. "And did you see those bedroom eyes she was giving you."

John took a big swig of his beer. "Yeah man and she was practically rubbing her tits up against you when she was pouring your beer."

Mike leaned back in his chair, waving both hands. "Get the fuck outta here."

"No face it, you're the man," replied Carl.

"That's bullshit man," added one of the guys. "The only reason that chick is interested in Mike is because she knows he has a girlfriend. It's like Murphy's Law or something."

John put his mug down on the table in polite defiance. "Now how the hell does that chick know that Mike has a girlfriend?"

"What are you fuckin kidding me? They have a built in sensor for that kind of shit."

Kevin shook his head. "That's true man. Chicks can smell pussy on another guy."

John put his head by Mike's shoulder and started sniffing. "C'mere man, let me smell."

Laughing, Mike pushed his friend away. "Get the hell outta here will you."

By 2:30pm, everyone had had enough of the bar. Kevin and Carl – who were already drunk – decided to go to another bar. Another guy was going to pick up his girlfriend and head out to the beach. Everyone else was heading home. During the car ride, John and Mike made plans to meet each other later on that evening and shoot some pool. Diane was supposed to be going out with two of her friends that night as a girl's night out, so Mike decided to do the same. Mike said he would call Dave to see if he also wanted to go. Even though it was summer, Mike had not hung out much with his friends. Most of his spare time was spent with Melissa and Diane – not that it bothered him. Mike enjoyed spending most of his time with Melissa, Diane and his mother. However, being able to hang out with a couple of his buddies for the night sounded appealing.

With Iron Maiden blasting on the tape deck, they pulled up to Mike's house. While climbing out of the car, Mike told John that he'd give him call in an hour. Still singing the words to Run To The Hills, Mike walked up to the front door feeling good. It was a beautiful summer day. He only had to work a couple of hours. He had a few drinks with the guys at work. It was still only three o'clock. And on top of it all, it was Friday. It was turning out to be one of those days when everything fell perfectly into place. After walking into the house, Mike yelled for his sister, who had finished summer school the previous week. He knew she was home because of the music blaring from her room, but there was no answer. He yelled her name again, but still no answer. Figuring the music was too loud for her to hear anything he blew it off and went into the kitchen to get a drink of water.

        In a laid-back mode, Mike then set-up camp on the couch in front of the TV. His only thoughts were if there was anything good on to watch. Flipping through the channels it seemed, as usual, that there wasn't, but that did not stop him from searching. However the search was cut short when the phone rang. Figuring that Melissa would never hear it over the music, Mike jumped up and went to the kitchen. It was one of Melissa's friends from summer school. "Missy, it's for you," he shouted to no avail. He then put the phone back up to his ear. "You're gonna have to hold on while I go get her. She has her music blasting."

        With that, Mike put the phone on the kitchen counter and went to go get Melissa. Singing along to the music while climbing the stairs, Mike realized how glad he was that his sister did not listen to the crap she used to. Respectful of her privacy, Mike knocked on the bedroom door. "Missy, Ashley's on the phone." After a few more knocks, each harder than the one before, he finally pried open the door. Instantly, Mike had an uneasy feeling as Melissa was nowhere in sight. When Mike walked over to the other side of the bed, he found her lying there in a fetal position with vomit around her mouth. Immediately the world came to a screeching halt. The music that blared on the stereo fell silent. The air disappeared. His heart stopped beating. Frozen in a black hole of fear, Mike could at first only stand there praying this was some kind of cruel joke. But then, as reality forced its way into the moment, Mike realized that it was not pretend. "Missy," he screamed, falling to her side. Then, in unexplainable panic, he rolled her over and saw that her face was a light blue. Frantically, he checked to see if she was breathing; she was not. He checked to see if she had a pulse; there was none. As he tried to revive her, he suddenly noticed a portable mirror with white powder sitting on the nightstand. Next to it was a vile and rolled-up dollar bill. This couldn't be happening, he thought – but it was. "Missy," he cried, "I'm gonna get you help. You just wait right here." With his heart now racing uncontrollably, Mike ran to their mother's bedroom and dialed 911.

"Hello," said a confused voice on the other end of the phone.

"Is this 911?" he asked frantically.

"No," said the now more nervous voice. "This is Ashley."

In the panic, Mike had forgotten that Melissa's friend was still on the phone. "Get off the phone," he yelled. "I have to call 911!" As everything moved in slow motion, Mike hung-up the phone and tried again. This time there was no dial tone. Finally, after two more attempts, it clicked in his head that the downstairs phone was still off the hook. Feeling now like he was going to have a heart attack, Mike flew through the hall and down the stairs. Once again, he dialed 911, only this time it worked.

"911 Operator," said an eerily calm woman's voice.

"My sister! My sister's not breathing," he yelled hysterically. "I think she might have overdosed!"

"What is your address sir?"

After almost forgetting it himself, Mike blurted it out. "Please hurry, she's in bad shape!"

"An ambulance is on the way sir."

As the operator began to ask another question, Mike dropped the phone and ran back upstairs to Melissa. His heart still palpitating uncontrollably, he hoisted his sister's listless body on the bed and again tried to revive her. The results were the same as the first time. He could feel no heartbeat, no pulse and her face was turning a darker blue. "No!" Mike screamed while pumping his trembling hands against her motionless chest.

"Missy, please wake up! Please!" Hysterically, Mike repeatedly pleaded and begged for her to wake-up, but there was no answer. Her eyes just kept staring back at him like two abandoned ships sinking helplessly at sea. Still, Mike refused to relinquish his grip to an elusively fading hope. "It's going to be ok Missy. The ambulance is on its way. We're gonna get you help." Clutching Melissa in his arms, his tears dripped onto the cold skin of her face. As the tape that was playing on the stereo suddenly ended a petrifying silence befell the spinning room. Yet the rapid thumping of Mike's heart was so intense that his entire body was now encased in its pounding sensation; so much so that his head felt like it was going to explode. Mike wanted to wake up in bed covered in a cold sweat to find that the last fifteen minutes was nothing more than a nightmare. He wanted to knock on his sister's door once more and have her open it with a waiting smile. Instead, the initial shock was giving way to a very cold and devastating reality.

Suddenly, there was a loud knock at the front door. It was the paramedics. Mike promised his sister that he would be right back and then flew down the stairs. In a panic, he opened the door to find two EMTs with a stretcher and other medical paraphernalia. "Hurry, hurry, it's my sister," he shouted. "She's upstairs!"

"You said you think she might have overdosed on something?" One of them asked as they raced up the stairs.

"Yes! I found a mirror on her nightstand with some coke or something on it. She's not breathing. Please, you've gotta help her! She's only eighteen!"

As one of the paramedics went to open his medical kit, the other went to Melissa's side. However before even checking for vital signs, he looked back up at his partner and shook his head. Mike could see the utter look of defeat on his face. "No! No!" Mike shouted as holding onto hope turned into wishing for a miracle. "You can revive her! You've got to help her! Please, she's my baby sister!"

Perhaps only for Mike's sake, the paramedics tried to revive her, but it was too late. It had already been too late when Mike found her on the floor. Melissa Julia Patterson had died earlier that morning. An autopsy would later reveal that she suffered a massive heart attack as a result of ingesting a fatally toxic batch of crystal meth. Unbeknownst to her at the time, the same batch had already taken the lives of two other teenagers, one in New York and one in New Jersey. Ultimately, it would kill seven and send thirty-three others to the emergency room that August. It was a story that would play out on the front page of the newspapers and on the news. In the end, Melissa had become another statistic.

The hardest thing Mike ever had to do in his life was to make that inevitable phone call to his mother. He knew that she was at work thinking nothing more than about coming home and deciding what to cook for dinner. There was no reason in the world for her to suspect that it was anything but an ordinary summer day. However, as soon as she picked-up the phone and heard Mike's quivering voice on the other end, she knew something catastrophic had happened – and knew that it was about Melissa. Yet when Mike told her that Melissa had died, she collapsed. Her body went into shock and shut itself down. Her co-workers rushed to her side. One of them picked up the dangling phone only to find out what had happened. Fearing that she had had a heart attack, another coworker called an ambulance. But Betty had merely fainted and would come through a minute later only to realize that the phone call was not a bad dream – it was real.

Four days later, Melissa's wake and funeral were held. All of Mike's friends were there as well as Diane and her family. Betty's co-workers had come to show their support. Melissa's ex-boyfriend Tom was there. Of course, Allison was also there, with her parents. One by one they went up and kneeled by the open coffin to pay their homage. Some said more than others, some stayed longer than others, but each said goodbye in their own way. Betty's co-workers prayed not only for the soul of the girl they had only known through family photos, but also for the well-being of their friend. Brian, who had known Melissa since she was born, cried profusely, wondering how such a bright, young promising little girl could have ended up never seeing her nineteenth birthday. When Diane went up she whispered in Melissa's ear that she hoped the eighteen year-old had found peace.

Besides Betty and Mike, Allison was the most visibly shaken. With buckling knees she made the ominous journey up to the open black casket, but seeing her best friend lying there lifeless was too much for her to bear. Immediately she fell to her knees with tears flowing like water from an open faucet. "No Melissa! Please wake-up!" she screamed loud enough for everyone to hear. "Please, you can't be dead! You can't be dead!! Please, I won't move! I'll stay in New York so we can be together!" Finally Allison's mother had to come and pry her daughter away from the coffin. "Mom, she can't be dead," Allison cried in her mother's arms as every eye in the room filled with even more tears.

Melissa was buried in the same cemetery as Katie was, six years earlier. Against the backdrop of a clear summer day, Mike and his friends woefully carried her coffin from the hearse to the waiting grave. Under a hot August sun the congregation of friends and loved ones watched as the now closed casket was hoisted onto the gurney that would soon lower Melissa into her final resting place.

Shaking and choking back tears, Mike stood by his sister for the last time and gave her eulogy. "I don't have anything written. The fact is that I didn't even know if I was going to be able to stand up here today. I had even asked Diane if she would do the eulogy if I was unable to. But I realized that no matter how hard it is for me to stand-up here, it's something that I have to do. I owe it to my sister.

Father Sullivan had said to me – as he said to all of you – that Melissa is in a better place now, which I'm sure she is. But make no mistake about it; what happened to her is a tragedy. My sister didn't die because god wanted her or for some greater cause. She died because of one thing and one thing only: drugs. But the drugs did not just kill my sister; they killed a part of the future. There was no telling what my sister could have accomplished in her life. There's no telling not only what she could have become, but also the joy she could have brought to others.

I wanted nothing more than for my sister to be happy, to enjoy life. I wanted her to grow old gracefully, to someday have a family of her own. I wanted to see her in the backyard of her own house, playing with her children. But now I know that'll never be. The bright, wide-open future of such a promising little girl has been replaced by a black hole that my mother and I will have to live with for the rest of our lives. Don't get me wrong, we'll carry many beautiful and fond memories of Melissa. I'll never forget the day she was born. I'll never forget all the times we shared growing-up. I'll never forget sitting together on the swing in our backyard or our recent trip to Montauk. God, I'm so glad we took together that trip together. But no matter how many wonderful memories I have of her – and there are many – I will always think not only of what was, but also what could have been.

Melissa once told me that she wished she could be somewhere far away. Well, she finally got her wish... but at what a cost." Choking with tears, Mike paused, virtually unable to go on. He then kissed the lifeless casket before it was lowered into the ground. "Goodbye Missy, I will always love you."